YOU'VE *goth* MY HEART

BY L. C. ROSEN

Jack of Hearts (and other parts)

Camp

Emmett

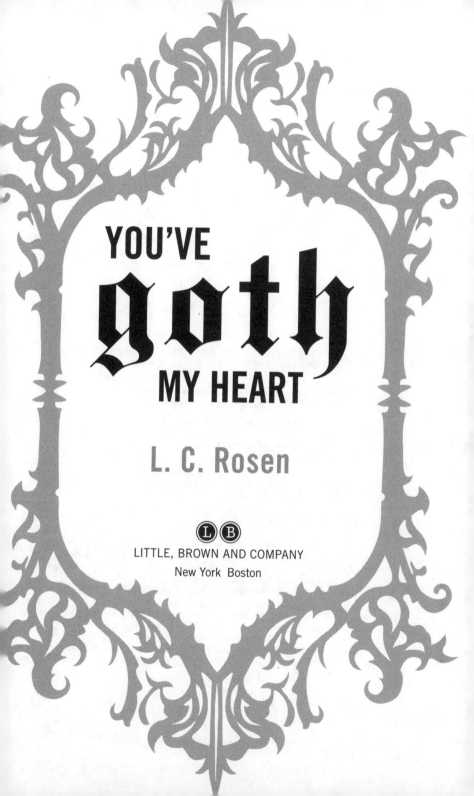

YOU'VE goth MY HEART

L. C. Rosen

LITTLE, BROWN AND COMPANY
New York Boston

This book is a work of fiction. Names, characters, places, and incidents are the product of the author's imagination or are used fictitiously. Any resemblance to actual events, locales, or persons, living or dead, is coincidental.

Copyright © 2025 by Lev Rosen

Emojis copyright © Cosmic Design/Shutterstock.com, Buch and Bee/Shutterstock.com, Kiseleva Natalya/Shutterstock.com

Cover art copyright © 2025 Colin Verdi. Cover design by Patrick Hulse.
Cover copyright © 2025 by Hachette Book Group, Inc.
Interior design by Carla Weise.

Hachette Book Group supports the right to free expression and the value of copyright. The purpose of copyright is to encourage writers and artists to produce the creative works that enrich our culture.

The scanning, uploading, and distribution of this book without permission is a theft of the author's intellectual property. If you would like permission to use material from the book (other than for review purposes), please contact permissions@hbgusa.com. Thank you for your support of the author's rights.

Little, Brown and Company
Hachette Book Group
1290 Avenue of the Americas, New York, NY 10104
Visit us at LBYR.com

First Edition: September 2025

Little, Brown and Company is a division of Hachette Book Group, Inc. The Little, Brown name and logo are registered trademarks of Hachette Book Group, Inc.

The publisher is not responsible for websites (or their content) that are not owned by the publisher.

Little, Brown and Company books may be purchased in bulk for business, educational, or promotional use. For information, please contact your local bookseller or the Hachette Book Group Special Markets Department at special.markets@hbgusa.com.

Library of Congress Cataloging-in-Publication Data
Names: Rosen, Lev AC author
Title: You've goth my heart / L.C. Rosen.
Other titles: You have goth my heart
Description: New York : Little, Brown and Company, 2025. | Audience term: Teenagers | Audience: Ages 14 and up | Summary: When sixteen-year-old Gray starts receiving anonymous messages from what seems like the perfect goth, he dares to hope it could lead to something real, but between his closeted ex coming back into the picture, and a possible serial killer targeting local gay teens, falling in love might just get him killed.
Identifiers: LCCN 2024053107 | ISBN 9780316575553 hardcover | ISBN 9780316575577 ebook
Subjects: CYAC: Romance stories | Text messaging (Cell phone systems)—Fiction | Serial murderers—Fiction | LGBTQ+ people—Fiction | LCGFT: Romance fiction | Novels
Classification: LCC PZ7.1.R67 Yo 2025 | DDC [Fic]—dc23/eng/20250514
LC record available at https://lccn.loc.gov/2024053107

ISBNs: 978-0-316-57555-3 (hardcover),
978-0-316-57557-7 (ebook)

Printed in Indiana, USA

LSC-C

Printing 1, 2025

FOR MY GOTHS—

Pat, Des, Rek, Laura, Molly, Rebecca, Alexis, Joe, Aire, Jeff, Greg, Erin, Phil, and Christina,

thanks for hanging out in graveyards with me

This is a story about Gray and Malcolm.

They just don't know that yet.

Summer

June 14

Unknown number:
So that band I was telling you about is
Night Club

> **Gray:**
> Sorry what?

Unknown number:
The band we talked about?

> **Gray:**
> I love Night Club. But I don't
> know who this is

Unknown number:
We met at George's party last
weekend? You liked my makeup?

> **Gray:**
> I don't know anyone named
> George and I wasn't at any
> party last weekend

Unknown number:
He fake numbered me?

> **Gray:**
> Sorry

Unknown number:
This sucks

Unknown number:
I thought he liked me. I liked him

> **Gray:**
> And now he's never going to
> know how good Night Club is

Unknown number:
😄 yeah. His loss, right?

Unknown number:
Did you see their new video?

> **Gray:**
> Yeah it's pretty cool.
>
> **Gray:**
> Do you know Kerli?

Unknown number:
I LOVE Kerli

Unknown number:
The video for Savages is totally my aesthetic

> **Gray:**
> Me too!!
>
> **Gray:**
> I mean it's a little too hetero for me but if you're into that kind of thing

Unknown number:
I am not. But I like the video otherwise

> **Gray:**
> Same. I feel like if Lestat's Boyfriends does a video it'll be like that but way gayer

Unknown number:
That would be fantastic I want it now

Unknown number:
Ok so I guess this is weird but nice talking to you stranger who is not the guy I met at the party

> **Gray:**
> You too

June 22

Unknown number:
So I'm watching the new Lestat's Boyfriends video and I immediately thought of the weird person I don't know who said it would be like Kerli but way gayer and was CLEARLY psychic

> **Gray:**
> It's SO good right?

Unknown number:
IT IS

Unknown number:
And thank you! I feel like I have no one to talk to about this. I love the high note with the dripping blood and the mouth

> **Gray:**
> YES! And the wolf?

Unknown number:
The wolf! OMG

Unknown number:
I did not expect it to look so high budget if I'm honest

> **Gray:**
> They got the guy who directed that movie The Violet Window to direct it because he used their music in the movie

Unknown number:
Ooooooh that explains it. I loved The Violet Window and yeah totally similar visuals

Unknown number:
I like your taste wrong number

> **Gray:**
> Same, possible scammer/
> murderer/my ex trying to get
> back with me

Unknown number:
I'm definitely at least two of those
things but now I'm curious about
this ex

> **Gray:**
> He's closeted

> **Gray:**
> When his friends teased him
> about being single he started
> dating girls on the side so I
> dumped him

> **Gray:**
> Not going to force him out but
> he doesn't get to make me a
> dirty secret

Unknown number:
That sucks

Unknown number:
I mean I know being closeted sucks
too but that's not cool

Unknown number:
I know I don't know you but that
makes me so angry for you

Unknown number:
A friend of mine once got cheated on
and I got on a table in the lunchroom
and called out the cheater

> **Gray:**
> 😄 you got on a table?

Unknown number:
I was really angry!

Unknown number:
So good thing I don't know who you really are because I'd probably get on a table and yell at him too

> **Gray:**
> 😂

> **Gray:**
> I wish I were more angry but I just feel sorry for him

> **Gray:**
> I don't know why I'm telling you all this

Unknown number:
Because you don't know me so you can't accidentally out him to anyone this way maybe?

Unknown number:
Or it's my finely honed long con skills

> **Gray:**
> That's it

> **Gray:**
> Both of those reasons

Unknown number:
His loss right? You seem awesome

Unknown number:
You could be 50 but still there are awesome 50 year olds

Gray:
I'm sixteen

Unknown number:
Me too!

Gray:
Ok now I know you're a
scammer or a murderer

Unknown number:
Or we were brought together by some
dark fate

Gray:
It can be both

Unknown number:
Always knew my fate would be to be
murdered by a mysterious stranger
with great taste

Gray:
I thought you were the murderer

Unknown number:
That's exactly what a murderer would
say

Gray:
Maybe we're both murderers

Unknown number:
That would be so awkward

Unknown number:
We both show up in matching ski
masks to kill some teenage boy

Gray:
MORTIFYING ☠ ☠ ☠

Unknown number:
Assuming you're a boy

Gray:
I am

Gray:
We shouldn't joke, though.
Some guy our age went missing
a few towns over from me

Unknown number:
I'm going to put aside my
disappointment that we clearly don't
live in the same CITY by your use of
the word town and ask: missing?

Gray:
Yeah. A few weeks ago now? It's
been in the local papers but
hasn't made national news

Unknown number:
But not like his body has been found
right?

Gray:
Nah he probably ran away

Unknown number:
Probably

Unknown number:
I guess if I haven't heard about it
we're not nearby though

Unknown number:
Which sucks

Unknown number:
Impressed I'm making a missing
teenager all about me?

Gray:
I mean I was thinking the same
thing

Gray:
Where are you though?

Gray:
If you didn't have your number blocked, I could at least look up your area code

Unknown number:
Yeah, I'm big on privacy

Unknown number:
But is it weird I don't want to know who you are?

Gray:
I think that's exactly what a murderer would say to try to get me to tell him

Unknown number:
OMG so true

Gray:
I'm not falling for it

Unknown number:
I'm putting you down in my phone as Dark Fate

Unknown number:
Before I can even look at your area code to look it up so that we're on equal footing

Gray:
I'm putting you in as my future murderer

Unknown number:

June 27

Gray:
It's raining and no one is visiting
me at work and I'm boooooored

My Future Murderer:
What do you do? If you want to tell me

Gray:
Let's say...retail

My Future Murderer:
Should we lay down rules about what
we tell each other?

Gray:
Do you just want my TikTok?

My Future Murderer:
No! I like the anonymity

Gray:
Good me too

Gray:
You're like the only person I can
even mention my ex to

My Future Murderer:
You haven't even mentioned him to
your friends?

Gray:
Well he was closeted, I couldn't
tell them much except I was
seeing someone

Gray:
They helped me through the
breakup but without specifics it
was hard

My Future Murderer:
Well you can vent to me anytime.
I'll back you up

My Future Murderer:
He's trash

My Future Murderer:
Want me to murder him before I
murder you?

> **Gray:**
> Yes, that would be great. You
> know just what to say

My Future Murderer:
So rules? Should we set some?

> **Gray:**
> If you want. What kind?

My Future Murderer:
Just respect if we don't want to reveal
something yet

My Future Murderer:
Ask before you say something
revealing about yourself

> **Gray:**
> Ok that sounds good

My Future Murderer:
Anything you want to ask me?

> **Gray:**
> You east coast? From when we
> text I think we're same time
> zone

My Future Murderer:
Yeah

My Future Murderer:
Though that could mean Toronto and Florida

My Future Murderer:
I don't think I want to know more about where you are yet if that's okay?

> **Gray:**
> Sure

> **Gray:**
> You a celebrity or something?

My Future Murderer:

June 29

> **Gray:**
> Work is still boring

My Future Murderer:
Can you read at work?

> **Gray:**
> Yeah but I haven't seen anything lately that calls to me

My Future Murderer:
What's the last thing you read?

> **Gray:**
> The Historian by Elizabeth Kostova

My Future Murderer:
YES

My Future Murderer:
I love that book

My Future Murderer:
One of the best vampire books out there

> **Gray:**
> It's SO good.

> **Gray:**
> And so now anything I read will be a disappointment and I don't want to start anything

My Future Murderer:
You just have to switch it up go for something with a different tone

My Future Murderer:
You read The Fell of Dark by Caleb Roehrig yet?

> **Gray:**
> Got it the day it came out

> **Gray:**
> Finished it that night

My Future Murderer:
How about Cherie Priest's Boneshaker books?

> **Gray:**
> No though my mom loved them and has told me to read them before

My Future Murderer:
Your mom? 💀 💀 💀

> **Gray:**
> My mom is cool

> **Gray:**
> You think they'll be good? They won't pale in comparison?

My Future Murderer:
Steampunk zombie alternate history
adventure? Can't compare

My Future Murderer:
Trust me

> **Gray:**
> Ok I'll start them tonight

> **Gray:**
> Thanks

My Future Murderer:
Hey you're my Dark Fate right? Maybe
that fate is book recommendations

> **Gray:**
> Nice try but I still know you're
> going to murder me

My Future Murderer:
Aw I almost had you!

June 30

> **Gray:**
> Did you see that new movie
> Rhododendron yet?

My Future Murderer:
No! I'm going to it tomorrow

My Future Murderer:
I'll text you after?

> **Gray:**
> You'd better

My Future Murderer:
Or what? You're already going to
kill me

> **Gray:**
> I'll think of something

July 1

My Future Murderer:
Ok saw it thought it was amazing
except for the ending

> **Gray:**
> YES. SAME. My parents loved
> the ending

> **Gray:**
> (yes I went with my parents
> all my friends are away for the
> summer)

My Future Murderer:
Really? Why?

> **Gray:**
> They're more bloodthirsty than
> me

My Future Murderer:
See, this is why you're taking so long
to kill me. No stomach for it

> **Gray:**
> Gothic and Romance go
> together!

> **Gray:**
> It doesn't all have to be gothic
> horror

My Future Murderer:
Exactly! Let the murderous Victorian vampires have some non-tragic romance for once

My Future Murderer:
Monsters should get some happiness

> **Gray:**
> I like happy endings in movies

> **Gray:**
> I feel like they can't happen in real life, so let me pretend

My Future Murderer:
Don't believe in happy endings?

> **Gray:**
> Just hard to picture them these days

> **Gray:**
> So much can go wrong

> **Gray:**
> You see it all the time

My Future Murderer:
Yeah I get it

My Future Murderer:
I think they happen but it's hard to see them through all the bad sometimes

> **Gray:**
> Sorry to be such a downer

My Future Murderer:
It's ok

My Future Murderer:
You doing anything for the 4th?

Gray:
They have some fireworks where I am. There's a good view from the graveyard

My Future Murderer:
Oooh that sounds so romantic

My Future Murderer:
The ex isn't going to show up is he?

Gray:
No, he was never one for the romance of graveyards anyway

Gray:
Why?

My Future Murderer:
idk just curious

Gray:
What are you doing?

My Future Murderer:
Family time. My folks like watching the fireworks from the rooftop

My Future Murderer:
We're moving out of the city so last fireworks here which sucks

Gray:
You can go back

My Future Murderer:
I just hate that we're leaving. I love this city

My Future Murderer:
And my parents are pretty much just like we're moving cause we're moving and I don't want to but they don't care

> **Gray:**
> I've never had to move, but it really sucks that they're not listening to you

My Future Murderer:
Why couldn't they wait until I was 18? In college?

My Future Murderer:
I say I don't want to move and they say tough. That's like all we say to each other now besides them asking me if I've packed everything...

> **Gray:**
> You should ask them. Maybe there's a real reason for the move

July 2

> **Gray:**
> Are you going to see that movie that opens next week? Unseelie?

My Future Murderer:
The dark fairy one that's for kids much younger than us?

> **Gray:**
> ...yes 😳

My Future Murderer:
Definitely. Want to both go opening night and text after?

> **Gray:**
> YES

July 9

Gray:
Ok I saw it I thought it was amazing

My Future Murderer:
I completely loved it!

My Future Murderer:
Was skeptical about the mix of puppets and CGI, but it was gorgeous

Gray:
The purple light in the crystal cave? I want that in my bedroom

My Future Murderer:
I may have googled purple lightbulbs before texting you

My Future Murderer:
Are we nerds for geeking so hard on this kids movie?

Gray:
I mean, I grew up on The Dark Crystal. That and Labyrinth were playing in my house since as long as I can remember. Oh, and when the prequel series came out a few years ago? Family binge weekend. Party. Decorations. Themed snacks.

My Future Murderer:
Labyrinth, too? No wonder you're gay.

My Future Murderer:
Your family sounds amazing. I had to find those from gifs on tumblr

Gray:
That's so sad.

Gray:
I'm second generation goth—raised right

My Future Murderer:
So how were fireworks at the graveyard?

Gray:
Nice. Chill. How about the rooftop?

My Future Murderer:
Mom and dad are freaking out about moving. Barely let me watch them

My Future Murderer:
Is it weird if I say I think it would have been more fun in the graveyard with you?

Gray:
No. I bet it would have been fun

My Future Murderer:
Maybe someday right?

Gray:
Yes. We can bring all our own purple lightbulbs and shine them through the graveyard

My Future Murderer:
OMG WHY DIDN'T THEY DO THAT IN THE MOVIE?

Gray:

Gray:
Missed opportunity

Gray:
So, if we're meeting up in purple-lit graveyards should we maybe know each other's names?

My Future Murderer:
Your name is Dark Fate.

Gray:
I should probably change yours actually

Gray:
Another guy our age went missing from another town

My Future Murderer:
Seriously?

Gray:
Police said he's probably a runaway...but some people are saying it's a serial killer

My Future Murderer:
That's a little scary. Don't get murdered except by me ok?

Gray:
😂 only if you get here first

My Future Murderer:
I'm coming for you

My Future Murderer:
But not really, because my mom is yelling at me about packing

My Future Murderer:
Talk later?

Gray:
Yes. I might be asleep but...
whenever you want to talk

My Future Murderer:
Cool

My Future Murderer:
Sweet dreams

July 10

My Future Murderer:
Hi

My Future Murderer:
Just wanted to say hi

Gray:
😊 hi

My Future Murderer:
😄

July 11

Gray:
So you're not my first wrong
number

My Future Murderer:
What?

Gray:
My number has 333 in it

Gray:
People type it in accidentally
a lot

My Future Murderer:
So there have been others?
💔

> **Gray:**
> It's not really a big deal

My Future Murderer:
I get it. You live in a village

My Future Murderer:
Wrong number texts are the only way to meet new people

My Future Murderer:
I'm just another notch in your cellphone case

> **Gray:**
> Actually I have seven wrong numbers I'm texting with right now

> **Gray:**
> Which one are you again?

My Future Murderer:
The hot one

My Future Murderer:
Which reminds me I actually am meeting some friends for a final shopping trip so gtg

My Future Murderer:
Need to stock up on cool clothes before I have to do all my shopping at...outlet malls

> **Gray:**
>

July 16

My Future Murderer:
Sorry! I'm not ghosting, really. We just have to move, and then we're going on vacation, so it's gotten sort of crazy

                        Gray:
                        That's ok

My Future Murderer:
And they're yelling again

My Future Murderer:
This is going to sound gross, but I miss talking to you. So... I'm not ghosting you

                        Gray:

My Future Murderer:

July 20

                        Gray:
                        You move yet?

August 2

My Future Murderer:
I'm back! I'm so so sorry!

My Future Murderer:
I thought I'd text after the move but we were on vacation and I broke my phone the first day.

My Future Murderer:
Dropped it in the airport 😖

My Future Murderer:
Screen stopped responding and
parents said they weren't going to
pause vacation just to get a new one
but now I'm back and my new one is
black and I'm texting you on it

My Future Murderer:
I'm SO sorry. Seriously. I'll make it up
to you.

> **Gray:**
> Oh yeah how?

My Future Murderer:
Photos of Italian graveyards I took for
you?

> **Gray:**
> That's pretty good actually

> **Gray:**
> What did you take them with?

My Future Murderer:
I use my parents old digital camera.
Photos just look more messy and real

My Future Murderer:
I missed you

> **Gray:**
> I missed you too

My Future Murderer:
Weird considering I don't even know
your name

> **Gray:**
> Do you want to know it?

My Future Murderer:
Can we just keep anonymous a little
while longer?

My Future Murderer:
I'm just afraid like you'll see me
and then it'll all change or you'll be
weirded out and stop texting

> **Gray:**
> Why? Are you really fifty?

My Future Murderer:
No. Just...shy. I don't know.

My Future Murderer:
You're Dark Fate. I like knowing you
without knowing. You know?

> **Gray:**
> Yeah I get it

My Future Murderer:
But how about we reveal ourselves on
Halloween? FaceTime?

> **Gray:**
> That sounds perfect

My Future Murderer:
Cool. And we can talk until then right?

> **Gray:**
> Yes of course

My Future Murderer:
Good, because I know no one in this
new town

> **Gray:**
> Did you ever ask why they
> wanted to move?

My Future Murderer:
My dad wanted a lawn

                        Gray:
                        Seriously?

My Future Murderer:
Yeah. He's semi-retired now and wanted a lawn. So hello tiny middle of nowhere town

My Future Murderer:
He keeps saying it will be good for me to get some sun

                        Gray:
                        Is the house nice at least? Your room?

My Future Murderer:
Yeah it's okay

My Future Murderer:
I'm going to start exploring the town there's probably a graveyard at least right?

My Future Murderer:
Still I'm so jealous. Your parents sound so much better

                        Gray:
                        They do make me work all summer though. Family business.

                        Gray:
                        And yes every small town has a graveyard

My Future Murderer:
No wonder you're so bored you're texting a serial killer all the time

> **Gray:**
> Death would be a sweet release

My Future Murderer:
All the more reason to look forward to
Halloween

> **Gray:**
> Promising me a sweet release?

My Future Murderer:
Are you flirting with your future
murderer?

> **Gray:**
> Trying to

> **Gray:**
> Unless that's weird

My Future Murderer:
I like flirting

My Future Murderer:
But if you're hoping to get laid before
I kill you put in that request now

> **Gray:**
> Before please!

My Future Murderer:
Ok let me make sure I put that down
on my calendar app 😂 😂 😂

My Future Murderer:
I have to go but

My Future Murderer:
I can't wait for Halloween

> **Gray:**
> Me neither

August 5

> **Gray:**
> So how's country life treating you?

Halloween Date:
It would be better if my parents weren't trying to do stuff with me all the time

Halloween Date:
They're trying to show me it's not boring here like I said it would be

Halloween Date:
They are failing

> **Gray:**
> Did you see the graveyard yet?

Halloween Date:
No 😞

Halloween Date:
No time yet plus it's a long walk or a short drive so I need time

> **Gray:**
> Your parents didn't buy you a bike?

Halloween Date:
Please remember I am a city boy when I say that I don't know how to ride a bike

> **Gray:**
> They have bikes in cities

Halloween Date:
They also have buses subways

and sidewalks that aren't mere suggestions. I never needed a bike

> **Gray:**
> Am I going to have to teach you how to ride a bike?

Halloween Date:
Maybe

> **Gray:**
> Ok

Halloween Date:
Ugh we're going out to dinner. They hate when I text at dinner so good night for now

> **Gray:**
> Good night country boy

Halloween Date:
Don't even tease

August 7

Halloween Date:
Ok so the graveyard is amazing

> **Gray:**
> How did you get there?

Halloween Date:
I walked

Halloween Date:
Shut up

Halloween Date:
It was perfect. First place I was like
ok I can do this

> **Gray:**
> Do what?

Halloween Date:
New school, new town, apparently new
parents who want to do stuff with me

Halloween Date:
But at least the dead aren't new

> **Gray:**
> You're not good at change are
> you?

Halloween Date:
Not really

Halloween Date:
Who is though?

> **Gray:**
> Yeah. I don't think I've ever
> experienced real change

> **Gray:**
> There's even a local college I
> might end up at while still living
> at home

Halloween Date:
Do you want that?

> **Gray:**
> I don't think about it a lot?
> I mean...look the world is
> boiling and we're all going to run
> out of water or burn to death
> or die in a plague. What do we
> need college for?

Halloween Date:
Yeah, sometimes I think like that, too.
But then, what do we need eyeliner for?
Friends? Love, sex, strangers we text
when we're feeling lonely or bored?

> **Gray:**
> Yeah

> **Gray:**
> My best friends are really
> talented like they're going to go
> to like MIT and art school and I
> am so happy for them

> **Gray:**
> But when I think about me...I
> don't know

> **Gray:**
> It's bleak

Halloween Date:
So what?

Halloween Date:
Make the bleakness beautiful

Halloween Date:
I think you can do that

Halloween Date:
I mean I don't know what you should
do with your life but bleak doesn't
mean giving up.

Halloween Date:
Sometimes hope is the darkest thing
you can give in to. Hope is goth.

> **Gray:**
> Pretty sure it's not. It's like the
> opposite of despair which is
> definitely goth

Halloween Date:
Hope is goth if you're hoping for more decay more beautiful nights in graveyards more roses that have time to wilt

Halloween Date:
Hope is goth when the alternative is just putting on some sweatpants and laying on the sofa until the world ends

Halloween Date:
Even though we're all going to die we do it with emotion and with style

Halloween Date:
Even if it's all meaningless we give it meaning

Halloween Date:
We're all living in a graveyard and most people close their eyes to it. But we see it and we make the graveyard beautiful with purple light

Halloween Date:
That's goth

> **Gray:**
> Ok you convinced me

Halloween Date:
Really?

> **Gray:**
> Maybe a little

> **Gray:**
> But I'm not deciding about college right now

Halloween Date:
Yeah you can still have angst over that, angst is very goth

> **Gray:**
> If hope is so goth though why not hope your new life is going to be good?

Halloween Date:
I do! It just isn't yet

Halloween Date:
But I have Halloween to look forward to

August 10

> **Gray:**
> I thought of something else cool about living in a town and not the city

Halloween Hope:
Yeah?

> **Gray:**
> You probably just had an apartment in the city, right?

> **Gray:**
> So you didn't get to decorate for Halloween!

> **Gray:**
> That lawn your dad wanted is a canvas

Halloween Hope:
OMG you're right

> **Gray:**
> We decorate our place inside and out. People go nuts.
> I'm always in charge of the decorations I get a budget to decorate my darkest dreams

Gray:
It's the best thing I do all year

Gray:
You can get weird stuff online and in antique shops and stuff really make it like a haunted house experience

Halloween Hope:
I'm obsessed with this

Gray:
See? Upside

Halloween Hope:
Thank you

Halloween Hope:
My parents said yes!!

Halloween Hope:
Honestly they seemed thrilled I was excited about something

Gray:
YESSSSS

Halloween Hope:
I'm going to have to find ideas

Halloween Hope:
I'm going to go just throw myself into this now

Gray:
😄

Halloween Hope:

August 14

Halloween Hope:
It turns out that this town has like a
Halloween decorating competition!

Halloween Hope:
So I guess I'm entering that?

> **Gray:**
> We have that too! It's fun but
> there's not much competition

> **Gray:**
> I do it mostly for me

> **Gray:**
> Though it feels good to win, like
> people finally see me?

Halloween Hope:
Yeah I don't know if there will be
much competition here either

> **Gray:**
> Most people want to visit the
> houses not decorate

> **Gray:**
> So Halloween we can see each
> other's decorations?

> **Gray:**
> Our FaceTime date is going to
> be amazing even before you
> murder me

Halloween Hope:
Date?

> **Gray:**
> Should I not have called it that?

Halloween Hope:
You should definitely call it that. I'm going to call it that now

> **Gray:**
> Cool

Halloween Hope:
Yeah

Halloween Hope:
I'd better get to work though. I have to decorate and figure out how to dispose of your body

Halloween Hope:
Looking forward to our date though

> **Gray:**
> Me too

August 19

Halloween Hope:
All this prep for a new school is really getting in the way of my Halloween decorating

> **Gray:**
> Yeah school gets in the way that's why I start early

Halloween Hope:
I have to get my parents to take me to some antique shops.

> **Gray:**
> Check Instagram. There are theater rental places too

Gray:
But we make most of our own stuff

Gray:
My friends are way more talented than me

Halloween Hope:
I need some friends

Gray:
I'd help if I could!

Halloween Hope:
If you helped you'd know what it would look like before it's ready

Halloween Hope:
I want to surprise you

Halloween Hope:
My murder dungeon needs to be unlike any others you've been in

Gray:
Oh are we up to the part where we talk about our exes?

Halloween Hope:
This isn't the closeted one right?

Gray:
Ugh no he's not interesting enough to have a murder dungeon

Gray:
Remember when I thought he was you trying to pull something?

Halloween Hope:
And you don't anymore?

> **Gray:**
> Well now that you said that I do!

> **Gray:**
> But no way. He's not goth at all.

Halloween Hope:
How did you even end up together?

> **Gray:**
> Christmas party at someone's house. We were drunk, we'd never talked much before but then we were alone in the woods and then we were making out and...

> **Gray:**
> Next day he calls me begs me not to tell anyone and I told him of course I wouldn't! And then he asks if we can do it again

Halloween Hope:
And you said yes?

> **Gray:**
> There aren't many options in my small town. it's liberal but...

Halloween Hope:
But not that liberal?

> **Gray:**
> Gay adults are fine mostly. Gay teens...There's some out girls. There actually are two other out guys at school but they're a preppy couple

Gray:
Well at least I have a date in a few months with a mysterious stranger who says he's going to murder me

Halloween Hope:
*hot and mysterious

Gray:
So he tells me

Halloween Hope:
Oh, he is. And he's really good with his mouth

Gray:
😮 I'm not quite at sexting yet

Halloween Hope:
Fair enough—let's pretend I meant like 🤵

Gray:

August 22

Future Sire:
I found the most amazing thing and I REALLY want to show it to you but I also don't want to spoil the house

Future Sire:
But I'm excited!

Gray:
I'm excited too!

Future Sire:
It needs to be hung though. I don't know where to hang it outside

Gray:
Make the outside inside if you need to

Gray:
Like hang some cloth on the side of your house to make it look like a room

Future Sire:
That could work!

Future Sire:
Thank you

Gray:
My small town smarts are at your disposal

Gray:
It's my favorite thing to do

Gray:
Make the world like I see it in my head just for a night

Future Sire:
How do you see it?

Gray:
Dark but not gory

Gray:
Beautiful

Gray:
Sinister but beautiful

Future Sire:
Like the purple light in the crystal cave?

Gray:
Exactly!

Gray:
I gotta go though, sorry

Gray:
It's the full moon so my family is doing a moon ceremony tonight.

Future Sire:
Moon ceremony?

Gray:
Yeah my family is pagan

Future Sire:
Really?

Gray:
Yeah

Gray:
I'll tell you more tomorrow? They're calling for me

Future Sire:
Ok go moon

August 23

Future Sire:
Ok it's tomorrow

Future Sire:
What's a moon ceremony?

Gray:
Ok so

> **Gray:**
> Some friends come over and
> we all hold hands outside and
> summon the circle

> **Gray:**
> Which is like asking the four
> elements to come watch over us

> **Gray:**
> And then we ask the moon to
> come and give us her blessing

Future Sire:
And what is this for?

> **Gray:**
> We're asking for the moons
> blessing in the coming month

> **Gray:**
> Like moon energies that we ask
> to bless us

Future Sire:
Moon energies sounds funny

> **Gray:**
> Is this too weird?

Future Sire:
I mean it's new and kind of weird but
only in the way new stuff is

Future Sire:
It sounds cool

Future Sire:
My folks are Jewish but barely

Future Sire:
Though they have been looking into
joining the local temple

Future Sire:
They're totally different people now

> **Gray:**
> So no big gothic crosses then?

Future Sire:
😄 no

> **Gray:**
> How about pentagrams?

Future Sire:
Yeah I've got a necklace and some earrings

> **Gray:**
> Good that means you're already a little pagan

Future Sire:
So it's not like satan worshipping?

> **Gray:**
> Satan? Who's she?

> **Gray:**
> It's just lots of nature worship and sometimes old gods

> **Gray:**
> If we really know and appreciate the gods and rituals

> **Gray:**
> But its about energy I guess? It's hard to explain

> **Gray:**
> I just know it makes me feel renewed

Future Sire:
That sounds really nice

Future Sire:
So you're not just second generation goth you're a full on witch

Gray:

Future Sire:
But you're not planning on killing me on Halloween to raise a demon?

Gray:
I never said that

August 29

Future Sire:
So apparently starting a new school means a ton of reading and paperwork

Gray:
Not just summer reading?

Future Sire:
That's mostly it but I only got the book list a few days ago

Future Sire:
Great Gatsby + books of my choice + some articles I have to make a list of

Future Sire:
I think my schedule is mostly done though. They put me in a pottery class which might be fun?

Gray:
Have you done pottery before?

Future Sire:
No

Future Sire:
Do you do any art?

> **Gray:**
> Some video stuff sort of
>
> **Gray:**
> And my Halloween decorating
>
> **Gray:**
> I think that's art anyway
>
> **Gray:**
> And I think it's what I'm best at in the world. Is that silly?

Future Sire:
It's not silly it's awesome

Future Sire:
And that means I'm going to see your art on Halloween!

Future Sire:
That you show off every year!

Future Sire:
Aren't you nervous?

> **Gray:**
> A little
>
> **Gray:**
> This year anyway
>
> **Gray:**
> You might kill me after all

Future Sire:
Yeah but that's the fun part

September 2

Gray:
Did you start school yet?

Future Sire:
A few more days

Gray:
Same

Future Sire:
We're going to some B&B this
weekend which seems like bad timing

Future Sire:
I hope there'll be antique shops where
I can buy old medical equipment or
something for Halloween

Gray:
Happy hunting

Fall

1

I glance down at my phone but it hasn't chimed again so I go back to smudging my eyeliner in the mirror.

"Stop looking at your phone," Callie says, some sort of technical manual in her lap. She's stretched out on the worn Victorian settee across the shop that my moms put in when I was old enough to start working in the store, so Callie and Lenore could hang out when it wasn't busy.

"Shut up," I call back to her, checking my makeup. It looks good. My dark brown curls fall over one eye nearly to my chin, and the hair in back is still short enough that it's not doing the duckbill thing I hate. I'm dressed for work, so a black velvet blazer studded with Victorian-style brooches over a black T-shirt that reads I'M GOING TO LOSE. I know I'm not meeting the stranger I call Future Sire until Halloween, but I try to look good in case one of these days he hits FaceTime instead of text.

I know he wants to wait, but I want to see him. More than see. I want to hold his hand and hear his voice and his laugh. Gods I want to hear him laugh.

"A third guy went missing over in Rye," Callie says, her eyes still on the book.

I roll my eyes and walk out from behind the register to look over the shop: Ceremony. It's owned by my moms, and older than I am. It has big windows that look out on the street, which I usually get to decorate with teas and candles and whatever we have that month. Inside is warm, dark wood, dried herbs hanging over the counter where we mix stuff up for tea or spells. There are display cases and tables. It's cluttered but homey, and it smells so good. Not just like tea and herbs, though that's the big one, but smoke and incense, a little like dark chocolate, too ('cause Mama likes to snack on it), and Mom's perfume (she can go overboard with it), which smells like overripe berries.

I took over the register from Mama this morning, so her mix is still playing—Rasputina, mostly, some Switchblade Symphony. Old stuff, but I grew up with it and it's cool. It's good for the morning and afternoon, pretty tame. Mom's mix is all Siouxsie and the Banshees and the Cure, so it scares away some of the boomers who come in early but feels right to the college kids who come in later.

But now, in the early afternoon, it's usually empty. For some reason no one needs magicked candles or incense or crystals at 1 p.m. Though, it's also Labor Day, so I'm guessing it's going to be empty all day. Which is probably why my moms asked me to cover it until five.

"He's not a murderer," I say, not looking at Callie and rearranging the small polished crystals in their bins on one of the tables. There's some rose quartz mixed in with amethyst. "He's cool." She doesn't like my new text friend. Boyfriend? No, we haven't had our first date yet. But something.

"The missing guys are all gay," she says. "Dad says they all knew each other. So there's a pattern."

Callie's Dad is a county DA and works with the police. The few times she has texted me this summer she's always told me to be careful and updated me. She gets nervous. I think living with a dad who always sees the bad stuff will do that. I'm mostly used to it, but I've never been the focus of her nervousness before.

I walk over to her and she pulls up her legs so I can sit down. She's in burgundy jeans, and as always a button-down and vest—white shirt, black-and-gold brocade vest. Her glasses are gold-rimmed, perfectly round, and her braids are up in a high ponytail, cascading down the side of the settee, a few of the bird skull–shaped beads winking out at me. Her makeup is masterful today—gold and black in a pattern that, when she closes her eyes, makes it look like her sockets are empty shadows with waves of light radiating out from them over her deep brown skin.

"You were off at space camp and Lenore was at the commune. It was boring here."

"They don't call it Sleepy Hollow for nothing."

I roll my eyes. It's an old joke. "But he was really fun to talk to, and texted more than you did."

"Space camp is a lot of work."

"Lenore doesn't get service at the commune—her excuse is better," I say, shrugging.

She shakes her head but smiles at me over the book. I've known Callie since I was four. Her mom came in looking for an Orisha candle, and though my moms didn't have any, they special-ordered some for her. Despite the Christianity and the paganism, my moms and her mom and dad ended up getting along, and suddenly we were having playdates all the time. I don't really remember a time without Callie. I'm lucky we grew together instead of apart—that's what Mama always says. Some people grow together, some grow apart. And Callie and I, and our families, have grown together. Maybe because my moms are two of the few queer people in town, and Callie's parents are two of the few Black people.

"I just don't think he's who he says he is," Callie says. "You need to be careful."

"We're just going to FaceTime," I promise. "I don't even know if he's nearby." I stand up and walk back to the counter with the register and grab a dustrag from underneath, heading to our glass display cases to polish one of the large black candlesticks. "Although, come on, being a serial killer victim? That would be pretty cool."

"Call me selfish," Callie says, "but I don't want you to die."

I sigh dramatically. "You ruin all my fun."

I close the case as the little bell over the shop door rings. I glance over, but it's not a customer. It's Lenore. She's wearing a white fifties-style dress with a Peter Pan collar patterned in spiderwebs to the waist, the same red as the buttons down the full skirt. In her white-gloved hands is a black wicker picnic basket overflowing with bloodred cloth, and her jet-black hair is side-parted and sweeps perfectly down to her shoulders, where it fans out a little. She wears black eyeliner and a bright red lip, as usual, and that unreadable Mona Lisa smile, also as usual. With her Latina mom's dark, almost black eyes and hair and her Irish father's Snow White skin, she doesn't really need to wear much makeup to pull off her look, but she always goes above and beyond—she's so put together she almost looks inhuman.

"Hi!" she says, wrapping her free hand around me in a tight hug. I hug her back, careful to keep the dustcloth away from her dress. Lenore makes all her own clothes, and out of awe and fear, I try not to damage them. But she only got back yesterday from all summer with her dad at the art commune, so I hug her tightly. Callie is up and hugging her a second later.

"I missed you!" I say.

"Me too!" Callie says.

"And I missed both of you!" Lenore says. "Which is why I have provisions for later." She lifts the picnic basket. "So we can have a reunion picnic. But they could stand to stay chilly. Will your moms mind if I use the fridge upstairs?"

"I doubt it. Mom is already up there, so you can ask."

"All right." She heads behind the counter to the door to upstairs, where my family lives. Then she turns back. "But once these are stored, we're having a chat about falling in love with serial killers."

"Callie already started that," I say.

"It's perfectly normal to have the hots for one," Lenore says. "I'd have a hard time saying no to Mr. Lonely Hearts Killer Harvey Glatman if he came back from the dead. But love, Gray? He probably only cares about your heart for the nutritional content."

"All right, all right," I say, waving her upstairs. "I get it, I'll be careful. And I'm not in love. I just like him."

Lenore raises one perfectly manicured eyebrow at me and goes upstairs.

"I think you should tell my dad," Callie says, sitting back down on the settee.

"I don't know where she of all people gets off lecturing me about who I have a date with," I say, ignoring that suggestion. I do not need to make my barely there love life into a sting operation.

"Cody is an asshole," Callie says, "but she knew who he was when he asked her out and he's never killed anyone."

"That we know of. I mean, Lenore could easily be a ghost and we'd never catch on. And besides, she keeps going back to him."

"That's her business," Callie says. "You don't get to control her love life, no matter how much you might want to."

"So why do you get to control mine?"

"I don't!" Callie puts her hands up in mock defense. "I just want you to be careful. Just like if she told us she was getting back together with Cody we'd be like 'It's your choice, but be careful 'cause you keep doing this and he keeps breaking your heart.'"

I go behind the counter and put the rag away. "Okay, well, you've said it, so now—"

"Said what?" Lenore asks, the door opening behind me.

"That being involved with a stranger online is a bad idea. Callie said it, I have heard it, I will now continue with my life, so you don't need to say anything."

"Oh, I don't know," Lenore says, lifting herself gracefully

up onto the counter and crossing her legs. "I wouldn't say it's a bad idea. Just dangerous. And dangerous means you need to take precautions."

"I know about condoms."

She raises an eyebrow. "I mean knives."

"I know about those, too." I gesture at the case of athames on one side of the store.

"I just think if you're going to continue this, you need to be ready for anything. Lies. Heartbreak. Murder." Her eyes widen ever so slightly.

"I mean, he and I joke about one of us being a serial killer all the time."

"That's exactly what a serial killer would do," Callie says, walking over to us. I glare at her. "And this isn't joking. There are real missing teenagers."

The missing guys bother me a little, but no bodies have been found, there's no blood, no signs of struggle or break-in or anything. Just kids who go out one day and don't come home. Even the newspapers aren't really sure what it means, so they haven't made too big a deal out of it. I've been more careful walking around alone at night, but I don't think they were all lured away by months of wrong number texts.

"What are their names?" I ask.

"Who? The missing guys?"

"The only gay guys I know are me, the two other guys at school, and Closet Ex. And I'd know if any of them were missing. You said they knew each other, so if I don't know them, I'm safe, right?"

She narrows her eyes. I've never told her who my ex

is; I didn't want to out him, and she respected that, but she doesn't like logic being used against her. She scrolls through something on her phone. "Dad says Samuel Burbank, Ethan Horowitz, and Perry Foster."

I start to laugh. Callie glares. "What?" she asks.

"I do know one of them," I say.

"That's not funny. That means you have a link, you could be next."

"They haven't been murdered or kidnapped," I say, confident. "They're all having an orgy in the woods."

Lenore and Callie look at me like I've lost my mind.

"Maybe not an orgy," I concede. "Since there's only three of them."

"What are you talking about?" Callie asks, hands on hips now. She's really not amused, and for a moment, I feel bad.

"Perry," I say. "We all know him. Poly Perry."

Callie stares at me blankly, but Lenore's face flashes with recognition. "Oh!" She turns to Callie. "Freshman year. That trip we took to Rye Playland? He was the guy who was flirting with Gray and then they texted for a few weeks after?"

"He was poly. Had a boyfriend. And I thought maybe I could get into that. We were texting a little, but then he said if we wanted to go out on a date, his poly boyfriend had rules...and he sent them to me. It was a fourteen-page document."

Lenore snickers. "I remember there was one about how long you could have your tongue in his mouth while kissing."

"They were very precise," I say, cackling. "It seemed like drama waiting to happen, so I said I didn't think it would work out. But while we were texting, Perry told me his dream was to go live in a cabin in the woods with like twenty other guys, totally off the grid, perpetual orgies." I shake my head. "Good for him, following his dream."

Callie is still frowning, but it's not as deep. "You don't know that's what's happened."

"It totally is," I say, confident. "He was out as queer to his parents, but not as poly because he thought they'd disapprove."

"That's not a reason to run away," Callie says.

"Maybe your parents are cool with you having orgies in the house," I say, "but not all of us are that lucky."

She laughs in spite of herself, then frowns again.

"What we're saying," Lenore says, just as I realize this is like an intervention and they've discussed it already, planned it, "is that we want to be there when you talk in person."

I sit down on the stool behind the counter. "If that's what it takes you to stop scolding me about this, fine," I say. "But it's just going to be FaceTime."

"You don't know," Callie says, hands on hips. "He could be local—as in the local serial killer who's targeting gay teens."

"They're in the woods making out as we speak," I fire back.

"If it's just FaceTime, it's fine," Lenore says, head swiveling between us. "But if he asks you to go meet him somewhere then we're coming."

I sigh. "Fine, but you'll sit at another table or something."

"We will scope him out and if we think something is off, we'll come over and drag you away," Callie says.

"No, come on," I groan. "This is like a first date, let me have at least a chance at getting laid by someone who will look at me in public."

"Between this and the closeted guy whose name you won't tell us, I think you do this to yourself," Callie says with a grin. "But I promise only if he's giving off seriously bad vibes."

"I like bad vibes," Lenore says. "So I'll make sure she only goes over if it's murder-y vibes. The harmful kind. Not the sexy kind."

I look up at Lenore. Her taste in men is not great, so if she's the one who decides if they interrupt my date, I should be safe. That's even if we can ever meet in person. I feel like we could be near enough—small town, Halloween decorating contest...but there are small towns in Georgia, too. Vermont is practically made of them. Whole swaths of America are just small town after small town...what are the chances he's in Westchester? There's no harm in agreeing to their demands when I'm probably not going to be able to meet him without getting on a train or plane for a few hours.

"Fine," I say. "But you both have to think he's dangerous or whatever word you want to say is bad enough to stop me going to see his haunted house."

"Deal," Lenore says, extending her hand. I shake.

Callie starts laughing. "*Haunted house* sounds like his dick."

"I can hope," I say. "Now can I tell you how cool he is?"

Callie and Lenore exchange a glance. "We'll allow it," Callie says.

"We like all the same stuff, and he's funny and smart and has great taste, and I like him," I say. "We even saw a movie together, kind of. *Unseelie.*"

"I wanted to see that," Lenore says, "but going to the movies with Dad is such a chore. I want popcorn, he gives me a ten-minute lecture on capitalism and GMOs and..." She shakes her head. "Sorry. You were saying?"

"Just that we saw it at the same time and talked about it after and loved the same stuff. We talked a lot. He's...I don't know. I like him. He's not..."

"A closeted guy who won't let you be his boyfriend in public or tell your friends his name?" Callie asks.

"That is definitely a plus," I say. "Although at first I did think it could be Closet Case, trying to get back with me."

"You said Closet Case was mid," Callie says, narrowing her eyes.

"Yeah, but he could be faking it." I look away. I really don't want to out Steve, so I haven't told them much about him. Not even a description. "Or he could have, like, studied up to win me back." I try to imagine Steve doing that. He's definitely a planner, and he was kind of desperate to get back together after I ended it, but he also wouldn't stop dating girls, so it's hard to imagine him putting in this much effort when he could have done something much easier.

"That seems like an extreme length to go for someone you won't even hold hands with in public," Lenore says. "But it would make me like him more."

I shake my head. "This is a different guy, and I like him and talking to him makes me happy."

Lenore and Callie are quiet for a moment, and then they both smile.

"You like him," Lenore says, poking my shoulder. "Awww, Gray likes a boy."

"Isn't that what we've been arguing about?" I ask. I love them and they love me and we all love driving each other crazy, apparently.

"So if this new texting guy isn't a serial killer, or your terrible ex, or some other kind of scam, he might actually be pretty cool," Callie says. "I'm happy for you—possibly."

"See?" I raise my hand at her. "Was that so hard? That's all I've wanted you to say for the past hour."

"If he's not a serial killer I'm happy for you, too," Lenore says. "Maybe even if he is. Imagine if he is, but he falls in love with you too much to kill you and then you take off on a murder spree together. Wouldn't that be romantic?" She clasps her hands under her chin.

"Sounds like a lot of work," Callie says.

The door chimes as someone enters; Lenore immediately hops off the counter, and she and Callie start inspecting the goods like they're customers. The new guy is our age, and cute, with pale skin, thick dark eyebrows, and short, precisely parted bleached white-blond hair. He's wearing a sheer black top studded with black sequins, so large it can only be described as billowy, and very short black shorts. He doesn't take off his sunglasses, but I *know* he must at least have some eyeliner on, to match that brownish lipstick. I don't recognize him, but he could be a freshman at a local college. This time of year a bunch of first-timers tend to show up and check the place out. Not many are this good-looking, though. I try not to stare as he browses, but when he bends over slightly to look at something on a bottom shelf, I can't help it.

My online stranger and I have a date, but until we meet, there's no harm in checking out other guys. Especially local ones with great style.

"Can I help you?" I ask.

He walks over and looks me up and down, but I can't read his expression well enough to tell if he likes what he sees.

"I'm looking for scary stuff, but glamorous," he says. His eyes scan the room and he frowns. "I'm thinking this isn't the right place?"

My attraction to him begins to fade at the bitchy remark. Now I know his type: some rich kid from the city who thinks everything in the suburbs is beneath him. Maybe LA. I don't know anyone from LA, but the haughty vibe he has makes me think of it. I've dealt with plenty of these snobby guys before—the ones who drive into town expecting some Headless Horseman theme park and are disappointed to find it's a regular town. The ones who don't appreciate how amazing Ceremony is. It's got style and substance; it's magic, and we don't sell sleek TikTok nonsense, we sell gorgeous, glamorous, *scary* stuff, a lot of which I pick out myself. He's a snob if he can't see that. No matter how good he looks in those shorts.

Still, I'm a professional. "Well, we don't have Halloween stuff out yet, but we are a spell shop and mysticism store, so what we have are real ceremonial items. We have some lovely candlesticks over there that definitely have an eerie vibe, and if there's something specific you want I can special-order it for you."

"Right," he says, looking over at the candlestick I pointed out. He walks over to it, tilts his head, but then shakes it. "Uh, this is cute, but it's not for me. I'm used to...more options, I guess." He smiles, and I notice that the part where his lipstick shadows into the pink inner lip looks soft as velvet. I want to smack him. "When is your Halloween stuff in? Maybe it'll be better."

"Three weeks," I say. I don't say an onyx candlestick with skulls carved into it isn't *cute*. I picked that one out for inventory myself. I have one just like it in my room.

"And there'll be like, actually scary stuff?"

I force myself to keep a pleasant, professional smile on, even as my neck starts to feel warmer and warmer. I've dealt with annoying customers who want the shop to be something else, who are looking for gift cards or antique clocks or something. But we sell herbs and candles and custom-blended teas and athames and crystals and wands. I love this store.

"Well, we sell actual, authentic spells," I tell him. "Some people find those scary. Black candles that drip red, crystal balls—"

"Okay," he interrupts, clearly disappointed. "Well, maybe in three weeks." He walks for the door and waves without looking behind him. "Thanks." I watch him go, hating how good he looks in those shorts.

The door shuts and I cross my arms. "What an asshole," I say.

"You mean what an ass?" Callie asks as she and Lenore come back over to the counter. "You weren't exactly subtle about the staring."

"Oh," I say, hoping I'm not blushing.

"What if he's your texter?" Lenore asks, grinning. "All that chemistry."

"What chemistry?" I ask. "He was rude about the store. My store." I look around the room. Anyone who can't see how amazing this place is couldn't possibly be my texter. "Besides, you know what the chances are of some random guy who just happens to walk into my store being the random guy I met online?"

I look at Callie for the answer.

"Infinitesimal," she confirms. "Especially since your texter is some old guy in a basement."

"Or destiny!" Lenore says.

I groan, shaking my head.

"But actually, you know who I think that was?" Lenore asks, getting out her phone. It's in a case that's just pictures of black cats. "Amanda Lash."

"No way," I say, immediately taking out my phone and going to Amanda Lash's TikTok.

"Yes," Lenore says. "I've been catching up since I got service back. She posted a video of her out of drag like two weeks ago and…found it." She holds up her phone.

Amanda's looks are glam and varied, from black leather and kohl to dark mermaid looks with a bejeweled face to

Wednesday Addams. The video is a makeup tutorial, and at the beginning he does look a lot like the guy who just called the shop "cute" in a tone so condescending it made me want to hex him.

"Why would Amanda Lash be in Sleepy Hollow?"

"We get a lot of ghost hunters and goths for the fall," Lenore says.

"No, he said he'd be back in three weeks," Callie says. "He lives here." She wiggles her eyebrows. "So maybe your serial killer has some competition? For your heart, I mean. Romantically. Not in the murder department."

"Ugh, no," I say. He was hot, but so rude. "That guy was the worst. No competition there." I sigh and look down at my phone, which is still open to Amanda Lash's TikTok. "I can't believe she was a bitch about the store. This place isn't *cute*. It's amazing. Unfollow," I say, pressing the button.

"Yeah," Callie says, taking out her own phone and doing the same. "What a bitch."

"Fine," Lenore says, hitting unfollow. "He was sort of a snob about it. But I will miss her looks."

I smile down at the freshly clicked unfollow, asking me to follow again, and close TikTok. It's petty, but so was he. As I'm about to put my phone away, a new text comes in.

Future Sire:
I'm really nervous about school
tomorrow

Gray:
Why?

> **Future Sire:**
> I don't know anyone
>
> **Future Sire:**
> I've seen people our age around and
> they have these pre-formed cliques
> and I know I'm too late to join one

"Is that him?" Lenore asks.

> **Gray:**
> Haven't you read the articles?
> We can still make friends
> through our thirties
>
> **Future Sire:**
> I'm just not good at it
>
> **Gray:**
> Says the man who made a date
> with a wrong number

"If you're going to text him in front of us, I'm going to read," Callie says, leaning over the counter to peer at my texts. "You call him Future Sire?"

"It's a joke," I say. " 'Cause he might be a vampire serial killer."

"That's sweet," Lenore says.

> **Future Sire:**
> That's different
>
> **Future Sire:**
> It's easier when you can't see the
> person

> **Gray:**
> You'll be in classes you'll have
> to talk to people
>
> **Gray:**
> Just compliment someone on
> their outfit
>
> **Gray:**
> That's a good start

"Their outfit?" Callie asks. "Tell him to bring booze for the whole class or something."

"I'm not telling him to get kicked out."

> **Future Sire:**
> Maybe
>
> **Future Sire:**
> I'm going to go back to online
> shopping for the haunted house
>
> **Future Sire:**
> It's the only thing that calms me down
> besides talking to you
>
> **Future Sire:**
> I'm a shopaholic and whatever the
> word is for being addicted to talking to
> strangers online

"The word is suicidal," Callie says.

"Stop reading it," I say, pulling the phone away but laughing. "Seriously, you're being rude, he's vulnerable. It's like reading his diary."

"Fine," Callie says, stepping back.

> **Gray:**
> Well since I'm the stranger the word is genius
>
> **Gray:**
> But you'll be fine new kids come to school every year and they always find friends within a month
>
> **Gray:**
> Just relax
>
> **Future Sire:**
> Yeah ok
>
> **Future Sire:**
> I've just never switched schools before
>
> **Gray:**
> It'll be fine
>
> **Gray:**
> And you can text me tomorrow and complain about it all you want
>
> **Future Sire:**
> Thanks
>
> **Gray:**
> Whatever you need
>
> **Future Sire:**
> Kiss for good luck?
>
> **Gray:**
>

I look up at Callie and Lenore, who are staring at me expectantly.

"Did he tell you his name yet?" Callie asks.

"Or how he plans to kill you?" Lenore adds.

"Shut up and tell us about your summer commune adventures." Callie and I flank her on the couch as she talks about Vermont, where they make their own cheese and all share one car. She doesn't mind the cheese-making, though apparently she got in an argument with an older woman who accused her of making her food too "ornate." Then Callie tells us about space camp and her time in the flight simulator and the math and engineering she did, which I barely understand, and the cute boy she made out with in the flight simulator after hours.

And then, finally, they let me give real details about the guy, about the jokes we shared and why I call him Future Sire. Then I throw in a story about a customer who came in looking for a spell to kill a man and how Mama guided her through the entire process of herbs and incantations before reminding her that any magic she did would come back to her as well. The woman was not amused. Mama smiled and sold her a spell for healing from being cheated on. Mama always knows what a customer really needs.

"All right, kids," Mom says from the door to upstairs. "You're off duty. You here for dinner, Gray?"

"No, we're doing a picnic at the graveyard," I tell her. "Same as every year."

She smirks. "Just checking."

When Lenore first met my moms, she went wide-eyed and afterward told me I was the luckiest boy in the world to have been raised by Morticia Addams and Eve from *Only Lovers Left Alive*. And I can see how she thought that. Mama is polished: pale skin, long black hair, perfect eyeliner and bright red lipstick, dressed in black. Mom has a mess of long bleached hair and wears skinny jeans and oversized shirts. She is...less polished. They tried to keep it a secret until I was "old enough," but it's always been pretty clear that Mom is my biological mother. We both try for the cool elegance of Mama in some way, but it never takes. Mom at least wears it like a rock star. Right now she's in an oversized white button-down and white flowing pants, but it's all kind of wrinkled and her skull pendant is askew. Her hair is up in a bun but sticks out at odd angles. At least her purple lipstick isn't smudged over her teeth.

"I'll get the picnic basket," Lenore says, hopping up and running upstairs.

"She looks like she had a nice summer," Mom says. I watch her go through the almost-subconscious ritual Grandpa taught her in their store growing up, selling art supplies in Boston: opening the register and counting the cash.

"She did," I say. "I mean, as much as you can on a commune."

"How does she keep herself from getting sunburned?"

"She has a big lace umbrella she carries everywhere," I say.

"And sunblock," Callie adds.

Lenore reappears with her picnic basket and we say goodbye to Mom and take off on our bikes, up Broadway past the Headless Horseman statue to the cemetery. It's not a long ride, but the sun is heavy on the horizon by the time Lenore has laid out the blanket under an out-of-the-way tree.

"Oh, this is nice," Callie says, lying on the blanket, which Lenore claims she didn't make, though I find that hard to believe. It's black-and-red plaid. "The breeze is perfect."

She's right. It makes it feel almost like autumn is really here. A few brown crumpled leaves even dot the shade around us.

Lenore opens the picnic basket: egg salad sandwiches on homemade black bread. "Black Pepper Blood Scones," dark red flecked with black. A fruit salad of grapes and melon. "Black Death Cake" of bitter chocolate. Spider cookies—three-dimensional spiders whose legs we can bite off—and some blackberry mead from her father's commune.

"Amazing," I say. "How do you make this even more elaborate every year?"

"I like to cook," Lenore says with a shrug. "I'm glad you both like to eat."

"I will eat anything you make," Callie says, reaching for a spider.

Lenore slaps her hand away. "That's dessert. And I'm glad you said that. It'll make poisoning you easier."

"Worth it," I say, grabbing a scone and biting it. It tastes like fire and butter and I love it. "This is so good," I say around crumbs. Callie, her mouth full of sandwich, nods.

We eat and drink, and when we're full and the sun is almost gone, the sky a mix of rose and black, Lenore takes out a few black candles and lights them.

"So what do you want this year?" Callie asks. This is our annual tradition the night before school starts. The picnic was Lenore's idea. The graveyard was Callie's. The telling each other what we want was mine.

The candles we came up with collectively.

"I want the same thing as last year," Lenore says with a sigh. "I know, I'm so predictable. But I want love. A man who isn't going to cheat on me every other week, like Cody. Someone sweet, and...different, maybe." She's quiet for a moment, but no one else will speak until she says "That's what I want," the official ending sentence. "I think about my mom and dad. How even when they were married, it was always fighting. And then I think about me and Cody, and how we were almost the same. I'm so scared that I'm doomed to be like my parents. And I don't want that. I want the stupid romantic comedy love I see in bad movies. Just, maybe, with a slightly darker veneer." She sighs, and I squeeze her hand. It was tough, watching her with Cody. Callie and I never knew what to say. We didn't want to tell her how much of a scumbag he was because she might get back together with him the next day, but she was hurting every other week from something he did. And then so happy the weeks in between.

Lenore exhales slowly. "Maybe I just want to be the sort of person who doesn't keep going back to a guy who cheats on me. But I don't want to be my parents after the divorce, either, Mom never dating, Dad dating too much. I want to know that love can be steady. Can you help me find that?" Callie and I nod. "And I want Ms. Downs to finally let me enter my cooking in the holiday art show.

Or sewing. It doesn't all have to be paint and clay, Margaret." She crosses her arms, annoyed at Ms. Downs. She's been petitioning to be in the school's seasonal art shows every year since junior high and hasn't gotten anywhere yet. "That's what I want."

"I hope you get it," I say. "And I'll help."

"Me too," Callie says. I look at her. "Okay. I want to win the science fair, for sure. I have to keep my record. And maybe I'd be up for making out with Bryce a little. We got pretty close at the end of the year and there was this moment when I thought he was going to kiss me, but then his mom called." She sighs. We heard all about this right up until she left for space camp. Bryce was second place in the science fair. "And to be clear, I'm not looking for some big overwhelming love. I don't think that exists, like you two do. But"—she pauses and pulls a little on my hand, embarrassed I think—"hormones are real. And they sometimes distract. I think Bryce could be a great method for removing distractions. Even easier to focus on my real work then. Like the science fair. That's the big one. That's what I want."

"I want it for you, too," Lenore says, a smile in her voice.

"And we'll help you get it," I say, chuckling a little, too. We're agreeing to help Callie get laid, after all.

"Oh, shut up," Callie says, laughing, too. "Your turn."

They look at me, and suddenly my mind is blank.

What do I want for this year?

"Well, I want online guy to be actually our age, and hot, and not a creep, and for us to hit it off and be boyfriends," I say, then laugh at how stupid and childish that sounds. "I mean, I want...someone I can love with without feeling like they're ashamed of it? Someone who doesn't make me feel like I'm a dirty secret. And maybe that's this guy, or maybe Closet Case messed up my idea of what a good relationship should be...but then I want to un-mess it. I know romances end in tragedies. I know the world is ending and it feels like everything is bad and getting worse. And there's beauty in decay as much as in growth. Balance is important. But I'd like love that's balanced...differently. And I want to figure out what I'm going to do after high school. My parents want me to go to college. I don't even know what I'd study, but you guys are going off to MIT and art or culinary school—don't say I'm wrong, I know you're getting in—and what do I do? I want to know that, y'know? And that's what I want."

"We want it for you, too," Lenore says.

"And we'll help you get it," they say, overlapping.

"Like, I can tell you right now what you are," Callie says. "You're the planner. You come up with the theme for the haunted house every year. You took Lenore's end-of-summer picnic when we were twelve and made it into a tradition. You...well, I can't speak for Lenore, but you help me see things outside myself. When I get hyper-focused, you make me see the big picture or the details or whatever."

"She's right," Lenore says. "And you're creative. What-ever happened to film? Aren't you in the film class this year?"

"Yeah," I say, "finally. But I doubt Mr. Stine is going to understand my taste in movies."

"So make him," Callie says.

"And maybe make a film of your own this year," Lenore adds. "You always talk about that."

I lie down on the blanket and look up at the night. "I don't know what it would be about. And my ideas are big, and like, to do them we'd need crazy special effects and digital stuff and cameras and..."

"We can do some of that," Callie says. "I mean, not the digital stuff, maybe, not without some really expensive programs. But camera stuff is cheap and easy now. Special effects can be old-school. I bet Lenore could make some great monster masks."

"It'll just end up cheesy."

"Do a documentary," Lenore says. "About this guy. Meeting a man who could date you or murder you."

"I...That wouldn't be cool to him," I say. "And what would I even film? The texts?"

"The meeting him. Your haunted house. Making it, preparing to show it to him. Wooing him with it."

"I...kind of like that." I wince as I say it. "I like showing how we do the decorations and then this year..." There's a narrative built in. A story. A good one, maybe, if things go well. "Oh no, do I have to do it now?"

"Yes, you do," Callie says.

They both lie down on the blanket next to me. There's a half-moon tonight, and the sky is black, aside from a few needle-sharp stars. Each of them takes one of my hands and we stare into the black.

"It's beautiful," Lenore says. Callie and I murmur in agreement. It's good to have them back. To have real friends who get you and want good things for you. But it feels a little like someone is missing. I can feel my phone in my pocket. But I don't text, because this is about us and while he's my friend, he's not *their* friend. Yet.

"It's going to be a good year, so help me," Callie says.

"If this year tries to misbehave, we'll just cut it open," Lenore agrees.

I sit up. "We should head back before you two start trying to attack the space-time continuum."

We pack up and pedal home, peeling off one by one until it's just me.

At home, Mom and Mama are watching TV on the sofa. The house looks a lot like downstairs, with red curtains and black trim on pale gray walls covered in weird art and photos of old medical specimens and a purple tapestry with a pentagram from their college days.

"Have a good picnic?" Mama asks, turning around.

"Yeah, it was good."

"You ready for school?" Mom asks.

"I am prepared to learn, I guess." I shrug.

"You guess?" Mama asks, her lips twitching into a smirk.

"Junior year!" Mom says, throwing her hands up in mock excitement. "Upperclassmen! That's cool, right? Beat up a few freshmen, take their lunch money?"

I snort despite myself.

"Don't give him any ideas," Mama says. "Honey, do you want to talk about it?"

"I..." I don't. Not with them. I'm talked out. "I'm okay," I say. "I'm going to bed."

"Sweet dreams," Mama says.

My room isn't big, and is mostly my bed, with its canopy of torn black lace and chains. The sheets are black, but not satin, because Mama said satin is tacky.

On my walls are posters from my favorite movies, overlapping to create a wallpaper, and my windows look out on the street in front of the shop. It's quiet.

I lie down in bed and take out my phone.

> **Gray:**
> My friends and I do this thing before school every year where we talk about what we want
>
> **Gray:**
> I kind of wished you were there tonight

I wait for a moment, but the *delivered* never turns to *read.*

> **Gray:**
> Anyway I hope you get what you want this year

Future Sire:
I hope you do too

Future Sire:
And I wish I were there tonight

Future Sire:
What did you wish for?

> **Gray:**
> It's not a wish

Future Sire:
Sorry

Future Sire:
What did you say you wanted?

> **Gray:**
> Some dark romance and a little guidance maybe

Future Sire:
Maybe our not-wishes overlap then

> **Gray:**
> Maybe 😉

Future Sire:
What kind of guidance do you want?

> **Gray:**
> My friends wishes were like winning fairs and getting into great colleges. I don't even know what to wish for

> **Gray:**
> And I have no idea what I want my year to be

> **Gray:**
> My life to be

> **Gray:**
> It feels so ridiculous to think about

> **Gray:**
> And because of that it's like I have no future

> **Gray:**
> I see their futures like laid out for them, like amazing lives just waiting to happen and for me I see nothing
>
> **Gray:**
> I see me working in this little town for the rest of my life
>
> **Gray:**
> Sorry, that's too heavy
>
> **Future Sire:**
> No I get it
>
> **Future Sire:**
> But I also bet you're wrong
>
> **Future Sire:**
> Like, what do you love doing?

I lie back, wondering that myself.

> **Gray:**
> I love working on the Halloween decorations. I really do. I love making the space different and putting like a living story out there.
>
> **Gray:**
> Sometimes I think about wanting to do film because of that. Like put my vision on screen. But it's different. A screen is flat. It never feels right
>
> **Gray:**
> But I do like film class.

Future Sire:
Maybe there's a film you can make
that'll feel like the Halloween
decorations.

> **Gray:**
> That's kind of what my friends
> said to do.

Future Sire:
They sound smart

> **Gray:**
> But like a documentary about
> making the decorations and...
> how I'm excited to show them
> to you, this stranger. So sort of
> about us, too.

> **Gray:**
> Would that be ok?

Future Sire:
I guess?

Future Sire:
Would you show any of my texts?

Future Sire:
That might be weird

> **Gray:**
> No I can do it without that

> **Gray:**
> I guess I'd just need to talk
> into the camera and then film
> building the house and try to
> make it really special for you

Future Sire:
Aww

Future Sire:
I like the phrase "for you"

Future Sire:
And yes you can do it I don't mind

Gray:
Thanks

I smile at the phone. It really is a good idea. I do the concept for the Halloween house every year, and then the three of us work to make it happen. I just need to set up a camera. Maybe interview Lenore and Callie. It wouldn't need special effects. It wouldn't be a cool dark gothic story like *Unseelie* or *Purple Window*, but it would be... something.

Future Sire:
Will you interview me? At the end?

Gray:
Yes if you'll let me

Future Sire:
Ok but not until after our date

Future Sire:
I want to focus on you that night

Gray:
You're trying to get out of the interview by killing me first aren't you?

Future Sire:
 maaaaaybe

Gray:
That's ok

> **Gray:**
> If I die before it's done it'll
> become a famous movie
>
> **Future Sire:**
> I wish we were going to the same
> school tomorrow so I could hang out
> with you in the hall
>
> **Gray:**
> You better text me after
>
> **Gray:**
> I'm going to sleep now
>
> **Gray:**
> Good night
>
> **Future Sire:**
> Good night

I stare at my phone in the dark, wondering if he'll text again, until I fall asleep.

2

Every day starts with homeroom. My homeroom advisor is Ms. Overbury, who, despite her excellently morbid name, does not appreciate my style choices. Every year when we meet to go over class schedules or "have a little sit-down" about future plans, she always asks me if I think I'll make friends dressing the way I do. I always tell her I already have friends.

"Gray, hello." She looks me up and down and sighs before forcing herself to smile. "Still dressing like that?"

"Style comes naturally to me," I say.

"Just remember to dress more...normally for college interviews next year, okay? You want them to take you seriously."

"Ms. Overbury, I'm a gay teenager who doesn't come from money and has under a hundred thousand TikTok followers. No one is going to take me seriously no matter what I'm wearing."

I smile at her sigh. She's not a bad person. She doesn't want to burn me. She just thinks I'm making life more difficult for myself. I admit, on top of a red tee and black pants with a tuxedo stripe of safety pins, I did go heavy on the eyeshadow and eyeliner. That was just to give her something to sigh about. But I'm not wrong. No one would take me more seriously in a polo shirt, even her.

"Did you have a nice summer?" she asks, desperate not to end our first conversation of the year on that note.

"Mostly just worked." I shrug. "It was okay."

"Well, that'll be good for your college fund," she says with a smile. Our advisors are supposed to help with college applications and stuff, and I'm one of her special projects, since I haven't told her where I want to go to college, because I don't know, because what's the point? College for what? The only thing I'd maybe want to study is stuff like my Halloween decorating, which they don't offer as a major, and if they did, I'd just end up back at my moms' shop four years later, with a new exciting lifetime of debt. But her smile is already straining, she wants this to be a nice interaction so badly, so I just nod.

I go sit at my usual desk at the back of the classroom. No phones allowed in school—of course we all use them during lunch and free periods out of sight of the teachers, but I can't whip mine out in front of Ms. Overbury to talk to my stranger.

More students file in, and I nod at them, exchange hellos. I'm not really close with anyone at school, aside from Lenore and Callie. Other people tend to get nervous around me, and that means they either smile at one of my morbid jokes and then gossip about me, or they get angry. So Callie and Lenore are the only ones who really know me.

And maybe Steve. I don't want to see him. I've been

imagining it, so I'm prepared: walking by him in the hall, our eyes meeting, lingering a little too long, or maybe brushing shoulders when he walks by me, like he used to. I can handle that. It's over, and I have this new guy, who at least promised to screw me before he kills me so Steve won't be the last guy I slept with.

The bell rings and everyone looks expectantly up at Ms. Overbury, who smiles the way the really enthusiastic greeters do at Walmart around Christmas.

"Welcome back! I hope you all had wonderful summers. I went to Aruba and went snorkeling for the first time! But you can ask me for my photos later." She giggles. "First, we have some announcements." She lifts her glasses on their beaded necklace and reads from a handout. "We're going to have a few active shooter drills this year. Next week there will be an assembly where we learn what to do. Spirit Week will begin on Monday the twentieth, so get your red-and-white clothes ready! And that means that homecoming will be on Friday the twenty-fourth, followed by the homecoming dance that evening. So start getting the nerve up to ask someone!"

I smirk. I wear red for Spirit Week every year, but for some reason my red never gets me much praise.

"Okay, and"—Ms. Overbury frowns—"as some of you may know, some teenage boys in the county have gone missing over the summer. They've probably just run away, but just in case, the police are reminding everyone to be careful walking at night. Find a buddy, or get your parents to pick you up. Also, if any of your friends have been acting strange, you should tell an adult. Your parents, or me, if you feel comfortable with it." I think about telling everyone about the orgy in the woods Poly Perry is having, but I know Ms. Overbury wouldn't like that.

"Well, that's scary," she continues. "But less scary is that student board elections are next week! All the candidates must register by the end of this week and be prepared to give their platform speech at the assembly on Monday."

There's a knock on the classroom door, and we all look over expectantly. It's weird for homeroom to be interrupted.

"Come in!" Ms. Overbury says.

The door opens, and Ms. Cain, who works in one of the offices and whom we barely see, comes in, followed by the kid from the store. Amanda Lash.

"Hello, Ms. Overbury. This is your new student, Malcolm Gabay."

Ms. Overbury looks Malcolm up and down, her smile becoming more forced.

"All right, thank you, Linda." Ms. Cain nods and leaves. "Well...welcome, Malcolm. I'm your advisor, Ms. Overbury, and...why don't you go sit next to Gray, there. I'm sure you two have a lot in common."

Malcolm moves toward the back. Today he's in a skintight white button-down with a red cravat and a long, flowing black skirt. His ears sparkle with rubies and diamonds, and he has a purple cat-eye and black lipstick. As he walks by my classmates, some of them stare, but no one snickers, which makes me happy. It's a killer outfit, one riding crop short of Victorian dominatrix. If he hadn't been such an ass about the shop, I'd probably be flustered by how hot he looks. But I'm not, so I just look down.

"Anything else, anything else?" Ms. Overbury mutters, looking over the paper. "Oh, please remember, no peanuts on school grounds. We have several students with allergies this year."

"You're from that store, right?" Malcolm whispers to me.

I turn to look at him. "The one that's cute but not scary?" He winces. "Yeah, my parents own it."

"Ah," he says, pursing his lips and looking away.

The bell rings, and Ms. Overbury claps once. "Remember, if you need anything, come see me!"

Everyone packs up their stuff and heads out the door. Malcom walks to Ms. Overbury.

"I have history next," he says. "Do you know where room 203 is?"

"Oh, well, I have to ... Gray?"

I sigh. My hand is on the door, but I'm too late. "Will you show Malcolm to room 203?"

"Sure," I say without looking back. I head into the hall and wait until Malcolm follows me, and then I walk toward his classroom. He doesn't say anything, which is fine by me.

And then it happens. Just like I knew it would. Steve, walking toward us. He didn't get ugly over the summer, sadly. He's still tall, broad-shouldered, blond. He's in a T-shirt for some sports team I don't know and basketball shorts and I think about the time he met me wearing those shorts with nothing underneath and how they contoured—

Stop. I make myself stop. I walk, Malcolm a step behind

me. There are other people in the hall, and we whorl around each other, like the water in a riverbend. I can feel Steve see me, but I won't look. He walks toward me, but I keep my eyes forward, not taking him in. His backpack is slung over one shoulder. He angles slightly, heading toward me. Some of his friends are with him, talking and laughing.

His shoulder is about to brush mine. So I dodge. He misses. And then he turns to look at me, and I stupidly stupidly turn back and our eyes catch and he looks sad, and what the hell am I supposed to do with that, Steve?

I keep walking.

Deep breath. We keep walking and I keep my eyes forward until we get to Malcolm's classroom.

"Here," I say.

"Thanks," he says. "And, um…" He looks me up and down, probably judging my clothes or something. I tap my foot.

"What? I need to get to class."

"Right," he says, nodding. "Never mind." He goes into his classroom and I run down the hall to mine before the bell rings.

I try not to think about Steve. I broke up with him, I remind myself. It's sad that he can't come out, but I get it. His parents are religious. The guys on the soccer team aren't homophobic-homophobic, but they throw *gay* around like it means something bad, they make fun of me and the other gay guys in the locker room. Steve told me he really hated it. I asked him why he didn't tell them to stop it, then. He said he didn't want the attention.

He's hot, which started the whole thing, but then he was unexpectedly sweet, too. He liked watching me put my makeup back on after he and my sheets had taken it off, when my moms were out, or working downstairs, thinking he and I had a science project together.

He's always been big on plans. Not just how to meet me in secret, but for the future. He'd go to college in California, far from his parents, and then he'd become an architect in LA and build me a house with Gothic arches and gargoyles. He had this whole future planned, for both of us, as long as I could stay hidden now. Stay out of sight until it was safe.

And I could. I understood. I didn't mind.

Well, I minded a little. He didn't stand up for me in the locker room. Not the makings of a good boyfriend. If that's what we were. But that's the word he used, after a few months: "My secret boyfriend."

The word *secret* sounded sexy. But then he asked out Jenny Appleton and they held hands in the hallway and I was supposed to be okay with that, he thought, because she was saving herself, so all they did was kiss sometimes.

"Not like what I do with you," he said, in the woods half a mile from school. His eyes traced my body, comfortable and hungry, and it made my body warm, 'cause I knew what he meant.

We had a system. I'd fan open my notebook in science class: *Meet me in the forest after school.* I'd done it after I saw him holding her hand in the hall and had to fix my makeup because it kept running off.

"It doesn't matter," I told him. "I thought we were..."

"We are," he said, taking a step forward. "She's just my beard."

"She doesn't know that."

"Why do you care about Jenny Appleton all of a sudden? She says you're a freak."

"It's not about her," I said. It wasn't. She thought I was a freak, fine. I thought she was a Jesus freak. "It's about me. I don't want to be..."

"My boyfriend?" It was the second time he said it. He left out a word this time but it hovered between us.

So I said it. "Your dirty secret."

"Isn't that what you've been this whole time?" he asked, stepping forward again, taking my wrists and pulling them from my chest, wrapping them around his back. I looked up at him. He was so handsome. "You've been my sexy"— he paused, kissed my neck—"dirty"—another kiss, on the ear—"secret." He went for my mouth and I pulled away, shaking my head.

"This is different," I say. "This is weird. It's like we're having an affair, not just a secret relationship."

"Come on," he said. "It doesn't matter." He grabbed at my hands again. He was the JV goalie, good with his hands. Fast and slow as needed, strong or gentle. He pulled me toward him. "You and me, we can be real boyfriends. Just a few more years."

It was the *years* that really did it.

"No," I said, and I turned and walked away.

He chased after me. "What? What do you mean, no?"

"Dump her, or I dump you," I said.

"I can't. People will talk."

"Say you didn't know she was saving herself. Say you want to play the field, get laid."

"But then people will think I'm a loser when I don't."

I kept walking. He finally understood and stopped.

"I...!" he shouted. I could feel the other words waiting to fall into place, and if they had, maybe I would have turned around. But they didn't. So I kept walking. And he held still.

But of course we have environmental science together. Luckily Mr. Rigman does assigned seats and doesn't put us at the same table. Except I'm next to Jenny Appleton, who scoots her chair away from me and raises her hand. I know she and Steve broke up like a week into the summer. It shouldn't matter, I remind myself. Steve and I are over, and I have a date scheduled...in two months.

"The bell hasn't even rung yet, Jenny," Mr. Rigman says, checking off names on his attendance sheet as students walk in.

"Can I have a different seat, please?"

I smirk. She hates me that much.

"Why?" Mr. Rigman asks.

"Gray's family worships the devil, and I'm afraid his presence will have a corrupting influence on me," she says, her voice thinning into a whine.

Mr. Rigman looks up at her, then his eyes dart over to me. I shrug. This is hilarious. "We don't worship the devil. We don't believe in the devil."

"Sounds like you were misinformed, Jenny," Mr. Rigman says. "Gray will be your lab partner, so I advise you to get over this."

She turns pink and then glares at me, like it's my fault.

"If you were really a good Christian, you'd try to save my soul," I tell her, smiling. "We could be besties, braid each other's hair, swap makeup tips. Maybe you could get me to switch from black lipstick to…what is that? Wet N Wild in Cat's Asshole Pink?" I tilt my head, still smiling. "That's what loving the sinner but hating the sin would really look like."

"Freak," she says softly, turning to her notebook. Her mom will call the principal, and she'll get switched beside her bestie Madison, and I'll be with Esme Goldbaum, my lab partner last year. She's cool, plays bass in a punk band, very chill.

Steve is seated a row back across the aisle, and I can feel his eyes on me during class, like a heat lamp being flicked on and off. Maybe he's afraid I'll say something to her. Or maybe he's hoping for something from me. A sign. I keep my handouts and notes in a neat, stacked pile.

Mr. Rigman goes on about how the world is ending, but how there's hope for the future if we all just make changes. I almost raise my hand to point out that it's not about us, it's about the huge corporations, and they're not stopping anytime soon, but he seems so sad, his lecture a little desperate, like he's trying to convince himself.

And then I remember what my stranger told me. That even if the world is ending, you can still find hope. That hope is goth. I don't know if I believe it. I mean sure, the end of the world, all of us already at our own funerals—that's goth. But I've always been more about the aesthetic, anyway. Callie is the one with the philosophy: The universe is unimaginably vast, and we're so tiny that nothing we do—including destroying the earth and all dying—matters in the slightest. She says that's what comforts her. Maybe that's goth, too.

When class is over, I start packing up my books and turn around and there's Steve, handouts all fanned out in front of him, almost wildly. I frown, turn away, and walk quickly, in case he's following me, to film class. Film is only a dozen students, Lenore included, and we sit next to each other in the back. Today she's in a pencil dress in dark blue, with a scoop neck trimmed in black lace, a very lifelike spider brooch pinned to it.

Lenore likes film because she has a YouTube channel where she shows people how to make stuff—food, clothes. But she's bad at explaining, and half the time it's just silent footage of her sewing or stirring. She's working on it, though. I take film because it feels like the closest thing school offers to what I want to do? It's not perfect, but... it's fun to play around with. For Halloween one year I wanted to do a tech haunted house, screens everywhere with creepy interlaced videos. It was way too expensive, so we couldn't, but that's how I got into it. It's also why Callie's documentary idea is good. It's sort of showing both sides—the work, the experience of being inside it, but not in a way that's forcing something on you. Well... maybe not. I don't know. Maybe I can't pull it off.

After class I ask Mr. Stine if I can do the documentary as my final project.

"A documentary?" he asks, sitting at his desk—off to the side of the room, so it doesn't block the screen. "Sure. Unexpected from you, with your wild fantasy scripts, though. What would it be about?"

I pause. He'll probably think my stranger is a serial killer, too. "Setting up the haunted house in my parents' store? For the competition?"

He nods. "Okay. Look, go through the syllabus, look at the final assignment requirements. The final film has to incorporate at least three of the fundamental visual techniques we're going to learn, and it needs some kind of narrative arc. If it's just footage of your friends decorating the store..."

"It won't be," I say. "There's more."

"Well, okay. Just read the assignment. And since you won't be able to redo anything after Halloween, make sure you have lots of footage to play with in editing."

Lenore is waiting by the door for me. "He's going to let you do it?"

"Yeah." I let myself break into a grin. Then I realize what I've committed to and suddenly go a little shaky.

"Did you tell him about the serial killer you've been talking to?"

"No," I say. "I just said it'll be about decorating the store."

"Well, I'm sure the plotline will be a fun surprise for him," she says as we walk to the cafeteria. "Especially if you go missing before you can turn it in."

Callie is already at our cafeteria table in the corner away from the windows. She's in a red vest over a black button-down shirt and black pants and is wearing a bowler hat over her braids. Her eyeliner is red and on her left eye comes down into a tear of blood. We sit down with our bagged lunch. Callie and I barely pack lunches—I just brought crackers and a soda today—because most days Lenore brings new recipes to test. Today it's that dark black bread, filled with tahini and vegetables.

"I'm concerned they're too sweet," she says, handing us each a sandwich.

"They're not," Callie says after a bite. "The bread makes it work."

I nod in agreement. "Another success."

"Look," Callie says, nodding behind Lenore and me. Malcolm is standing in the middle of the cafeteria, doing the new-kid social-anxiety thing. He's a jerk, but what he's going through gives me a lump in my throat; I turn back.

"His name is Malcolm," Lenore says. "He's in my chemistry class."

"And my homeroom," I add.

"We should invite him over."

"He can sit with the mean girls," I say, nodding at the other side of the room where the popular girls are throwing fake smiles at each other.

"I know he was rude, but maybe he didn't mean it in a rude way," Callie says.

"Doesn't matter," Lenore says. "He's leaving."

I turn just in time to see him walk out of the cafeteria.

"Oh well," I say sarcastically. "He shouldn't have been

so rude in the store. And he didn't apologize in homeroom. He's one of those rich mean goths who thinks he's better than everyone else."

"Don't we think we're better than everyone else?" Callie asks.

"Lenore is better than both of us." I say.

"Oh, you," Lenore says, swatting me on the shoulder.

"He's just worried if he didn't say that, you'd stop bringing us food," Callie says. We quickly forget about Malcolm and talk about how we should decorate the store.

"I want two beating hearts," I say. "At opposite ends of the store. Or maybe we do two rooms again like last year. And I want them just slightly out of sync with each other. Can we do that?"

"I can definitely make something that pulses and makes a loud heartbeat sound," Callie says.

"I think I can craft some realistic hollow hearts. Your mechanisms will have to be small, though," Lenore says.

"And we'll need fake blood, of course, and I think I want to do the thing we did two years ago with the false entrance so when people come in they have to go around a corner?"

They nod as I go on, trying to figure out the story of the haunted house this year. Separated hearts, cursed to stay alive until they come together, at which point they'll destroy the world. It's a good story but hard to tell in house format. We throw ideas around until the end of lunch. As I take my tray over to the trash and put it away, I spot Steve, texting. I tense up, waiting for my phone to vibrate with a message, in case he *is* the stranger. But nothing comes. He catches me staring and smiles, then glances at his friends and stops.

Callie and I have Victorian literature together. Ms. Mullins is an eldergoth, like my parents, with wild black curls and heavy eyeliner. She's even come into the store a few times. I take whatever class she teaches. She makes learning fun.

"*Dracula*!" she shouts, jumping up onto her desk. She's wearing black boots that go up past the hem of her dress. "An epistolary classic!"

"We'll also be covering *Frankenstein* and *The Strange Case of Dr. Jekyll and Mr. Hyde* this semester. I know the theme might seem to be horror," she says, raising an eyebrow in our direction, "but I encourage you all to look beyond that at what they're saying fear is. Is it the unknown? Power? Ourselves? What scares you?"

Some other students look nervous, but Callie and I clutch hands in excitement. Victorian lit has all the good stuff.

Afterward, we head off for our other classes, which though not as much fun as English, breeze by until the end of the day.

"So," Lenore says to us as we meet at our bikes after school. "I have news. I have been asked to the homecoming dance."

"Already?" I ask. "That was fast."

"I know," Lenore says. "I found it a bit suspect, honestly. But he said he'd always watched me and you only live once and so on. It was sweet. He's sort of wholesome. Makes my teeth hurt. But he wasn't Cody. So I said yes."

"Does he have a name?" Callie asks.

"Oh," Lenore laughs. "Right. Steven. Steve O'Daly. He's the goalie on the soccer team?"

At first, my ears start to ring, and then I swallow, and it sounds way too loud. Then everything that's happening finally hits me and my blood actually goes cold. I shiver.

"I don't know him," Callie says.

"Sure you do," Lenore says. "Tall, blond. You know who I mean, right, Gray?"

"Yeah," I say. "I better get going, though. I have a shift at the store."

"We'll come," Callie says. "I can do work there."

"No, no, that's okay," I say. "I um...I'm probably going to do stockroom stuff."

Lenore looks at me funny. "Are you okay?"

"Just really tired," I lie. "I'll text you later."

I hop on my bike and pedal off, wobbling a little because I'm shaking all over. My Steve. Lenore. If I tell her, I out him. If I don't, I let her be used for...what? Why would he ask out one of my best—only—friends?

All I want to do is get home. All I want to do is talk to the stranger on my phone.

3

Future Sire:
School sucks.

Gray:
Just got home. Was about to text you

Gray:
Yeah it kind of does

Future Sire:
I did the whole don't know anyone so nowhere to sit at lunch I guess I'll eat in the bathroom thing

Future Sire:
I felt SO pathetic

Gray:
That sucks I'm sorry

I remember Malcolm doing that, too, and suddenly feel a pang of guilt for not having waved him over. But he probably would have turned his nose up at us anyway.

> Gray:
> Hundreds of kids must have done that today

> Gray:
> I'm sorry you were one of them

> Gray:
> You could always sit with me

Future Sire:
If I saw you I don't know if I would

> Gray:
> Why not?

Future Sire:
I don't know. I'm shy

Future Sire:
I don't think anyone even noticed me to invite me over

> Gray:
> Tomorrow just sit with people who look cool

> Gray:
> Make them be your friends

Future Sire:
Yeah

> Gray:
> I wish I could give you a hug

Future Sire:
Me too

> Gray:
> Maybe grab your ass while I'm doing it

Future Sire:

Future Sire:
Your first day back go ok?

> **Gray:**
> Yes

> **Gray:**
> No

> **Gray:**
> It was and then something bad happened

Future Sire:
What?

> **Gray:**
> The closet-case ex? He asked out one of my girl friends

Future Sire:

> **Gray:**
> Yeah

> **Gray:**
> I don't know what to do

Future Sire:
Is it possible he's bi?

> **Gray:**
> He always said he tried and tried to be into women and never could be

> **Gray:**
> So

> **Gray:**
> And even then it doesn't feel good having my friend date my ex and not know it

Future Sire:
Yeah

Future Sire:
I don't know what to say

> **Gray:**
> Can I just out him to her? Make her promise to keep it quiet?

Future Sire:

> **Gray:**
> Yeah feels not ok

Future Sire:
Can you tell your friend he's not a good guy but not go into why?

> **Gray:**
> Maybe

> **Gray:**
> I wish there were something easier

Future Sire:
Maybe you should actually talk to him

> **Gray:**
> No

> **Gray:**
> I feel like this could be so I have to talk to him? He was using our old signal today to try to get me to meet him

Future Sire:
You have a signal?

> **Future Sire:**
> Very espionage
>
> > **Gray:**
> > Had
>
> **Future Sire:**
> So...I hope this isn't offensive but
> couldn't you like do a spell?

I lean back in bed. I mean, yeah, I know some basic spellwork, but I don't do it very often. It's complicated and both my moms always tell me I have to be careful, have to have good intentions. But I have good intentions, right? Not wanting Lenore to get used?

> > **Gray:**
> > Spells are weird. You don't want
> > to do anything that could hurt
> > people because anything you
> > do will come back to you three
> > times over
> >
> > **Gray:**
> > Well mama says three times
> > over, mom says the universe
> > balances things by biting you in
> > the ass
> >
> > **Gray:**
> > But maybe
>
> **Future Sire:**
> You have two moms?
>
> > **Gray:**
> > Yeah did I not mention that?
>
> **Future Sire:**
> I'm so jealous of your life

Future Sire:
I mean aside from the whole ex drama
you're dealing with

Future Sire:
And growing up in the country

                               Gray:
                               It's a small town not the
                               country

Future Sire:
All looks the same to me

                               Gray:
                               Snob

Future Sire:
Ouch

Future Sire:
I thought it was part of my charm

                               Gray:
                               It is

                               Gray:
                               I'm just...

Future Sire:
Yeah

Future Sire:
And honestly the town I'm in, it's not
so bad

Future Sire:
Dad really loves his lawn

                               Gray:
                               See? And you'll make friends at
                               school and I'll figure out this ex
                               drama

Future Sire:
Let's hope

> **Gray:**
> If we fail we'll fail beautifully right?

Future Sire:
Yeah. Hope is goth.

Future Sire:
Like me hoping my parents will relax with the bonding time

> **Gray:**
> What are they doing now?

Future Sire:
They want to help me with Halloween. They keep talking about spooky plants.

> **Gray:**
> Spooky plants?

Future Sire:
They're really into plants now. The lawn.

> **Gray:**
>

> **Gray:**
> But it's nice they want to help

> **Gray:**
> You can hope they'll have some good ideas

Future Sire:

> **Gray:**
>

> **Gray:**
> But I should probably text my friends
>
> **Gray:**
> I sort of bailed when she told me the ex had asked her out and then I should talk to my moms about a spell maybe
>
> **Gray:**
> Sit with cool people tomorrow! Talk later

Future Sire:
I will!

I sigh, then open my group chat with Lenore and Callie.

> **Gray:**
> Sorry! My stomach suddenly freaked out.

Callie:
You didn't look great

Lenore:
It wasn't my food, was it?

> **Gray:**
> No, definitely breakfast. Thought I'd gotten the mold off that pear, but...

Lenore:
So we can come over?

> **Gray:**
> Yeah I'll be in the store soon I want to ask Mama something

Callie:
Be there soon

Mom was working the counter when I got home, which means Mama is probably in the garden. Our building has a nice backyard, gated off by a black picket fence taller than me. On one side is a bonfire pit with chairs and a picnic table, and on the other is Mama's garden, and the tiny little greenhouse. This is where she grows a lot of stuff for the shop—rosemary, mint, chamomile, mugwort, flowers, and vegetables. She's got a green thumb and rotates everything with the seasons, so even now, in the run toward autumn, it's huge and blooming.

I find Mama pulling chamomile, wearing black gardening gloves and the big Halloween witch's hat she wears as a sun hat. She glances up and smiles as I walk over.

"How was your first day?"

I shrug. "Kind of okay. Something bad happened at the end."

"Bad?" She falls back, sitting in the dirt and looking up at me.

I sit down next to her and she puts her hand over mine. "I was hoping you might know a spell to help."

She cocks an eyebrow. "What kind of spell?"

I start doodling a pentagram in the dirt with my finger. "Well…something so that the truth comes out? I… have a secret. Not my secret." I wipe the pentagram away. "Someone else has a secret and they want me to keep it, and I know I have to, but they're also hurting people by not telling them."

"Hurting people?" she asks. "How?"

"Well…" I tilt my head. Steve isn't hurting Lenore, not yet at least. The thing about Lenore is she'd probably think it was funny to be his fake girlfriend if she knew. But she's looking for love, and after everything with Cody—his cheating, his love-bombing, his pulling away—she deserves something better. Steve isn't it. "If they keep doing what they're doing without telling the truth, they could hurt someone."

Mama takes the hat off and fans herself with it. "So they're not hurting anyone yet?"

"Not...badly?" I try. But I know that if he were really hurting Lenore, I'd tell him to tell her the truth or I would. Right now, it's just the potential to hurt. And that's not enough to out him for. Maybe I can get her to not want a second date. "Is there a spell to make someone dislike someone else?"

Mama stands up, brushing the dirt off her black dress. She reaches a hand down to me and I take it, standing next to her.

"You want a secret revealed, so no one gets hurt, but you don't want it to hurt anyone and if it's revealed it will hurt someone, but keeping it will also hurt someone?"

I nod.

She sighs. "Tricky. But you know how these things work. You work some magick, maybe it works, maybe it turns out perfect, but reveal someone else's secret, three of yours will be revealed."

"Yeah," I say, kicking the dirt.

"Don't kick the earth, she's your friend. You don't need a spell, you need a reading. Come on, let's get the cards."

I follow her inside, to the little breakfast nook with the bay window that looks out over the garden. There's a round table there, almost directly across the room from the altar, a small table with some magickal tools like an athame, a wand, candles, a few symbols, objects of importance like the handfasting ribbon my moms used during their wedding. Mama keeps her cards here, too, in a wooden box carved with the phases of the moon. She brings them to me and sits at the table, shuffling.

Mama is a great card shuffler; it's like they're a liquid she stirs in her hands. She puts them on the table in front of me.

"What am I asking them, though?"

"Ask them for guidance. That's always the best thing."

I shuffle awkwardly, thinking about wanting guidance— on Steve and Lenore, on the Halloween decorations, on my stranger. I know I should focus on just one thing, but there's so much going on it's like my brain is a tornado.

I'm not sure how shuffled the cards are by the time I'm done, but I get them back into a stack and feel like they're where they need to be. I hand them back to Mama, who starts laying out cards. Mama is an expert reader, but I've never been great at it. I kind of know what each of the major arcana mean, and if they're reversed, I know it's like...the opposite of that. Well, no, only sometimes. And then with the minor arcana I know the suits, and what they represent, but it's so many cards. I have to check the booklet constantly. But Mama makes it look easy.

"This is a sort of vague reading," she says, glancing up. "Were you focusing?"

I can't meet her eye. "Sort of?"

She smiles. "Mmmm...well, they'll give you the advice

you need, I'm sure." She taps the High Priestess. "Trying to balance things, truth and lies in this case, or maybe truth and pain. What the cards are saying, though, is that when the truth is revealed…" She taps another major arcana. The Tower. Not great.

"Disaster," I say.

"Not necessarily. It's more like…a painful change. But maybe a needed one…but the two of wands—does this have to do with your love life?"

"No," I say quickly. But it sort of does. "Not really. Someone else's."

"Well, it feels like there's some secret in your love life, that's what I'm seeing. And when you figure it out it won't be pleasant."

I frown. My love life? The only secret there is…I swallow. There's no way my texting stranger is actually a serial killer, right?

"Sorry, honey," she says, patting my hand. "But what I see here is the suggestion that you shouldn't tell truths that aren't yours to tell. Maybe if you give me more details, I can give you some motherly advice? I don't just do magic, you know."

I think about telling her everything—about Steve, and Lenore, but I know what she'll say: I should gently guide Lenore away from him, tell her I think it's a bad idea to date him, but not tell her why. But I know Lenore. She'll needle me, and maybe get Callie involved, and then they'll get it out of me. I can't keep secrets from them. It's why they know about Steve at all. In fact, if I were to say Steve was a bad idea, they might figure it out on their own, and then I might as well have just outed him, which is not cool at all.

"Sorry, I don't think I can."

She squeezes my hand reassuringly, but the corners of her mouth dip, disappointed, and I feel a heavy drop of guilt in my chest.

"I won't tell anyone," she says.

"But the cards said they're not my secrets to tell, right?"

She nods and squeezes my hand again.

"I'm going downstairs, Lenore and Callie are coming over. We'll do homework or something."

"All right. Tell Mom we're doing takeout tonight, I don't want to cook. The Chinese place, unless you or she have strong objections."

"Sounds good to me." I stand up. "She's going to want the kung pao tofu, same as she always does. I don't even need to ask."

"Mmmm," Mama says, sweeping the cards back into a pile. "Why try to be psychic when you can just ask, though?"

I laugh. "Okay. Thanks for the reading, Mama."

"Anytime, honey."

Downstairs, Mom is behind the register dancing to *The Rocky Horror Show* cast recording. She gives me finger guns to "The Time Warp" while doing the movements.

"Mama says Chinese for dinner, cool?"

Mom nods, still dancing. "Kung pao tofu."

I smile. "I know."

"How was the first day?"

"It was okay," I say. "Kinda got weird at the end. But Ms. Mullins was already standing on the desk."

"Amazing, love her," Mom says. "*Dracula, Jekyll and Hyde, Frankenstein* this year, right?"

"Yeah." I nod. "There are others on the syllabus, too, but those are all on there."

"*Carmilla*? Before *Dracula*, lesbian vampire. Good stuff."

I shake my head. "I didn't see that one, but maybe I can get her to add it as extra credit."

"Oh, for sure," Mom says, giving me the pelvic thrust.

The bell over the door rings as Callie and Lenore walk in. Mom, horrifyingly, does not stop dancing, but instead turns her pelvic thrusting on them.

They immediately join in.

"Okay," I say, stepping between my mother and my friends. "Enough of 'The Time Warp.' We have homework."

"Well, then, get to it," Mom says, still dancing. "Don't mind me."

I roll my eyes but go over to the velvet sofa, and Callie and Lenore follow.

"Sorry again," I say, rubbing my stomach. I hope I'm not overselling it.

"You should have just said," Callie says. "Lenore was worried you were upset with her."

"I was not," Lenore says, not very convincingly.

"Sorry, it just felt like the more words I spent explaining it, the worse the situation would become." I feel even worse for not telling her. I hate this lie. I hate Steve for making me tell it. I should never have gone to that party.

Callie snorts. "Poetic."

We start our reading, Callie with her legs stretched out

across our laps. Customers come and go: a lot of college kids, but plenty of nice housewives who come in for tea and the essential-oil air fresheners. A few approach Mom and whisper, and Mom pulls out some premade spell kit: herbal blends, crystals, a candle.

Mom also comes over with a tray of her homemade cinnamon sandwich cookies with a blood orange marmalade filling. I watch Lenore eat her cookie daintily and wonder how angry she'd be if she knew what I was keeping from her. After Lenore and Callie have gone home and the store is closed, Mama heads out to pick up the food.

Then Mom stares at me for a moment, her normally intense eyes amplified, taking something in about me.

"So what aren't you telling them?"

That's the scary thing about Mom. Mama can do magic—but Mom might *be* magic.

I sigh, and she smirks, then goes into the storage room behind the counter. "Come help me unpack." It's not very big, and there are three big boxes in the corner.

"Is that the Halloween stuff?" I ask, excited.

"Yes it is. Nice avoiding the question."

"I don't want to talk about it," I say. "I already got a tarot reading from Mama."

"And?"

"Reply hazy."

She nods, grabbing a knife from a shelf and cutting open the top box. "Hate those." She pulls out a few vases I chose, long elegant things with skulls and crossbones, like elongated poison bottles, in dark glass. "These are great," she says, handing them to me. "Well, look, it's your life.

But keeping stuff from your friends doesn't end well, in my experience. Either they find out or it eats you up inside and you act funny. Sometimes both."

"I want to tell them...but it's not my secret. The cards told me not to."

"Screw the cards, do what feels right. That's the energy you put into the world. Being the best person you can be." She hands me more vases to shelve.

"I just don't know what that is."

"Well, that sucks. I'm here if you wanna talk it through more."

"Thanks."

"Oh, these are great," she says, pulling out bags of twinkle lights, not the usual chintzy Halloween kind with plastic jack-o'-lanterns, but anatomical hearts in deep red.

"The lights inside them pulse," I say. "This is one of their new artists. I'm totally stealing a strand for my room."

"Niiiiice," Mom says, opening a package and plugging them in. "Yeah, get these strung up so people can see them. That'll make them buy, for sure. Good choice, kid."

I smile, proud. I bet my texting friend will love them, too. I bet he'd love all of this. I should...no, that could ruin the surprise of the haunted house. Still, I bet he'd love it. They're stunning. If Malcolm comes back into the store, he'll regret being a jackass.

We keep unpacking the rest of the new stuff, and we finish just as Mama comes home, carrying bags of food. We follow her upstairs, where I set the table and Mom puts on *Dracula's Daughter*, this old creepy movie they love, which makes Mama laugh. Then she grabs Mom around the waist and dips her slightly, kissing her. I shake my head like it's gross, but really, it's nice to see. I like that my parents are like, stupid in love, still, and kind of funny and gross about it. I want that, too.

"All right, dessert later," Mama says, letting Mom out of the dip. "Dinner first."

"And vampires," Mom says.

"Always vampires," Mama agrees.

4

Mama always says to sleep on things, and she's right. In the morning, I know what I have to do. So in science class, after Jenny and Esme have switched seats and Esme and I have exchanged cool, wordless nods of approval, I fan out my papers, glancing up at Steve. He smiles at me slightly. I need to know what he thinks he's doing, asking out one of my best friends.

It's hard to focus on anything else the rest of the day. Thankfully, classes are still ramping up, so aside from Ms. Mullins leaping onto the desk to talk about Freytag's pyramid and how each letter in *Dracula* has its own arc, nothing much exciting happens before lunch. Which is bad, because all I can think about is Lenore. I wish I could at least tell Callie, but I can already hear her saying *Tell her—Steve lost the right to stay closeted the moment he started trying to have it both ways.* But she's straight and doesn't know what the closet is like.

At lunch, Lenore has brought potato salad and little cucumber sandwiches on bloodred bread. She looks perfect in a soft pink dress right out of the fifties and bright red contact lenses. Callie is in full skeletal makeup, but gold, not white, like her bones are glowing. I asked her once why she bothers doing all the makeup for school, and she said it was something that made her look forward to waking up. I almost feel bad sitting with them in a Drab Majesty T-shirt and torn black jeans with just basic black eyeliner on.

"Are you okay?" Callie asks me, mid–potato salad.

I open my mouth, not sure what to say, wanting to tell them everything, but I'm interrupted.

"Hi, you don't mind if I join, do you?"

Malcolm. He is also, of course, dressed better than I am, in a black fishnet button-down over a white crop top and huge holographic pants. He sits down next to me. Callie, Lenore, and I exchange silent looks.

"I know, I'm new, it's weird, but you seem cool, and I don't want to eat lunch alone," Malcolm says, a little quiet.

"Of course," Lenore says. Callie shrugs. I glare. Lenore puts her hand on mine. "It's always great to get to know new people."

I don't see us getting to know him making us like him, but Lenore always gives people chances and she makes my lunch—not to mention I'm kind of lying to her right now—so I don't want to tell her no. And besides, this is exactly what I told my texter to do, too, right? Go up to people who look cool and sit with them. So at least Malcolm is making smart choices. Kind of weirdly smart, actually. For a moment I wonder if Lenore was onto something, if Malcolm could be my texter. But no. No way. My texter is much, much cooler than him. Better taste. Nicer. Just so much better than Malcolm.

I'm annoyed to realize he smells good—like the clove incense we sometimes burn in the store. My texter might be superior to him in every way, but I wouldn't mind if he smelled this good.

"I love your makeup," he says to Callie.

"Thanks," Callie says.

"You want a sandwich?" Lenore asks. "I made plenty."

He shakes his head, white hair flopping slightly over one eye. "That's okay, really."

"If you don't take one, she'll be offended," Callie says.

"And you wouldn't like me offended," Lenore adds with a sinister smile.

Malcolm laughs nervously and takes a bite. "Oh. This is really good."

"You shouldn't sound so surprised," I say, angry on Lenore's behalf.

"He doesn't know me," Lenore says. "It's all right to be surprised the first time. It is *he*, right? Not *they*?"

"Yeah, *he* is fine," he says.

"Are you Amanda Lash?" Callie asks suddenly.

We watch as Malcolm goes from pale to bright pink for a moment. He looks down at the table. He has a burger from the lunch line, some soggy fries. "Yes," he says finally.

Callie nods. "Cool. I like your looks. We all do."

She looks at me. I guess this is happening. Giving the asshole a second chance. Fine. Hopefully that means they'll give *me* one if everything about Steve comes out.

"Please don't tell anyone," Malcolm says. "Like…I know I

have a look, and people here"—he glances around—"I mean, I don't know. New town. Being a teen goth drag queen feels like something to ease people into. And even when people are cool about it, like...I wasn't going to tell you because people can be weird. They can ask for me to do their makeup or—"

"I do my own makeup," Callie says.

"And it looks fierce," Malcolm says, smiling. "It's just weird. I try to keep it...not secret, but like, it's not my opener."

"Well, sorry we blew your cover," Callie says. "But don't worry, no one else talks to us anyway."

"That's not true," Lenore says. "People talk to us. Steve has been texting me planning our date. He wants to go somewhere I'll like and didn't balk when I said the grave-yard! Maybe he's the one."

I literally bite my tongue to keep my face from moving.

"Well, point is, we won't tell," Callie says.

"Yeah," I say.

"Thanks." Malcolm smiles in a shy kind of way, not the way I'd expect a fashionable, semifamous goth to smile. Not the way I'd expect the guy who told me my store wasn't scary to smile. One corner of his mouth goes up, and he suddenly has dimples. I look down at my food, feeling very warm.

"So," he says. "Are you guys entering the Halloween decorating contest thing? I know it's kind of tacky and childish, but I thought—"

"It's not," I interrupt. "It's a lot of fun. We enter every year. We work together to decorate my store."

"Oh." He nods. "A store? The one you were working in?"

"Yeah," I say.

"Where you sell all the stuff other people use to decorate their homes?"

I nod, not sure why he's asking.

"So isn't that kind of unfair?"

I frown. His tone is surprised, but it's that slightly high voice again, the same one he used in the store.

"How is it unfair?" I ask flatly.

Lenore and Callie turn to him, too, faces neutral.

"Oh." He frowns slightly. "I just mean, other people have to pay for their decorations, and you have all that stuff there already, plus you have access to things I probably don't, right?"

"Lots of stores participate," Lenore says. Her voice sounds light, but there's a warning bell in it.

"Well, sure," Malcolm says, not hearing the bell, "that's cool. It's just, I mean, feels like you have an advantage."

None of us says anything. He shrugs and takes another bite of his sandwich—the one Lenore offered him.

"Anyway, I'm decorating my home. Or my yard, at least. I think it'll be cool."

"Well, then get ready to lose," Callie says, smirking. "We always win."

Malcolm frowns again, not nearly as cute as his smile, almost a sneer, and then shrugs. "We'll see. I'm guessing you've never had much competition before."

"Oho," Callie says, her competitive streak now less of a streak and more of a flashing neon sign. "It is on. No discussing what we're doing to the store when he's around, no secrets."

"I wouldn't steal anything from you," Malcolm says, smiling again now. "I won't need to."

Callie cackles. "All right, you talk a big game. We'll see on Halloween."

Lenore smiles. "Now you've done it. Callie loves a competition."

"How's the science fair project coming along, anyway?" I ask, eager to move the subject away from the Halloween contest. Everything Malcolm says just annoys me more.

"I've picked my topic, and it's a weird one," Callie says. "Antigravity makeup."

"What?" I ask. "Isn't makeup like…normally antigravity?"

"No," Callie says. "I mean, some. Gels at least have enough cohesion that they probably won't just float out of the jar, but I mean like fake blood, prosthetics, stuff like that. We talked all about it at space camp—how they need to run drills for when people are injured, but they have to do it without fake blood floating around. I make that stuff all the time, so I thought, maybe I can make some that works in space. There's so much the makeup has to get through, though—extreme heat, application issues, glue, storage, and it needs to be easy to clean up but still behave like real wounds. Like if the fake blood gets everywhere after a test and it's hard to clean, that's bad. Some fake bloods can even screw with equipment." She shakes her head. "It might sound silly, but I think if I really get into the science of it, it'll be weird enough to make sure Bryce doesn't stand a chance." She slams her fist into her palm.

"Well, I think that sounds wonderful," Lenore says. "But how will you test it?"

Callie nods. "That's the hard part...there are those airplanes that simulate antigrav, but it's not really the same, and also they're way too expensive. I think I'll just have to show all the science—the chemistry and physics of it all."

"I can be your model," Malcolm says. "I mean, if you want," he adds quickly. "I just mean, I've worn a lot of those prosthetics."

"So has Callie," I say. "And I thought you didn't want anyone knowing you were Amanda Lash?"

He shrugs, looking away.

"That's cool," Callie says. "I'll let you know if I need it. It might be good to have someone like actually putting it on while I talk for my judges' presentation. I was just going to put it on myself, but..."

"You're actually going to make it?" Lenore asks.

Callie grins. "That's the plan."

"Your own makeup SFX line," I say, smiling. "Step one for world domination."

"Step two, doomsday laser." Callie nods.

Lenore laughs. "Well, let us know if we can help."

"Yeah," I say. "I might be able to get you some ingredients through the store."

"And I get sent free makeup stuff by some companies," Malcolm says, "if you think that's good for testing stuff, or just comparing? I usually just sample stuff for TikTok, I have a lot left over."

I stare at Callie. She smiles at Malcolm. Why is she smiling? I get he's hot and knows how to do great makeup himself, but this guy has implied he does makeup better than her and now is offering her his rejects.

"Sure," she says. "I never say no to free stuff."

"Cool," Malcolm says, smiling.

I'm relieved when the bell rings—I really don't want to sit much longer with this guy who we're apparently giving a second chance to, which he is using to insult us and imply we're cheating in the Halloween competition.

"I have to talk to Mr. Stine about my project after school," I tell Lenore and Callie as we walk to our next classes. "I'll meet you at the store after?"

"Sure," Lenore says. "I need your help picking an outfit for my date!"

Callie laughs. "Like you ever need help picking an outfit."

Her date. My body feels like it's caving inward. I can't stand lying to her like this.

The rest of the day goes too fast and too slow all at once, questions and information seem to whiz by me in blurs, things I can't even see right, much less focus on, while the clock hands move slower than I've ever seen them. When school finally ends, though, I feel anxiety well up inside me, like a rose about to burst right out of my chest.

The woods are a quick bike ride away from school, but I wait until I know Callie and Lenore are gone before leaving. On the way out, I pass Malcolm, who's walking somewhere, but he doesn't wave or anything, so I don't wave, either.

The woods are part of Tarrytown Lakes Park, sort of behind the high school, surrounding the reservoir, but honestly, *woods* is a big promotion. There are trees, maple and beech and all the others, but not clustered together the way proper woods should be, not twisting over each other, branches leaving dark shadows. These are nice woods with bike trails and walking paths, and not too much privacy. But Steve and I have a spot, on the south side of the reservoir, in the middle of a peninsula jutting into the water, where there are a few large rocks and the trees are thick enough that it feels kind of private.

He's already there, waiting for me.

"What the hell are you doing?" I ask, getting off my bike. It's the first thing I can think of. But he just smiles and shakes his head and walks over to me, and suddenly his arms are around me, his face nestled in the crook of my neck.

"I missed you," he says.

For a moment, it feels familiar, his large hands, the muscles in his arms. Sometimes we would each put in one of my earbuds and dance, silent disco style, and this is like that again. I wait too long to pull free.

"Steve. We broke up. Or...ended it. Whatever. We're not doing this anymore."

"No, no." He takes my hand and pulls me back toward the rock, where he sits in the dirt. "I know. I'm sorry. But I really have missed you."

I sit down across from him. His face is that weird mix of happy and sad, guilt and joy. It makes me feel sorry for him, and also sort of powerful, that I can make him so happy. It makes me feel bad somehow, too. He shakes his head. It's kind of goth, actually, this feeling, this weird mix of pleasure and pain, and the way he seems so happy, thinking of the ashes of our relationship.

"Steve...," I say. "Is that why you asked out Lenore? To get me to meet with you?"

He looks up at that, smiling. "It's more than that."

I rock back slightly. "You like her?"

"What?" He looks confused. "I mean, not like that. I wish I were bi, trust me. I mean, she's cool, and the guys on the team thought I was so cool for asking her out. Brave. Said she's freaky. I don't know if my parents will like her, but maybe I just make sure they don't meet her, just like, know I'm dating a girl, y'know?"

The pity is draining into the dirt. "She's my friend."

"I know, that's why it's so smart, right? I date her, we all start hanging out. You and me, and your friends, right? I mean, that's why you broke up with me, right? You wanted me to meet your friends, hang out in public...you wanted all the stuff I was giving Jenny, right? You were jealous. Well, now I can give it to you."

I sigh, the pity creeping back in. "I wasn't jealous—"

"Gray," he interrupts, looking at me with this expression he's used on me before. He'd say my name and tilt his head down, bright blue eyes looking up at me, his thick eyebrows sort of heavy, and it would mean I was safe with him, I could tell him whatever. And I did.

"Fine, I was jealous, but it was more than just that."

"You didn't want to be my dirty secret..." He sighs, picks up a twig from the dirt, and pushes it in, a little tree. "I know. But this way you're less secret, right? Like people will know we're hanging out."

"But Lenore will think—"

"I'm going to keep it light with her, I promise. It'll be chaste and sweet. We'll hold hands, maybe a peck on the lips, but I'll tell her I'm saving myself or something…" He snorts a laugh. "I'll come up with something."

"It's not that—" I start.

"This summer, I was away at soccer camp, and there were all these guys around me, and some were pretty cute, and one was even out. And I like…wished I could have his life. No one hassled him. I think if my parents…" He shakes his head.

"I know," I say. "It sucks your parents are who they are."

"He was cute, too," he continues, not even hearing me. "I thought about maybe trying something, but…he wasn't you. I just kept thinking about you. So I thought about what would make you happy but keep me safe. I mean, that's fair, right? Wanting to stay safe?"

"Yeah, but—"

"I know I need to win you back. I watched that movie you always talked about, *Dark Crystal*, it was pretty cool. My mom said it was 'devilish,' but I liked it. And I listened to the music you told me about, too—I really liked Night Club."

My eyes snap up at this, searching his face for some hidden meaning. He's not my texter, right? There's no way… but if he's been thinking of me, making plans…

"Gray." He takes both my hands, squeezing tightly, almost pulling me onto him. "I'm so sorry. And I'm sorry my situation is so messed up and I can't just be cool and out like you deserve. But I miss you, and I know you care about me, so…this is what I'm going to do. To win you back. I love you."

I swallow. We never said that to each other. I felt it, I thought, a few times, working on our fake science project in my room, his fingers laced through mine as he would kiss the top of my head. Those were moments when I thought that he was someone who got me—opposites attracting, meant to be. He was sunny, and filled with plans, and always had a way to turn my cynical little remarks around. Shadows can only be cast by light, I told myself. He was the light that let me be a slice of darkness, cradled in his warmth.

But he couldn't see the bright side in being out. And I couldn't blame him, not with the stories he told me about his parents. But not blaming him didn't stop the light from turning colorless, cold.

He takes my silence as a positive and pulls me close for real now, like we're going to kiss, and for a moment the memories make me just want to fall back into him, live there again. But that place doesn't exist anymore. Maybe never did. I wrench my hands free.

"I'm seeing someone," I say. It falls out, a wall I'm trying to put up.

He makes a face I've never seen on him before, except once, at a game, when another player crashed into his chest and knocked him over. More than a flinch. Real pain. Then he shakes his head, smiles.

"Who?" he asks. "You were here all summer. There's no one to meet. Maybe that new guy."

"Malcolm. Not him."

"Then who?" He smiles like he's caught me in a lie. And the truth is, he has. I haven't *seen* anyone. Just words on a phone.

"Have you been texting me?" I ask. If it is him...I don't know how I'll feel. Furious? Heartbroken? I feel kind of nauseous considering it. Dizzy. It would be a betrayal, but also...I like the guy on the phone. And I liked Steve, and... what a mean thing to do, but his plans weren't always kind.

"No," he says, his face still. "You didn't block me?"

"From another number?"

He ignores me. "Who are you dating?"

I stand up, wipe dirt off my pants. It catches in the rips, falls down my legs, sticky against my skin.

"Don't do this to Lenore. She wants to fall in love. Don't hurt her."

"Relax." He stands up, too. "I won't hurt her."

I have my hands on the handlebars of my bike. "You already are. You're using her. That's cruel."

"I'll cancel the date," he says. "Just tell me who you're seeing. Or that you're lying because you're angry. I'm sorry, Gray."

I pedal away. I know the conversation isn't done, but I just can't be around him anymore—the guilt I feel, the bubbling happy memories—it's like a whirlpool. Was I wrong for ending it? I don't want to look back, but I do, and he's standing at the side of the trail, body slumped. But when he sees me he puffs up and shouts:

"I'm going to win you back!"

It makes something flutter in my chest, a breeze rattling the dried petals of a dead flower. This isn't fair. Being in this situation, and now my own heart betraying me. None of this is fair. I'm out of the park before I realize I'm crying.

5

Back at the store, Mom is behind the counter, Bauhaus blasting on the speaker. An old guy with a ponytail is looking at candles, and a middle-aged woman is perusing teas. Lenore sits with Callie on the sofa, and when I smile at them, the guilt bites into me.

"You okay?" Callie asks, looking up. "You look like that time we went on the Double Shot at Playland."

"Mr. Stine take back his okay on the project?" Lenore asks.

I shake my head. "No, we just had to go over all the requirements because I'm going to be filming most of it so early. I think I feel a little overwhelmed, is all," I lie. I hate this.

"Really?" Callie asks, suspicious.

"Maybe the texter went creepy," Lenore guesses.

I shake my head quickly, but then I think about Steve saying the same thing the texter did when he first messaged me. Maybe he is creepy.

"It's not that," I say. I open my mouth to tell them.

"Hey, kiddo," Mom calls. "I need to go do the books, so you're on." She waves us over. "Also hi, how was school?"

"This annoying guy sat with us at lunch."

"He wasn't so bad," Callie says.

"He liked my cooking," Lenore adds.

"New can be fun," Mom says, then messes up my hair. I pull back, trying to fix it. She smirks. "I'll be upstairs. Your mama is at the garden center."

"Okay." I take her place behind the counter, Lenore and Callie leaning on the customer side of it. I'm allowed to hang out and do homework when it's empty, but if there are customers in the store, I need to be behind the counter. "Oh, Mom," I say before she's through the door, "can you bring down my video camera? It's on the shelf to the left of the Crimson Peak poster. I need it for homework."

She raises an eyebrow. With Mama, that's usually a sign that she's curious, or doesn't believe me. With Mom it's because I have The Audacity.

"I'm working," I point out.

She rolls her eyes. "Fine, Your Majesty."

She goes upstairs and I turn to Callie and Lenore. "I have to start filming, talking about the decorations and stuff we're going to do. You're okay with me filming all of it, right?"

"Yeah, and we have to start planning now," Callie says. "Malcolm could be competition. It's good to finally have some, but it means we have to up our game."

"I thought you said he wasn't so bad," I say to her.

"He's not. I mean...jury's out on him overall, but today he was cool. Doesn't mean I'm not gonna kick his ass decorating-wise."

Lenore smirks. "This is the woman who wants to make out with her competition in the science fair. Have you seen Bryce since school started?"

"Oh, sure." Callie grins. "He asked me out."

"Really?" Lenore clasps her hands excitedly.

"I said maybe."

Lenore drops her hands with a sigh. "Only maybe?"

"Not until after I beat him in the science fair."

Mom reappears, hands me the camera, and kisses the top of my head. "Don't film customers." And then she's gone again.

I check the viewfinder. It's easier to look at Lenore on a screen, like she's a character, not a friend who I'm betraying. I'll deal with that later, I remind myself.

"So," I tell them, filming. "We already picked out a concept. Two hearts, separated, and when they meet, the end of the world. Beautiful darkness consuming everything out of love." It catches slightly when I say it and I think about Steve, about him liking Night Club, and about my texter. I don't like how linked the two are in my mind now.

"Right," Lenore says to the camera. "I'm going to make hearts. Poured rubber, I figure."

"I want to watch you do that, it might help with my prosthetic research," Callie says, then turns to the camera. "And I'm going to make the pump, so we need to design them together, make sure everything fits right. Gray, you said you wanted the heartbeats to be slightly out of pace with each other?"

"Yeah, I want them to sound irregular together, not too rhythmic, like footsteps running toward something."

"I like that."

"So beyond the showpiece," Lenore says, "what have you thought of?"

I haven't. I came up with the idea because of me and my texter, but then Steve asked out Lenore and it's been a lot. Who can be creative when all you're thinking about is how it feels like everything is pushing in on you?

"I'm not sure," I say. "I know I want people to have to walk between them, and this sense of them getting closer, impending doom..."

"How about stained glass?" Lenore says. "I learned how over the summer. Stained-glass windows, backlit, showing this story?"

"Oooooh, yes," Callie says. "I can make the lights flicker and stuff, like a storm, too."

"Yes," I say, feeling inspired, the image of it stretching out. "We make the opening area feel like a cathedral, this heart up above you—or no, let's get it closer, on an altar maybe—beating, stained glass telling you what it is, how doomed we are, and then you journey out...into the rain and realize that the other heart, once thought lost, is close, and getting closer."

"A cathedral, in that little space?" Callie asks.

"That will be difficult," Lenore says.

"Forced perspective, maybe," Callie says, sounding uncertain.

"I could try to make the windows work with that," Lenore says, not sounding too sure. "It's hard to get them really small, though. And it would need to be so precise."

"We could use 3D mapping," Callie says. "I'll have

to"—she frowns slightly—"ask Bryce for help, though, since 3D mapping is his thing. He's an expert." Lenore and I smile. Callie glares.

"You said we had real competition this year," I remind her. "So if he can help us..."

"And I bet he'd love to help," Lenore says.

"Shut up." Callie sighs, but she's trying to hide a smile, and not doing it well. "But fine. It could work. We use foam blocks for the interior, the mapping will let us visualize how to cut and assemble them, and how to do the stained glass...it could be really cool."

We keep chatting, pausing as I ring up the guy's candle and the woman's tea. A few more customers come in and shop as we figure out a plan. Cathedral, then rain in the woods outside. Stained glass for the store windows, too. I show them the stuff from the back room and we try to figure out how to use it—some set up outside, or relics on a shelf in the cathedral. It is still a store, so having stuff people can buy will make my parents happy.

By the time they leave I feel really good about the haunted house design...if not about anything else. But it took my mind off everything for a while. And it distracted them from my apparently obvious distress. I'm so angry at Steve for doing this to me.

I sell a bunch of premade spell kits and candles to college kids. Then, while it's empty I film the whole shop, inside and out, to make sure I have footage for the film.

I do my homework and eat dinner with my parents, sometimes texting Callie and Lenore about haunted house stuff. My stranger doesn't text me, and I don't text him.

His silence makes me even more sure he's Steve, that the trick is played out now that we've talked. But also, then why say he'll win me back? I can't keep my thoughts settled. I feel miserable, and not in the fun, pining way. Goth misery is supposed to be beautiful, sad, aching...this is just nausea. Any choice I make is bad, and every moment I don't make a choice is bad, too.

It's not until I've turned out the lights and gone to sleep, the whole house quiet, that my phone buzzes with a message.

Future Sire:
You awake?

If it is Steve, is this more of a trick? And if it isn't... then I should answer.

Gray:
Falling asleep

Future Sire:
Ok well just wanted to say thank you for the advice

Future Sire:
I think I made some friends

Gray:
That's cool

Future Sire:
They seem cool

Future Sire:
Night Club listeners, probably

I frown. Night Club again. Is this Steve telling me it's him? I don't say anything.

> **Future Sire:**
> Oh and my parents showed me these cool plants actually?
>
> **Future Sire:**
> So... I don't know
>
> **Future Sire:**
> It was cool and I wanted to tell you

I stare at the phone, not sure what to think. I want to hug him. I don't want him to be Steve. I don't answer.

> **Future Sire:**
> Talk tomorrow

I put the phone down. I was...kind of rude. It's just impossible to not think he could be Steve, and I...I don't want that to be true. A lot of goths love Night Club. I *did* tell Steve to listen to them. I sigh and get out of bed. It's late, but my brain is knotting itself into spiderwebs. I need to shake it loose before bed. If that's possible.

I'm surprised to find Mom in the living room, watching a David Bowie music video, earbuds in. When she sees me she takes out an earbud.

"You okay, kid?"

"Just can't sleep," I say. "I was getting a glass of water."

She pats the sofa next to her, and I sit down.

"I can't sleep, either," she says. "It happens."

"Yeah." I cross my arms.

"Wanna talk about it?" She tilts her head.

"What?"

"Something has been bothering you since yesterday. Is it school? A teacher, other student?"

"No," I say quickly. "Well, not like that..." I sigh, and my arms drop. I can't keep going like this. Everyone can tell, and it's making me feel trapped. "It's..." I need to get this out of me. If I hold it in anymore I think I'll burst. "You can't tell anyone."

"I'm going to tell your mama," she says. "Unless it's about her. Is it about her?"

"No...that's okay. I should have told her yesterday. I just feel...this is someone else's secret. So I shouldn't be telling anyone."

"Except it's hurting you to keep it," Mom says, leaning forward. "I promise we won't tell."

"There's this guy at school, Steve. We worked on a science project last year, you remember him?"

"Tall, blond, kinda a jock?"

"Yeah," I sigh. "It wasn't a science project...we were kind of...a thing." I feel myself blushing and hope the dim light from the TV hides it. "But he's closeted. His family is super religious and he can't be out, so it was secret."

"That's always rough," Mom says. "And not to change the subject, but when you mean a thing, you mean you were having sex?"

"Mom," I sigh.

"I just need you to promise me you were being safe."

"Yes," I say quickly. "That's not what this is about."

"Okay, just being a mom. Go on."

"So...he was worried that not dating girls was making his friends and his parents suspicious. So he...started dating this girl. While still seeing me. Which I didn't love. So I ended it."

"Oooof," Mom says. "I'm sorry, kid. That was not kind of him."

"That's not even the issue. It sucked, but I get why he was scared. And I thought he got why I didn't want to see him under those circumstances. But then, at the start of this year...he asked out Lenore."

I look up at her, seeing if she gets it, and she leans back, shaking her head. "Teenagers really love tormenting each other, don't they?"

"I can't tell her without outing him. And she wants to find a boyfriend who isn't Cody, and I want that for her, but Steve says he only asked her out for an excuse to hang out with me, so..." I put my face in my hands, trying to hide that I'm starting to cry again. "What do I do?"

Mom rubs my back. "Well, first off, you realize this isn't your fault. This is Steve, who sounds kind of messed up. Except about liking you. That's the only good thing I'm seeing."

"He was nice when we were together."

"I'm sure. But what he's doing is unfair to you, and unfair to Lenore. And he's telling you he's putting you in this situation for you, so he's making you feel like the position he's putting you in is somehow your fault. It isn't.

These are all his own choices. And it sucks that he can't come out. But that doesn't mean he gets to do this to other people."

I nod. "Yeah, I know." It sounds weak, though. I mean, I do know it. It makes sense as Mom says it. But it still feels like maybe all this could be fixed if I had just done something different. If I'd never hooked up with him, maybe.

"Well, you work on believing it. I can explain how to fix the rest of it."

I look up, staring at her. "What?"

"Tell Lenore that Steve has said homophobic stuff to you. She won't want to date him."

"But what if he finds out?"

"Then tell him that's the price he pays for putting you in that situation. You didn't out him—you didn't put him in danger from his parents. If anything, they'll probably approve of him more. Yeah, some kids might think less of him, but...he's left you no other option. You can't let him hurt your friend. You can't out him. So you come up with something else."

"I lie." I lean back. Mom pulls her hand away, and I stare up at the ceiling. It flashes with colors from the TV, pale and watery.

"I know, it sucks. Mama would probably disapprove, tell you to tell Lenore everything or maybe not do anything. But this is tearing you up, clearly, and if you felt like you could tell Lenore the truth, you would have done it already. This is the alternative. A lie to cover another lie. Not something I'd recommend in most circumstances, to be clear, but this is a unique one. And one day, when he's out, you can be honest, and apologize and explain why you lied, and Lenore, being your friend, I think will understand. And probably thank you. Goddess, that poor girl has uncannily bad taste in men."

I turn it over in my mind. It's not exactly the simple, right thing to do. It's a not great thing among the really bad options. But it would probably work.

I lean over and hug Mom, tucking my head under her chin. She squeezes me back tightly.

"Thanks," I say softly.

"No problem, just being a mom." She pauses. "Which also means I'm going to have to tell you to schedule an appointment with Dr. Chang so he can give you a full STD panel and a prescription for PrEP."

I half sigh, half laugh. "Mom."

"Just, now that you're sexually active."

"Well, I'm not active now."

"You know what I mean. I'm not saying don't have sex. If you think you're ready, adult enough for that, then that's on you. But part of being an adult is being smart and careful. So condoms, PrEP, testing. Just promise me that and I'll never talk to you about this again."

"I promise," I say quickly. "Just make this stop."

She laughs. "Okay. Now, go get your water and go to bed. It's late, you have school."

I squeeze her again before standing. "Thanks." And then I realize it. "Are you okay? Why are you up?"

She smiles. "I'm good. Just the insomnia of old age. Your mama is so lucky. She just lies down, folds her arms over her chest like a corpse, and she's out."

"That's usually what I do, too."

"Well, I gotta exhaust my brain with music videos and books. Consider yourself lucky. Now go to sleep."

"Thanks, Mom. Good night."

"Good night, kid."

I feel better when I wake up. My chest doesn't feel tight with the anxiety of no good choices. I know Mom's idea is the best one I have, even if it's not perfect. Nothing here is perfect, but this is what Steve has sort of forced me to do.

So I feel pretty good as I get dressed, even doing a full face: bloodless foundation, smeared black eyeliner, gunmetal lips. It's warm, so I put on a black tank top that ends just below my belly button and just above the trail of hair below it, and a black lace button-down, plus some loose black pants covered in zippers. I put some pins on the button-down, even if they pull at the lace, and look at myself in the mirror. It's not my best look, but it's a step back up from what I've been doing. A step closer to feeling like me. Which is good, because I need to be me if I'm going to fix stuff today.

Every day our schedules are different, and today I don't have film or English before lunch, so my plan is to tell Lenore at lunch, but by the time I sit down, Malcolm is already there. Lenore and Callie are talking to him like this is normal, so I guess...we're friends with him now? I still think he's a snob, and not in the fun way, but maybe that can be okay as long as he's not a snob about us anymore. And seeing as we're the only ones talking to him, he should know that.

I don't love it, but…

"Hi," Malcolm says as I sit down. "I like your outfit."

Okay, maybe he's not so bad. "Thanks," I say. "We all look amazing. It's a requirement at this table."

We do look pretty good today. Callie is in a red vest and gray button-down, with red eye shadow on one side, white on the other, gold blush, contouring galore, and a little star drawn on her cheek. Lenore is in a vintage schoolgirl pinafore over a white button-down, which looks like windowpane check until you look closely and realize the stripes are snakes eating their own tails. And Malcolm—well, yeah, he looks good, in a chunky black-and-white-striped mohair sweater, oversized enough that he's just wearing black tights and knee-high boots. He's done makeup today, too, though not a full Amanda Lash look, with eyeliner and black glittery eyeshadow that makes his amber eyes pop.

"I'll keep that in mind," he says, smiling. "Thanks for letting me sit with you again."

"I brought enough treats for you today, too," Lenore says, taking out what looks like dried millipedes, but which she explains are chocolate with almonds.

"Oh." He shakes his head. "That's all right."

Lenore raises an eyebrow, looking a little offended.

"Sure," she says simply. Callie and I dig in, exchanging looks. Maybe we don't like this guy. He just keeps blowing his chances.

Everyone is quiet for a moment.

"Sorry," Malcolm says suddenly. "I…get sort of nervous and things don't come out right. I'm allergic to almonds is all. I didn't mean to sound like"—he shakes his head—"I'm sorry. It's a nervous thing. I'm new. I'm nervous."

Lenore laughs suddenly. "That's all? All right, no more almonds at lunch. Is it bad that they're in front of you?"

"No, it's only if I eat them, it's not so bad that someone eating them next to me will make my throat close up or anything."

"Any other allergies?" Lenore asks. "For real this time?"

"Just almonds. It kind of sucks, no almond milk, no marzipan. So if you want to keep making stuff with it, don't worry about me, I don't want to be a bother."

Lenore pats his hand. "Relax. Callie can't do raspberries. Do you know how good raspberries are for bloody-looking food? Almonds are nothing. I'll figure it out."

"Thanks," Malcolm says, smiling a little. I wait for him to apologize for how he was in the store, too. If he gets condescending and rude when he's nervous, that would make sense. I look at him expectantly, but he meets my eye for a moment, then turns away and doesn't say anything. I pop a millipede into my mouth and bite down. Well, he doesn't get an invitation to the real friend group—the one that hangs out at my very frightening family store—until he apologizes. Probably not fancy and expensive enough for his tastes, anyway.

But I guess I'll have to learn how to tolerate him at lunch. I know if I said anything Callie and Lenore would tell me I was overreacting. And besides, I have more important stuff to tell them.

We talk about music and movies for the rest of lunch. Malcom has good taste: Creux Lies, Drab Majesty, Night

Club, Virgin X, even She Past Away. And he saw *Unseelie* over the summer and liked it. But also as we talk, it's clear how much disdain he has for the town. He misses the city, he misses the life there, the clubs, the fun. What is there to do here? We've all said that, too—Sleepy Hollow is, well, sleepy—but it's different when you live here. The way he says it, an outsider, just makes me feel small. It reminds me of the way he looked around Ceremony, like it was such a disappointment. And Ceremony is me. Why is he acting like he likes us when he was so rude about the store? It feels like liking us is just fake now, or even some secret joke, like his compliments are secretly insults, like he'll go home and text his city friends how trashy we all were.

Once again, lunch does nothing to make me like him.

On the way to English, I get Lenore alone by our lockers. "So, I need to tell you something."

"You don't like Malcolm? That's pretty obvious."

"What?" I shake my head quickly. I didn't expect to be talking about this, and it's like a splash of cold water. "No. But why is it obvious?"

"The glare you keep giving him at lunch."

I roll my eyes. "I'm not glaring."

She smirks. "Sure. You're just annoyed a cute boy is finally sitting at our table when you have your online guy. You could have asked Malcolm to homecoming."

"I wouldn't do that even if I didn't have my texter," I say. "He was so rude about the store."

She nods. "I know. Like, does he actually like us, or is he just sitting with us because we're the closest to acceptable to him? I feel like he's so annoyed about being here at all, and we're part of that...but we'll see. It's just lunch. Plus gives me one more taste-tester." She smiles, sinister.

"Yeah," I say, feeling a sort of swell of pleasure that we're on the same page. "But that's not what I wanted to talk about. It's Steve."

She looks up. "Don't like him, either?"

"I wasn't sure if I should say anything," I say, weighing the lie in my mouth. But it's the only way, right? "But last year, he sort of led some douchebags at a party in doing the"—I sigh—"the fag cough near me? Y'know, where they cough, but they're saying *fag*?"

She frowns. "Why didn't you tell me the moment he asked me out?"

"I just know it's important to you that you find a guy who isn't Cody, and I felt guilty that I might be ruining that."

"Gray, no." She looks annoyed, genuinely annoyed. "I would never date a guy who would go after my friend like that." She takes out her phone and types rapidly. "There. Date canceled. And with plenty of time to find a new one."

"Really?" I ask. "That simple?"

"It's not like I was in love with him," she says as we start walking to class. "I barely know him. Not being Cody isn't exactly a high bar, but it's all I really know about him."

"I'm sorry," I say. "For not telling you." Those words are heavier, they're the truth, and they taste so sharp I tear up saying them.

She hugs my waist as we walk. "It's fine. I'm glad you're so eager for me to find love! Especially now that you have your anonymous murderer. I can't die alone, you know. I want to die like you will—being stabbed to death by the stranger you love."

"I don't love him," I say quickly.

"Mmmmm." She gives me some knowing side-eye. "Well, I'm still going to homecoming. I started on a dress. So you and Callie will have to come with me."

"Callie hates homecoming. But I'll go."

"Maybe we can get her to go with Bryce."

"She said not until after she beats him in the science fair."

Lenore throws a hand up in the air. "That's not for ages! Why wait for love?"

In class, she leans over and writes in my notebook, skulls doodled all around it: *Why wait for love?*

6

In science, Steve fans out his pages and isn't even subtle about trying to make eye contact with me, his expression practically shouting *What the hell?* I sigh. He's probably terrified, and for a moment, I think about letting him stay that way as payback, but I nod slightly. At least I can tell him I didn't out him.

Science goes too slowly, especially as I keep hearing Steve's foot tapping on the floor. Even the teacher tells him to stop. But then I have history and film, and having told Lenore the newer, better lie, I'm totally focused on the classes, not stressing out anymore.

After school, Malcolm is standing with Callie and Lenore at our meeting place. Surely he won't head over to my sad little store with us? I can't imagine he'd deign.

"Hey," Callie says. "Malcolm was just telling me some of his favorite fake blood brands, for the science fair."

"Cool," I say, nodding.

Malcolm nods back, but for a moment, we're all in awkward silence.

"I should head home," Malcolm says. "I have work to do on my haunted house."

"Why bother when we're going to kick your ass?" Callie asks, smiling.

Malcolm laughs nervously. "That's what you think, but you've never dealt with me before." His voice gets steadier as he goes on, cockier, but not in a fun trash-talking way. In a genuinely condescending way. He forces a laugh, maybe to cover that, and walks away.

"Was that more of his nervous thing?" I ask, skeptical.

"Should we invite him to the store?" Callie asks.

I glare. "The store he's too good for? I think not."

"I mean maybe he was just nervous when he was in there," Callie says. "He seems cool."

"Then he should apologize. He wasn't cool when he first met us. And besides, we're talking about our haunted house there, right? Can't give it away."

She tilts her head, considering. "True."

"What's true?" Lenore asks, walking up to us.

"Callie wants to invite Malcolm to hang out at the store." It comes out more annoyed than I mean it to.

"Oh." Lenore scrunches her face like she's smelled something burning in her kitchen. "I don't think we're there yet. I can't tell if he really likes us or is just settling, you know?"

Callie shrugs. "If you say so. I like him, though."

"We'll see," Lenore says.

"I have to go run one errand," I say to them, grabbing my bike from the rack out front. "Meet you at the store?"

"Sure," Callie says. "What do you have to do?"

I shake my head. "Something...stupid. Ex stuff."

"Ah," Lenore says, exchanging a look with Callie that I can't quite interpret. "Abandoning your online stranger for a more familiar bad choice? That's my whole romantic life thus far."

I feel a pang of guilt, like I'm the one who took away her chance at something new.

"Just returning a thing," I say.

"Okay," Callie says. "See you in a bit."

I wave goodbye as I pedal off. So Callie actually does like Malcolm. That annoys me. Like, I-want-to-shake-out-my-hands-and-scream-a-little annoys me. Maybe he's really only a snob when he's nervous. But he was rude and hasn't apologized and I don't like him just sitting with us like we're props.

I get to the woods first this time. When Steve walks up, his back is hunched like his backpack is heavy, baseball cap shadowing his eyes. It's a bright day, and even surrounded by the trees, there's so much light it feels more exposed here than other days.

Closer, I can see he's tearing up.

"Did you tell her?" he asks, his voice a sharp whisper.

"No," I say, hands up, like I'm trying to calm down an animal. "I told her you teased me for being gay once. She doesn't want to date you, you're not outed. Everyone is happy."

His face contorts with a bunch of emotions I can only half read: relief, frustration, rage, sadness. "I'm not happy.

I wanted to do this so we could spend time together, and then we could..."

"Steve," I say, trying not to sound too pitying. "I told you, I'm seeing someone."

"Who? Someone secret, like me?"

I pause. I know he'll consider it a joke if he knows. "He's not from around here."

"Long-distance?" He half laughs. "You'd do that over me?" He folds inward, leaning against the rock, crouching slightly, and I suddenly want to go and give him a hand, pull him up. But I know if I do that, he'll kiss my wrist, he'll take it as a sign.

"Steve...I can't. I can't be with you if you're dating girls for appearances."

"But you'd be with me otherwise?" he asks quickly. "The other guy is fake?"

"I..." I lock eyes with him. "No. Unless it's secretly you pretending to be some cool goth guy to win me back."

"What?" He looks confused as he tries to put that together. I said too much. His eyes go wide as he figures it out. "You don't even know him!" He shakes his head and then laughs. He always had a good laugh, low and sexy. "What, some torso on Grindr stole your heart?"

"No, it's not like that, he's—"

"He's someone you don't even know!" He throws his hands up. "You don't even know what he looks like. He could be some grandpa, or like a killer—" He freezes. "Those guys that have gone missing."

"He's not a killer," I say quickly.

"You don't know that," Steve says, stepping forward, looking around, suddenly protective. His eyes fall back on my face and for a moment I think he's going to reach up and cradle my cheek. "You don't know anything about this guy. You thought he could be me! He could be anyone, Gray. You have to stop talking to him. Please, Gray, don't do anything stupid just because I..." His hands rise and fall for a moment, emotions puppeting him.

I turn away and grab my bike. "Steve, just...leave me alone, okay?"

He shakes his head. "I don't understand why you can't just wait a little. I'll be out in a few years. I have a plan, remember? The house I designed for us. Gothic arches and gargoyles."

I do remember. I didn't trash any of the sketches he did of it, either. They're tucked in the back of a drawer in my room. One gargoyle was so funny-looking that just thinking about it makes me laugh. Then I think of my stranger—not Steve, now. It's true, he could be a killer or a million other things. Something awful or ugly. But he's the one who told me—hope is goth.

"Just wait," Steve says again as I get on my bike. "Can't that be enough for now?"

I shake my head, though I feel terrible doing it. "I have to hope for something better." And then I ride away.

I ride fast so that the wind cuts at me, peels back my hair. It's not really cold enough to be sharp yet, but I try. I feel angry. Sad. And I know that if I can just make the air hurt a little on my face, then I'll feel a little better. I didn't want to do that. I didn't want to hurt him—never even wanted to end it last year, and thinking about that makes guilt churn in my stomach. Everything would have been good if not for his parents, or even his stupid idea to date girls. Where would we be then?

Or maybe it would have ended anyway. So much of what we had was just physical. We talked, we laughed, but it was always on the way to sex, or after it. His body, our bodies...I miss that. I hate that I miss it, but I do. And then my stranger, who has no body at all, as far as I'm concerned. He'd be perfect if he did. For a moment, feeling my legs burn as I pedal, I wish the stranger *were* Steve. I wish I could have it all together as one.

That's stupid. I've made my choice, right? Maybe that was stupid, too, though. Maybe the stranger is a killer, or some old guy in a basement. But he doesn't make me feel confused and angry the way Steve did. He doesn't make me lie to my friends, and hurt them. So that's got to be something better, right? Even if it turns out it is all a lie.

Hope is goth, right? Well, I hope it's not all a lie.

When I pull up to the store I almost ride past it. I want to keep going, to make my whole body ache and burn. But Callie and Lenore are inside and I'm supposed to work there for an hour after school unless I tell my moms otherwise. Instead I wipe my eyes, put my bike in the backyard, and then go into the store.

Mama is working the register and she cocks an eyebrow at me, but not with the sly smile she usually uses as accompaniment. "Everything all right, honey?"

"Yeah," I lie, my eyes darting to Callie and Lenore. Mama nods like she understands and floats out from behind the register in a black cardigan over a long black dress. "Well, the store is yours. I'll be upstairs working on online orders if you need anything. I'm going to make the farfalle with chickpeas for dinner. Unless you'd prefer something else?"

I shake my head. Letting me pick dinner used to be a way of helping me shake off a bad day when I was younger, but now it doesn't have the same effect. Controlling what I eat doesn't make me feel like I can control anything else in life. "That sounds great."

I take my seat behind the register and Mama waves goodbye to Callie and Lenore, who are sprawled across the velvet sofa. There are a few customers, all middle-aged women, passing candles around to smell.

"How'd the ex stuff go?" Callie asks from the sofa. "You look unhappy."

I sigh. "Not, like, great. But it's over." I hope it is, anyway. "So it's done."

"If you told us who he is, we could just kill him," Lenore offers, walking over to the counter. "I know ways to do it without getting caught."

I smile. "If it comes to that, you know I'll ask. But for now...no. I can't kill every asshole in the world. Then there'd just be the three of us left."

"Maybe four," Callie says, joining us at the counter. "Malcolm doesn't seem so bad, really, right? I mean he's got great style, he's helping me out with makeup stuff."

"He's lonely and latching onto us 'cause we haven't said no," I say.

"You're being too hard on him," Callie says. "We were

talking, and maybe we invite him to the shop, like as a test run, see if he apologizes for last time."

"What?" I ask, too loudly. The women smelling candles look over and I shoot them a fake smile. I'm still raw from Steve and now they want to invite Malcolm into my home to insult it again?

"As, like, a test," Lenore says quickly.

I shake my head. "Maybe after he apologizes for insulting it the first time."

"Just tell him it bugged you," Callie says. "Talk to him at lunch tomorrow."

I fold my arms. "Nope, not my job to make him apologize. He could have said something today."

Lenore and Callie exchange a look, but Callie finally nods. "Okay, but I still think he's cool. So give him a chance at school at least?"

The women approach the counter, each holding a large two-wick candle. Callie and Lenore step aside so I can ring them up, telling them what each candle scent is good for promoting—calm, focus, romance—as I wrap them in black tissue paper and put them in black paper bags. Telling a middle-aged woman she's buying a sex candle is always mortifying, but Mom and Mama taught me to do it this way, so I do, and only cringe a little on the inside. After they've thanked me and left, Callie and Lenore turn back to me, like we were in the middle of a conversation. But we weren't. It was over.

"What?" I ask.

They look at each other again, and Callie looks ready to say something, but Lenore speaks first.

"You can't force it," she tells Callie. "We'll talk at lunch. We'll see if he wants to be our friend or just *anyone's* friend. Friendships don't just happen overnight."

"Sometimes they do," Callie says. "Gray and I knew you were meant to be our friend pretty quickly." That's true. Lenore walked into school in the seventh grade, after moving here with her mom after the divorce. She brought cookies shaped like anatomical hearts for everyone in each of her classes. We all had history together. We were the only ones who ate the cookies. They were amazing to look at and better tasting, and we told her so, and invited her to eat lunch with us. She just slipped into our lives like we'd been waiting for her.

"I'm special," Lenore says with a shrug, her hair falling momentarily over an eye. "Once-in-a-lifetime."

"Well...I hope Malcolm is almost as special, then," Callie says. She turns to me. "I think he could be."

"Unlikely."

Callie rolls her eyes.

"Let's talk about the stained-glass design for the house," Lenore offers. "You said you could map out the forced perspective with a computer program?"

"Yeah," Callie says, going back to the sofa to grab her laptop from her backpack. "Bryce and I started it last night and I think it'll work."

"What else did you start?" Lenore asks, smiling sweetly.

"We just can't go too crazy with the design," Callie continues, ignoring her. "Otherwise the glass pieces will get too small. So time to decide exactly what each window should show."

We talk through the storyline on the windows for a while, Malcolm thankfully forgotten. It's nice, actually, working on the haunted house, the story, the decorations. It's going to be amazing, and it just consumes my brain. Except, when Lenore and Callie go home for dinner and I close up the shop, everything comes flooding back in. Steve kissing my wrist, crying, wanting to be with me. My stranger, who I don't know. Not even what he looks like. I like talking to him, flirting, but seeing Steve today has made me remember that while it's nice to hope for the best, you have to be prepared for the worst. What is the worst thing the stranger could be, though? An actual murderer, I guess. A serial killer targeting gay teens, just like Callie is afraid of—even if I know it's just Poly Perry living out his fantasies.

Upstairs, Mama and Mom are cooking, arguing over spices. I grab a can of Coke Zero from the fridge and a bowl and head up to my room, telling them I have homework, even though they know what I'm doing.

Scrying with Coke is a trick Mom taught me. Mama uses a black mirror, this beautiful slice of polished onyx that hangs on the wall in the living room. Mom uses it sometimes, but she doesn't like scrying much. Mama's always been more of the fortune teller, curious about advice from the universe. Mom just barges through. I don't know which of them I'm more like, but right now I want some guidance. I just feel like every choice I make is a bad one, and I want to know if that's true, or why, or...something.

Magick can be fancy and complicated, tarot cards on silk fabric, gleaming athames, polished onyx. But it can also be soda in a bowl.

In my bedroom I lock the door and find the spot on my floor where none of the lights shine directly on me. Then I lie down, pop the Coke, and pour it into the bowl. It fizzes, a noise I've always liked, like insects or a hissing snake. The bowl fills up, not quite to the brim, and bubbles for a few moments before settling into a flat black surface. Some people scry with crystal balls, or glass, or just plain mirrors. The idea is to stare into something that has depth, not a full reflection, but something you can lose yourself in staring at. Mama says a nice view will do, but it's easier with something like this, a bowl of dark liquid, that faint fizz still coming from it, the smell, sweet and chemical.

I stare into it and try to focus just on the surface. The way I've angled it, it doesn't reflect much. A faint hint of my face, but mostly dark, liquid, an endless void. I try to lose myself in that, unfocus my eyes so the hint of reflection is gone, my room is gone, even the bowl is gone, and it's just me, and the smell and the hiss and the black.

Eventually, it feels like I'm swimming in it. And this is when I know I can ask what I want, and hopefully some god or spirit will answer. But what's my question exactly?—I didn't work that out. I try to just let everything I'm feeling pour out of me.

"What am I doing wrong?" is what I hear my voice say.

It's not quite what I meant to ask, and hearing it just makes me feel silly. Am I doing anything wrong? I'm not sure if that question comes from my head or from the universe. I'm trying to do my best, right? So why does it always feel like nothing is quite right?

What would right feel like? Again, I'm not sure if the

question comes from me or somewhere else. And I don't know the answer. I think about my moms, the way they hold hands, cuddle on the sofa. I'm not sure I've ever seen them fight. They seem to have things figured out. They're also a lot older than me, though. Maybe there's time to get there. And in the meanwhile it's okay to just try my best to be—not optimistic, but...to see all the things I've done right. Maybe I can find that in my life. The choices I've made aren't great: everything with Steve, and talking to a stranger online isn't known to be a good idea. But I stopped Lenore from getting hurt. That's got to mean something. And maybe the stranger isn't a serial killer, right? What's wrong with a little hope?

I smirk and the surface ripples. Hope. Not because I think everything is going to turn out all right in the end, but because I know that even if things go badly, there's beauty in that. That's true. I hate where I am with Steve now, but it was really nice for a while. Terrible and wonderful all at once. And maybe today was like an echo of that, or like a reminder that the terrible was overwhelming the wonderful now, and there needed to be more balance. Is that hope? Or just something I've lost?

I don't know, and maybe the stranger will be terrible, too, but in the meanwhile, before he stabs me and buries my body somewhere, in the meanwhile, I really like talking to him. Even if everything he is is a lie, I can still find beauty in that lie for now, right? That's what goth hope is?

My phone buzzes and it's like my body flies backward out of the darkness and I'm back in my room staring at a bowl of Coke. I feel better, I think. My life isn't a disaster, exactly—or if it is, it's a beautiful one. I just have to remember to see the beauty.

I take my phone out of my pocket, sitting up and leaning against the side of the bed.

Future Sire:
Do you know what a corn cockle is?

> **Gray:**
> Is this a sex thing?

Future Sire:
😨 😂 it's a flower

> **Gray:**
> Your parents want to plant corn cockles?

Future Sire:
They do. Or maybe. They asked me what I thought of them.

> **Gray:**
> Do you like them?

Future Sire:
They're okay I guess

Future Sire:
Little flowers in pink or white from what I looked up

Future Sire:
I guess when they said big flower garden I was expecting something more dramatic though

> **Gray:**
> So counter them

> **Gray:**
> Find something big and
> dramatic

Future Sire:
I do like dahlias

Future Sire:
Some come in this bloodred color

I google *bloodred dahlia* and am thrilled by what I see.

> **Gray:**
> Yeah plant those

Future Sire:
😄 maybe I can talk my parents into
them

> **Gray:**
> You can

> **Gray:**
> And after that a poison garden

Future Sire:
🫠 I'll start with the dahlias

Future Sire:
Oh and I think I made some friends!

Future Sire:
And it's because of you

Future Sire:
So thank you

I smile and bring the bowl of Coke to my lips, drinking it.

> **Gray:**
> It's not because of me you're awesome

Future Sire:
There's one who's a musician from my English class

Future Sire:
She seems cool

Future Sire:
And I sat with people at lunch

Future Sire:
And I think they were cool with it

Future Sire:
I hope. I'll be eating lunch alone otherwise

> **Gray:**
> No you won't

Future Sire:
How do you know?

> **Gray:**
> Because you're friendlier than you think. You talk to me all the time and I'm a stranger you met through a random text

Future Sire:
Yeah but only because it's not in person

Gray:
Yeah and that makes it feel easier but actually it's a lot scarier if you think about it

Gray:
I could really be a serial killer or something

Future Sire:
You're not

Gray:
That's what you think

Future Sire:
Well then I deserve to get murdered I guess

Gray:
Ha. I was just thinking something similar

Future Sire:
This is sort of insane when you think about it

Gray:
My friends are making me promise to be nearby and in public if we ever meet

Future Sire:
We're just going to FaceTime. can't stab you through the phone, you're safe

I want to ask him where he is, but I know he won't say, so I just stare at the phone and think about him being close by. It would make Callie a lot more suspicious. Might even make me worry that Poly Perry was not having the time of his life. But if my texter is an actual teen boy... he can't be Steve. Not after today. I'm almost sure.

He could be Malcolm. Similar interests, new kid in town. But not similar vibes at all. Malcolm is a snob. My stranger is sweet and welcoming. Plus if he were Amanda Lash I'd know. He would have mentioned being a semi-famous goth drag queen by now, right? That's not something you keep from someone you're doing whatever we're doing with.

It's a big coast. Even eliminating places where the seasons don't change and people don't have Halloween decorating contests, there's still Massachusetts, Vermont, New Hampshire, Maine, Connecticut...

Connecticut isn't so far. I smile. It would be really cool if he were in Connecticut. Lots of people move from New York to Connecticut for lawns.

He could even just be in another part of Westchester. Rye has a Halloween decorating contest.

> **Gray:**
> Well I will hope you're kind of close I won't pry yet
>
> **Future Sire:**
> Ok
>
> **Gray:**
> Did I tell you we're reading like all these goth books in English this year?

> **Future Sire:**
> No! I'm jealous. My teacher is mostly
> making us read Austen.

We talk for a while longer about classes and books we love and I completely forget about my homework until Mom knocks on my door and tells me dinner is in five.

I realize I feel better. Steve wasn't fun today, but it's over, and I did what I needed to do, the best option out of a lot of terrible choices. And I don't regret any of it. I'm glad I dated Steve, and glad it's over now, too, and I can focus on my maybe-murderer. And if he ends up being a liar, then I'll try to be glad I felt good with him until whoever he really is reveals themselves—and maybe murders me. No regrets. Even if things go badly, there's still something beautiful there. We're all made up of past relationships and experiences and choices we loved or regretted. Each of them is a headstone, marking something buried in our past, and as we grow, we're building this big graveyard of all the things we were. And every graveyard is beautiful.

7

I decide to try to be nicer when Malcolm sits with us again at lunch the next day. Callie likes him and Lenore is giving him a chance, so I don't want to be the bitchy gay guy who won't let the other gay guy sit with us because we all have to immediately be enemies or lovers.

Lenore has brought more sandwiches, bloodred bread with some kind of beet salad like blood and guts, which Malcolm accepts this time, eating almost daintily, trying not to let the food fall out.

"So what do you all do after school?" Malcolm asks, his lips stained red.

Callie turns to me, lifting an eyebrow.

"I have to work at the shop most days, but they come hang out," I say. "We plan how to decorate it for the contest."

"I still can't *believe* that's allowed," Malcolm says, condescending again. "Well, I'm a professional creative. So this year you're up for some real competition for once."

"Bring it," Callie says approvingly. I nod, but inside I feel a tremor of nausea that isn't because my lunch looks like viscera. He really could beat us. And then what would my texter think? What if I show him everything and say *Yeah, we lost to Amanda Lash*. I try to picture it. I hear him asking *You know Amanda Lash?* and suddenly I have to put my food down—my hands feel like they're going to cramp. I want to run or yell or something. No one else seems to notice. Malcolm is still smiling that same condescending smile. He can't beat us.

"I'm not worried," I tell him. "I always thought your looks were more tryhard than terror, Amanda."

He looks up at me like I've thrown one of the sandwiches fully in his face.

"What?" he hisses.

"What? Are we not doing the competitive banter?" I ask. "You keep implying that we cheat."

He takes a breath and stands up without saying anything, then walks away.

"Oh my gods," I say. He's walking out of the cafeteria. "What a drama queen."

"I dunno, that was kind of harsh," Callie says.

"He called us cheaters. It was banter."

"Was it?" Callie asks.

"Yes, and don't forget, he's the competition. We shouldn't get too close to him."

"But—" Callie starts.

"He might be really cool," Lenore interrupts, her voice calm. "But he does seem to really want to beat us for some reason, and he thinks we should be disqualified. If we invite him to hang out at the store, he'll hear our plans. Let's just be careful, I think. At least until after we beat him in the contest."

167

Callie sighs. "Fine. We will...keep him as a lunch buddy. If he even wants to keep sitting with us after what you just said."

"I was giving as good as I got," I say. "If he wants to be competitive, he has to learn how to take it."

"I mean I think you were a little harsher," Callie says, glancing over her shoulder. "Fine, it's fine. Maybe we can get closer after Halloween." She turns back to us. "I'll talk to him later. Oh, and speaking of getting closer..." She's speaking low and quickly, like she doesn't want to make a big deal out of it. "I know I said I had to beat him at the science fair first, but"—she pauses dramatically—"Bryce asked me to homecoming. And"—she rolls her eyes—"I said yes."

Lenore's hands fly together, clasping in joy. "Does that mean—"

"Yes," Callie says. "I am requesting your help with an outfit."

"Hooray! And Gray. You're going to be my date to homecoming now, since I dropped Steve, right?"

"Sure," I say. "But I don't need you to make me an outfit."

She lays her hand over mine. "You do."

I laugh, pulling my hand back. "I have style."

"I'll make you something fantastic and you know it," she says. "Oh, I'm so excited. So much sewing. You can take today off, right?" she asks me. I nod. "Then let's all go to my place. I'll take some measurements."

"I'm going to go find Malcolm," Callie says.

"I really didn't think it was so harsh," I say. "I was just doing, like, catty gay guy."

"Yeah, but he doesn't know you, and your tone was..." She licks her lips, searching for the word. "You sounded angry. Anyway, I'm done eating. Meet you after school."

"I'll start planning looks!" Lenore claps her hands together, excited.

"I wasn't too harsh, really, was I?" I ask Lenore when Callie has left.

Lenore takes a sip of her soda. "No. But she's right that it might have looked that way." She glances after Callie. "It'll be fine. Besides, you don't like him, right? Why do you care?"

"I just don't want Callie to be annoyed with me," I say. Which is true. But I also don't want to actually be an asshole. He's the asshole. I'm the guy waiting for an apology.

"She's not."

"Okay."

We eat in silence for a moment, before Lenore claps her hands together suddenly. "I am so excited to make us some outfits."

Callie doesn't say anything about Malcolm when we meet after school, and I don't ask. I've already texted Mom and Mama asking for the afternoon off, so we ride our bikes to Lenore's place, which is a cute two-story house near the Headless Horseman statue, with a pothole out front that hasn't been fixed the whole time we've known her. Lenore's mom, Paola, works for a telehealth company from home, so downstairs, where her office is, is kind of off-limits until after five. We walk in quietly, waving at Paola through the open door to her office. She waves back, on the phone. Then we go upstairs.

Lenore's room, like everything else in Lenore's life, is an ongoing project. In one corner is a triple mirror, the kind tailors use for fittings. Her bed is on the other side, under the window and next to her desk. The rest of the room is a collection of wardrobes and shelves, with one small antique vanity squeezed in among them and a full sewing table in the middle with a fancy sewing machine on top. The furniture is all different styles, but Lenore has painted them all the same soft rose color, which matches the pink vine pattern on the black fabric she has lined her room in, tufted with brass buttons so the walls are bulging. The whole room is like a pillow that way—but also like a pincushion, because the tufting lets her pin things to the walls—sketches, articles, photos, things cut out of magazines or printed from the internet. She also has a never-ending supply of fabric, with scraps thrown over every surface, and bolts leaning against the walls.

I don't ask too much about how she can afford it all, but I know her dad's family owned a company that makes medical devices until he decided he was bored and went to live on the commune when Lenore was little. I think the divorce wasn't great, but her parents seem to function fine now, and she's mentioned having an allowance from her dad. It's probably nice to have an allowance without having to work at the family store, but considering how generous she is—bringing us food, making us clothes—I'm not really jealous. She does way more for me with her money than I could do.

We put down our bags and park on the bed while Lenore immediately goes to work. She opens one of the wardrobes and pulls bolts of fabric from it, spinning like a cartoon princess.

"I'm scared," I tell Callie. She snorts.

"Just for that, you're up first," Lenore says, pointing at the mirrors. A tape measure appears in her hand. I let her manhandle me, pulling my arms up, legs apart, shoulders back, calling out each number to Callie, who takes notes on a pad. Then she starts holding fabrics up to my face.

"You have to look perfect if you're going to be my date."

"Please don't make us match," I tell her. "Like some straight nightmare."

She smirks. "We'll see."

"Hey," Callie says, holding up her phone, filming.

"Please no," I say.

Callie laughs. "It's for you. For your film. While she measures you, tell us why decorating the store is so important to you."

I smile for a moment before Lenore spins me around and drapes some velvet over me.

"I think...it's not the most original thought, but Halloween is a chance to show the world who you are, right? Especially for people like us. We get to show off, and people are excited about it, as opposed to the rest of the year, where people think we're trying too hard or are creeps just because we have an aesthetic they don't love."

Lenore puts another fabric over my head this time. Sequins. Good thing she can't see my expression. I keep talking, though; I can use the audio over something else in the movie. "But with the store, with a space you invite people into, it's different, because you're saying *Hey, try being a part of this*. And part of it is that, and like showing people that we're beautiful and fantastic and all of that. But part of it, too, is I grew up in a goth house. No one takes my moms seriously, and I think they know that and are okay with it. They say they're understood by the people who count. But."

The fabric is taken off my head. My hair is in my eyes now. Somewhere along the line another bolt of fabric got wrapped around me, a sickly green.

"But. My people who count are just you two, and I keep thinking that if I make this perfect space maybe... I'll find more." Like my texter.

"That's sweet," Lenore says. "What about scaring people?"

"Oh well, yeah." I grin. "That, too. And this year..." I pause, lick my lips. This is what the movie is about, right? "This year there's this guy I've been talking to online. Stupid, I know, but I like him. A lot. And he's doing a Halloween decorating competition, too, wherever he is. I don't know his name or what he looks like. But so I'm telling this story about love, but scary. 'Cause it is scary. Even if I did know him I think it would be scary because I like him so much. I did not mean to say all that."

"It's the fabric," Callie says, dropping the phone. "Makes you feel wrapped up tight and safe. But it's good. You should use it in the video."

"So you're doing this whole haunted house for love?" Lenore asks. "To win the heart of your mysterious murderous stranger?"

"I..." I laugh. "I guess? No. I mean I'd be doing it anyway.

172

I love getting to make the world outside look like the world in my head, and how we make these things come to life is so cool. Like 3D mapping, stained glass? I'm going to learn so much just this year. And then we get to figure out how to do new stuff next year and build on the stuff we already know. I wish I could do this all year. So no, I'd love doing this anyway, guy or no guy. I just want this year to be really really great, to impress him. Because he...inspires me, I guess. And I want to show him that. I want to win for him."

Callie and Lenore look at each other, smiling a little.

"Shut up," I say.

"You're done," Lenore says, and I realize there's no more fabric wrapped around me and I'm just standing there, arms out.

"Wait, what did you pick?" I ask her.

She smiles, a little menacing. "I think it'll be more fun as a surprise."

Callie stands up next and we do the whole thing again. Lenore practically mummifies Callie—gold, burgundy, three shades of black. *She* gets to see it all.

"Do you know what Bryce is wearing?" Lenore asks.

"I'm with Gray on this, no couple matching," Callie says.

"To avoid it, then."

"I'll ask him. But probably something plain. He's not in our...what did you call it, Gray? Our outsider aesthetic."

"Yeah," I say. "Bryce wears polo shirts unironically."

"I like them," Callie says. "A collar gives you something to grab."

Lenore raises an eyebrow, and I laugh.

"Maybe I can send a photo of myself in my outfit to my texter," I say.

"Then he'll know what you look like before you know what he looks like," Lenore says, putting the fabrics away. "Seems dangerous. In the stupid mistake way, not the sexy way."

"Maybe he'll send me a photo," I say.

"He could just search for *goth teen* and send you what he finds," Callie says.

"I know how to reverse-image search." I lie back on the bed. "I just wish it were more concrete. The closet case, yesterday, he kissed me, like a tactic, and it was really"—I sigh—"not like, nice. But it made me remember what I miss with this weird anonymous texting thing."

"The physical," Lenore says, pulling fabric tight around Callie. "That's what always brought me back to Cody. Even when he cheated, he'd just pull me in and kiss my neck and I forgot all the bad stuff. So good for you for not falling for it with your closet case."

"Yeah." I look down, feeling guilty that my closet case was her chance to get over Cody.

"You didn't, right?" Lenore asks.

"I didn't. I told him it was over. He said he'd win me back."

Callie snorts. "You know what you should do? Tell him you're dating Malcolm. The two goth gay boys at school—everyone will be thinking it anyway."

"Absolutely not," I say.

"Actually, I can see it," Lenore says. "You'd be cute together."

"Ew, maybe if he had a different personality," I say.

"He's really not bad," Callie says. "Just awkward. Not so offended by what you said, either, just, like, embarrassed he said something that made you feel like you should respond like that. I think maybe the Amanda Lash persona makes him not good at the in-person stuff. He's probably better in the DMs."

I shrug. "Then he can apologize via DM."

"I'll tell him," Callie says, smirking. We turn to Lenore, who has thrown some fabric over her sewing table and is pinning paper patterns. The fabric is a dark, tarnished gold with a black toile design depicting skeletons doing everyday things, like riding the subway or waiting in line at a coffee shop.

"What are you thinking for outside the cathedral part of the haunted house?" Lenore asks. "You said the second heart would be outside, but what does that look like? Dusk like we did two years ago? You said rain, right?"

"Yeah. Rain, outside, dark..." I hadn't thought of this part as much, but from my scrying last night and the idea I had about us all being beautiful graveyards, something starts to come together. "Let's make it a graveyard. Filled with stuff, not just graves, and not like, junk, but like things that seem to match, maybe, but are broken apart. Like bookends on opposite sides of the graveyard. We can showcase stuff from the store."

"I like it," Callie says, nodding.

"The pairing idea is great," Lenore says, still pinning. "But we'll need more stuff. We should go antiquing this weekend."

"I can borrow my folks' car," Callie says. "But not until next weekend, I think. They're doing a weekend away in the city."

"Aww, cute old-people romance," Lenore says. "I can do next weekend."

"Yes." I smile. "There's that weird little place in Tarrytown, and what's the one that's basically just an old house falling apart, with the room filled with dolls?"

We help Lenore pin and cut for an hour before heading home. Mama is behind the register, selling a college student some tea.

"A boy came by looking for you," she tells me before I head upstairs.

"Who?" I ask, not sure who it could be.

"He didn't say his name. Left when I said you were off today. White, blond hair. He looked familiar." Mama is terrible with faces so she tends to say everyone looks familiar, just in case.

"Huh." I frown. "Thanks." Steve is the only guy I know who fits that description. Unless.

> **Gray:**
> Are you a blond?
>
> **Future Sire:**
> Sometimes. Why?
>
> **Gray:**
> Just trying to picture you I guess.
>
> **Future Sire:**
> Why

Gray:
Reasons

Future Sire:

Gray:
😮 Sorry

Future Sire:
No I get it, it's weird what we're doing

Gray:
Yeah and this thing happened with my ex where he like tried to get back together with me and kissed my wrist and obviously No but also it felt good you know?

I sit in bed, watching the ... appear and disappear, then reappear.

Future Sire:
I don't want to like keep you from pursuing anything.

Gray:
You're not I promise.

Gray:
And he said something about Night Club and for a day or two I thought maybe he was you?

Future Sire:
Is that why you haven't been as text-y?

Gray:
Yeah sorry. It was a lot.

Future Sire:
It sounds like it. I'm sorry that all sucks. I promise I have not yet kissed your wrist, but if given the opportunity...

      Gray:
      It's a great place to drink blood from so makes sense

Future Sire:
Exactly what I was thinking

Future Sire:
Do you have a thing for blonds? Is that why you asked?

      Gray:
      No, just a blond guy stopped by my place of work, it's stupid but I thought maybe it was you

Future Sire:
Now I wish I had gone somewhere besides straight home

Future Sire:
How would I even know where you work though? You think I'm a stalker?

      Gray:
      I mean we've already established you're a serial killer

Future Sire:
I thought you were the serial killer

      Gray:

Future Sire:

> **Gray:**
> You talk your parents into the dahlias?

Future Sire:
Yes!

Future Sire:
They were so excited I had an opinion

Future Sire:
But apparently they're not really a plant-in-the-fall flower so we won't see them until the summer

Future Sire:
My reward for finishing junior year in some weird new place I guess

> **Gray:**
> How is school going anyway?

Future Sire:
Good! Sort of. I'm so awkward I can't tell

> **Gray:**
> You can't tell?

Future Sire:
I haven't hung out with anyone outside lunch yet.

> **Gray:**
> Well it's only been a few days. Everyone is still getting settled in classes and stuff

Future Sire:
That's true

Future Sire:
Yeah ok I won't worry, hopefully it'll be cool. New friends. Why is it so horrifying?

> **Gray:**
> Putting yourself out there is
> always scary

Future Sire:
We're literally both texting a stranger
we are only mostly sure is not a killer

> **Gray:**
> True. But it's different in
> person. You said that right?
> Easier to open up to someone
> you don't know

Future Sire:
Yeah. Maybe I'll try getting their
numbers and texting. That might be
easier.

> **Gray:**
> Slide into those DMs

Future Sire:
Yes! The musician gave me her
number

Future Sire:
Oh, and this other cool one follows me
on insta, I'll DM her right now

> **Gray:**
> The pressure is on!

Future Sire:
Okay I'm going to try to think of
something

> **Gray:**
> I'm going to do homework

Future Sire:
I'll report back later

Thankfully my homework is mostly reading, and I finish it off just before Mama calls me down to dinner, so all night I can work on the decorating scheme. I've been focusing too much on the visual. If I'm making this for my texter, it has to be the best I've done. Fully sensory experience. And we met because of music—I need a soundscape. Something eerie and nature-based for the graveyard section, but more musical for the church. Rain tapping on windows over it, I think. I bet Callie can find music somewhere, but it makes me wish I knew an actual musician.

> **Gray:**
> Any chance you compose music?
>
> **Future Sire:**
> no
>
> **Gray:**
> I want a soundscape for my haunted house.
>
> **Future Sire:**
> Oh that's a fantastic idea I need that too now
>
> **Gray:**
> 😁 well now we both need a composer
>
> **Future Sire:**
> Now I have to find one to impress you
>
> **Gray:**
> You want to impress me?
>
> **Future Sire:**
> Yes obviously

Future Sire:
You're the expert, I'm new at this

> **Gray:**
> I think I'll be impressed no matter what

Future Sire:
No it has to be amazing

Future Sire:
No pity impressed

Future Sire:
I have to win

Future Sire:
People will die for it

> **Gray:**
> If people are dying from your decor, what makes it special when you murder me?

Future Sire:
Don't worry, no matter how many people I kill, when I finally do you, it'll be my favorite

> **Gray:**
>
> **Gray:**
> How did it go with your new friend anyway? Since you're apparently killing other people now
>
> **Gray:**
> Come up with something funny?

Future Sire:
YES!

Future Sire:
Well I don't know if it was really
that funny but she responded and
we talked for a while. I really do feel
so much better just texting than in
person in a crowded lunchroom where
everyone is looking at me like the new
freak I am

> **Gray:**
> Nothing wrong with being a
> little freaky

Future Sire:
True

Future Sire:
In fact I think I owe you a thank you
for encouraging me

> **Gray:**
> You're welcome

Future Sire:
😄 I meant I was going to send you a
sexy photo maybe

> **Gray:**
> Oh!

Future Sire:
I mean if you're okay with it

> **Gray:**
> I absolutely am just surprised

Future Sire:
Well, you said you wanted to see me,
and I'm not going to show you my face
or anything but 😈 thank you

183

The photo comes through before I can even lock my bedroom door.

It's not especially scandalous: a young guy, at a three-quarter angle, mostly showing off his ass in very tight red briefs. His skin is pale and olive. He's cropped it from around the belly button to the knees, so all I can see around him is a sliver of a bed. If this is him, he's hot; really great ass, thin but not gaunt. He's got some hair on his legs but nowhere else.

I am instantly turned on.

> **Gray:**
> Wow
>
> **Future Sire:**
> you have to say that

It might not be him, but... maybe it is. I lie down in bed and unzip my pants, pulling them down a bit as I imagine what the guy in this photo would be like in person.

> **Gray:**
> No trust me I mean it
>
> **Gray:**
> You want anything similar in return?
>
> **Future Sire:**
> I wouldn't say no

I swallow, unprepared and suddenly aware of how messy my room is, and how my gray briefs are kind of ratty.

> **Gray:**
> Give me a sec

I go through my underwear drawer and pick out the sexiest pair I own—black boxer briefs with tears like claw marks up each leg that I bought in a goth shop in New York last year. I wore them once for Steve but he said they were too horror movie. I slip them on and then try to find the best place to take a photo. My mirror reflects my desk, which isn't great, covered in books and my laptop, so I throw a red sheet over everything and then pose in front of the mirror. I'm still hard, but I decide I'm okay with that. I take a bunch of photos, then pick the best one and crop it. My finger hovers over the send button. This really could just be some creepy guy in a basement somewhere but... my face isn't in it. Not hard to find a photo of a twink in his underwear on the internet, and if you crop it, reverse image search isn't going to turn up much.

And it's a nice photo, more straight-on than his, the tears in the underwear cutting dangerously close to making it less artsy erotica and more flat-out porn, but it's hot. I cut it at the same places he did—just above the belly button, showing off my treasure trail of hair, and just above the knees. I hit send, then lie back on my bed, slipping the underwear off as I look back at his photo. I feel like my arm could wrap around his waist easily. And I would love to pull that ass close to me.

Future Sire:
I do not deserve this

Future Sire:
My photo isn't that hot

> **Gray:**
> Yeah it is

> **Future Sire:**
> I don't know
>
> **Gray:**
> If you want to send me another I won't mind but trust me when I say I'm enjoying this one
>
> **Gray:**
>
>
> **Future Sire:**
> Well as long as you're enjoying it
>
> **Future Sire:**
> I want to enjoy this but my parents just called me to dinner so I actually really need to stop enjoying it 😭
>
> **Future Sire:**
> But later
>
> **Future Sire:**
> Have fun with mine

I do. And fall asleep early afterward.

8

Malcolm becomes a fixture at lunch, acting like he never walked out. He and Callie seem to really click, referencing inside jokes and stories I don't know—and I don't mind that, not really, but it means we can't talk about our decorating plans at lunch. Even Lenore stops bringing in her more creative food for fear of accidentally inspiring the competition.

"Y'all need to relax," Callie says as we pile into her parents' hybrid for our antiquing day. "He's doing his own thing, he's not going to steal our ideas."

"How do you know?" Lenore asks, getting in the passenger seat. I get in the back, camera out so I can film the day. "He might look at one of my spider cookies and think *Spiders! That's what I need!* and that'll be all my fault."

"I think he would have thought of spiders by now," Callie says.

"It was an *example*. I'm just saying, we need to be careful. And it's tough not being able to use lunchtime. Maybe we can ask him not to sit with us a few days a week?"

"That would be rude," Callie says. "And besides, we're

gonna kick his ass. I like him, and he's talented, but we're awesome. So stop worrying."

"I guess that is a good point," Lenore says, turning to me. "We are—are you filming this?"

"I said I was going to," I say. "It's for my project."

"Well, let's not include the part where we complain about Malcolm," she says. "I don't want him being inspired by my cookies, but I don't want to hurt his feelings."

"You prefer bodily pain?" I ask.

"Only if he's very lucky," she says with a smile. "But I don't think I'm his type." She sighs. "I need to find myself a real romantic partner. Not a cheater, not a homophobe. Just someone to watch the sun go down while we discuss the beauty of death and crafts."

"Death and Crafts should be the name of your You-Tube channel," I say.

Her eyes go wide. "It should!"

"You have to get better at telling people what you're doing, though," Callie says. "I watched last night's video and it was just you at the sewing machine for twenty minutes. You didn't even look up."

"It's like ASMR," Lenore says. "I mean, not really because I don't have one of those mics, but it's...noise."

I laugh. "I think it has to be more than noise."

"Oh?" She arches an eyebrow. "How's your video coming, anyway? Or do you just film stuff and never edit it together or organize it because doing so would mean actually trying to create a narrative instead of just watching?"

"Ooof," Callie says.

"I create a narrative," I protest, but she's dead right. "I came up with the story for the store decorations, didn't I? In fact, why don't you tell us what we're doing today?" I ask Lenore.

"Looking for stuff for the graveyard. Unsettling pairs of antiques."

"And music, if we can," says Callie. "I've been searching all the free stuff and none is really what we're looking for, I think. It's all like violins or organs. Too safe."

"Yeah," I say. "We need something weirder. Unexpected so it's really unsettling."

The great thing about Westchester is it is swimming in antique shops. We don't even have to leave town before we find our first success: a pair of anatomical head busts, each one half of the head split in two, with various regions marked on the outside. They don't quite match, they're supposed to show different skulls, I guess.

"Phrenology," Lenore says on the way to the next shop, cradling the half-heads like babies. "An old racist belief that skull shape determined stuff like personality and intelligence. Invented by the same guy who invented BMI."

"Don't we still use BMI?" Callie asks.

"We do," Lenore says cheerfully. "Personally, I would have liked it better if the reason people died because doctors misdiagnosed them was because of phrenology, though. Or the humors! We should really try to bring back the humors."

"I don't know if you can bring back outdated science," Callie says.

"Please." Lenore shakes her head. "People do it all the time. But if we're going to go out because of bad education, let's at least make it the more aesthetically pleasing ones. Those old charts showing humors were art."

I snort a laugh as Callie pulls up to the next vintage shop. We don't find anything there, but at the one after that we find a pair of cracked lamp bases, each of their three sides with a different Victorian-looking painting of a poisonous flower. The shop after that is just clothing, but Lenore picks out a skirt for herself.

After that, we make our way to Cray Estates, a giant falling-apart Victorian mansion filled to the brim with oddities. It's run by a woman in her sixties who tells us that everything there belonged to her mother, who was a hoarder. It's all a little sad, but fun, too. We're helping her get rid of this stuff, and her hoarder mom would probably be glad it's going to people who want it, even if the whole manor feels like we're trespassing. It's another beautiful graveyard.

There's a room just filled with old dolls, half of them sliding down a collapsed shelf. The owner never repairs anything, or even puts anything new out. She just reads behind a table in the foyer, waiting for people to pay her and take things. Everything smells like dust. It's one of our favorite shops. Despite having come here several times, it feels like we always find new stuff, uncovered as the previous layer was sold.

The woman who owns the place nods at us as we come in, then goes back to her book. We start by looking in the dining room, tea sets and teapots stacked on top of each other on cheap IKEA shelves that line the whole room. In the center is a large old table, with two mismatched chairs, all for sale. Among the teapots we find a pair of black ones, not an actual set, but both black and small, one shiny and round with a rabbit on it, one small and black.

"They sort of work," Lenore says holding them up. "But I'm not sold."

"Neither am I," I say. "I love the idea of two teapots, though."

"Maybe a teapot and a cup and saucer—a pair that way," Callie says.

"Yes," Lenore says, and heads to the shelves of teacups.

"I'm going to check upstairs," I say.

Upstairs are a series of small rooms off a narrow hall, a few of them themed—like the doll room—but some more eclectic. I have a vague memory of a violin in one, so I'm hoping there might be more musical stuff in it.

There's a young woman in the room already, maybe a student at the local college, poking around. The room does seem music-themed. I flip through a bookcase full of sheet music. It's not really what I need, though. Then the girl picks something up at the far end of the room, and suddenly there's a haunting, tinkling music. I look up. She's holding a music box. It's out of tune, too slow—I'm not even sure what the song is. It's perfect. I watch her stare at it a moment and then I step forward.

"Excuse me—" I start, then stop, because stepping forward from the other side of the bookshelf, where I couldn't see him, is Malcolm.

"You going to buy that?" he asks over me, then looks at me, surprised.

The girl turns around, looking at both of us. "You can have it if you want," she says, apparently thinking we're together.

I reach forward to take the music box, and as she puts it in my hand, he reaches out, too, knocking it out of hers.

It hits the floor and shatters. I watch as one of the springs rolls away from the collapsed box. Splinters surround it like a fireball.

I feel rage start to swell up in me. This asshole butts into my friend group, insults my sacred space and my moms by extension, accuses us of cheating, and now he's actively sabotaging us.

The girl makes a face at the shattered music box on the floor, a little confused, a little embarrassed, and just shrugs and leaves. I turn to look at Malcolm, furious.

"She was handing it to *me*," I say. My voice sounds hoarse. My jaw clenches.

"She was giving it to both of us, because she thought we were together," he says, that same snobby tone as always.

"Then why did you reach out?" I ask, almost shouting now. I turn away from him, frustrated, and bend down to pick up the pieces. Maybe Callie can fix it.

"I was taking it," he says, getting down and grabbing pieces, too.

"*From me*," I say. "That was perfect for the soundscape for the store's Halloween decor."

"That's what you were using it for?" he asks. He's holding a few pieces, but I have the rest and I hold out my hand. He stares at me a moment, then sneers and puts them in my palm.

"Don't act like you weren't thinking the same thing."

He rolls his eyes. "Yes, I was."

"So you broke it because she was handing it to me. After you accused *me* of cheating."

"I never—" He cuts himself off, his jaw clenching. "I did not do that. Why do you think I'm such a bitch?"

"Because you are," I say, keeping my voice steady, even though I'm furious. I'm so angry that I almost close my hand around the pieces just to feel the sharp edges dig into my skin, but I know that could break them even more, so instead I look up at him and say, "You're one of the rudest people I've met, and you're not even funny about it. Just boring."

His face freezes, and for a moment I feel satisfied, like I finally got him back for his dig about my store.

"You're just some cheap suburban mall goth," he says. "I truly don't care what you think."

"What's going on?" We both turn to see Callie and Lenore in the door. Malcolm looks at them and his face turns pink, then back at me like he's going to say something, but instead he just runs out of the room, pushing through them hard enough that they both are knocked back. Callie looks after him, then back at me. "What was that?"

"It's—" I sigh. "We both went after this music box. He knocked it out of my hand and it broke." I hold out the pieces. "I said he was sabotaging us, he said I was being mean, I said he was rude, he called me cheap."

"We saw that part," Lenore says.

"He knocked it out of your hand?" Callie looks at the pieces I'm holding.

"He knew we were using it for the haunted house," I say, holding it out to her. "Fixable?"

"Maybe," she says. "I can't believe he did that."

"He already accused us of cheating and insulted my store," I say.

Callie tilts her head, considering. "Well...I'm sorry that happened."

"Yeah," Lenore says. "Ribbing and competition aren't whatever that was. He looked so angry. So did you."

"I am. Was." I take a deep breath, feel my body cool down a little as the anger leaves me. "Was," I repeat. "Let's go see how much a broken music box costs."

We go downstairs in silence and the woman behind the desk only shrugs when I tell her I broke the box and want to buy it. She charges me full price, and part of me thinks of billing Malcolm for it, but maybe Callie can fix it. Maybe the music will be even more haunting now.

Afterward, in the car, with Creux Lies playing, we're all silent as we drive home. It's late, and we all feel done with the day without even saying it.

"We should drive by his place," Lenore says. "See what he's doing. He's come into the store, we should get to spy on him."

"You don't think that's taking it too far?" Callie asks.

"He broke the music box so we couldn't use it," I say. "This is a real competition now, not a friendly one. Imagine if he wins." I hate the idea of it, of some city kid coming in from nowhere and kicking our asses and how I'd have to tell my texter about that and how mortifying it would be. This is *my thing*! The only thing I ever really want to do, the thing I'd make my life if I could. And Malcolm wants to take it from me.

Callie frowns. Lenore takes out her phone and pulls up the online student directory.

"He's on Pocantico—not too far from you, Gray."

Callie drives back to Sleepy Hollow and swings around the turn, creeping down the street slowly to look at the houses. "We might not be able to see anything from out here."

But we do. We know exactly which house it is immediately. A big white McMansion, with a giant lawn stretched out in front, only a few trees along the driveway. And there on the lawn, already set up, is a half-built set: huge wooden walls, some painted, a few with only outlines for paint on them.

"It looks like a street," Callie says.

"A Victorian street at night," Lenore says softly. "And look at those shops. That's a working door."

"He's building houses," I say. And he is. Not just one simple house, but a row of them. A whole different world.

The car creeps by slowly, all of us silent. Lenore even shuts off the music.

When we're finally past it, I take a deep breath.

"Okay," I say. He doesn't just want to take my dream from me, my future, but he could really do it. I shiver.

Callie and Lenore nod.

"He's real competition," Lenore says. "That was... amazing."

"We have to win," I say.

"Let's hope," Callie says.

We're quiet for the next few blocks, too, until Callie parks and we carry in our vintage store finds.

"Any luck?" Mama asks from behind the tea counter. The store is more crowded on weekends, and Mom is minding the register, where there's a small line.

I hold up the half-head bust I'm carrying, and Mama nods approvingly. "Phrenology?" she asks as I bring it toward her. "That means it's old. Could be valuable. Did you use the store card?"

195

I nod. If I use the store card, that means it doesn't come from my money, and it means my moms can sell it afterward. Mama takes the half-head bust from me and holds it up admiringly. "Oh, we might keep this one for the house," she says. "Anything else?"

We show off our finds, explaining that Callie can try to rebuild the music box, but not how it broke. Mama looks all of them over and has us put them in the back room. Mom is nearly done with the line of customers when we come back out. "Everyone want to stay for dinner?" she asks. "We were thinking a movie night. Maybe *Labyrinth* or *Häxan*, if you want a laugh."

"Always Bowie," Mom says quickly.

"I'll second that," I say.

Callie and Lenore text their folks and after Mom closes the store, all of us head upstairs to help cook and then watch David Bowie act with puppets. I feel like we're quieter than usual, all of us probably thinking of Malcolm's set—or at least that's where my mind is. He must have been working on it for ages already, he seems so far ahead. He also has all that space. We can build stuff, but we have to set it all up and hope it works perfectly in just one night. He thinks having a store is cheating, but he's the one with a whole yard to just build whatever he wants, and months to do it. And it looked really good. If he weren't the competition, I'd want to help him with his vision. And if he weren't an asshole.

After the movie, when everyone says good night, I go up to my room and look at my phone, which I silenced for the movie. My future sire has been texting.

> **Future Sire:**
> Today was kind of miserable.

> **Future Sire:**
> I feel like I did something wrong but I also know I didn't and it's making me a little insane

> **Future Sire:**
> I wish you were there

> **Future Sire:**
> Talking with you always makes me feel less like I'm losing my mind

> **Future Sire:**
> Everything has totally changed my home my parents my life and you're like the only thing that I've kept from my old life

> **Future Sire:**
> Oh god that sounded so needy please ignore me I need to go curl up and die now

> **Future Sire:**
> Good night though

I smirk.

> **Gray:**
> I was watching a movie, phone was off sorry

> **Future Sire:**
> It's okay I was just having a little meltdown but I'm better now and no I do not want to talk about it

> **Gray:**
> You sure?

Future Sire:
What movie?

Gray:
Labyrinth. My moms wanted to watch it and my friends came over for dinner so we all just piled on the couch and stared at David Bowie and his bulge

Future Sire:
It's hard to look away from

Future Sire:
Much like yours

Gray:

Future Sire:
I was thinking about what I'd like to do if I saw it in person

Gray:
Oh yeah?

Future Sire:
Yeah

Gray:
Do you want to tell me?

Future Sire:
Maybe but not yet

Future Sire:
I don't even know what you're into

Gray:
You mean if I prefer to be the fang or the neck?

Future Sire:
 Or just the lips, if you're not into biting.

> **Gray:**
> I've only been with one guy but I was usually the fang and I liked that

Future Sire:
That works out perfectly then

> **Gray:**
> Glad to hear it

> **Gray:**
> Hoping to bite you soon

Future Sire:
Me too

Future Sire:
I was thinking...can I call you my boyfriend?

I feel my cheeks color as I read the words, but I immediately want to say yes. He is already, right?

Future Sire:
 it's too much right?

Future Sire:
I don't even know your name

I smile. It doesn't matter.

> **Gray:**
> No I like it

> **Future Sire:**
> Really?
>
> **Gray:**
> Yeah
>
> **Gray:**
> I mean I know it's insane but
> why not hope it's not?
>
> **Future Sire:**
> And all of these texts are kind of like
> dates so we've been dating awhile

I laugh aloud at that. He's right. We've been dating forever. Me and my...boyfriend. I roll the word around in my head. Yes. My boyfriend.

> **Gray:**
> Yeah
>
> **Gray:**
> I love that

I think of texting Callie and Lenore but I can already imagine their reaction. I don't even know him, not really, and he could be a serial killer...I sigh.

> **Gray:**
> Weird we don't know each
> other's names though
>
> **Gray:**
> Should we trade those?
>
> **Future Sire:**
> No! Now I'm invested in keeping it
> secret until Halloween

> **Future Sire:**
> But it is weird
>
> **Future Sire:**
> In a good way
>
> **Future Sire:**
> I know so much about you it feels like

I laugh, thinking of the underwear shot I sent.

> **Future Sire:**
> Including your dick-print
>
> > **Gray:**
> > I was just about to say that
> >
> > **Gray:**
> > About knowing you I mean
> >
> > **Gray:**
> > But I guess also the other thing
>
> **Future Sire:**
> You remember that scene in The
> Violet Window when the two deer
> just sort of come out of the different
> sides of the woods and see each
> other, and we know they don't know
> each other, but they just start walking
> together?
>
> > **Gray:**
> > When Jez is watching all the
> > animals flee?
>
> **Future Sire:**
> Yeah and we see how all the animals
> are just suddenly like we know each
> other because of that spell and we
> know what to do

Gray:
The deers' antlers create that web and they crossfade to the attic.

Future Sire:
That's how I think of you. Like another deer in the woods. And I don't know you but suddenly I do and I know I can run away with you and be safe

Gray:
That's how I think of you too

Gray:
My deer boyfriend

Gray:
Deer Friend!

Future Sire:
Yes! Let's be deer friends

Future Sire:
But that's a moose

Gray:

Future Sire:

9

The next few weeks go by fast. Deer Friend and I start texting more, like the summer again. It's funny what we tell each other—he knows my thoughts on *Dracula* and how I feel about Callie and Lenore and my moms without knowing any of their names. He knows I work for my parents' business but not what it is. He knows all my feelings on art, the world, relationships—big topics, but none of the little details of my life. I don't even really tell him about my days anymore, just about thoughts I'm having. It feels like our connection is somehow above the daily, the mundane. It's more than that, it's magic.

I don't mention it to Callie and Lenore; they would make fun of me, and I'd deserve it. But it makes me a lot happier as the days go by. Also, Malcolm stops sitting with us at lunch, which is fantastic. He sits with Esme and her punk friends, and they always seem to laugh and have fun, so it's not like he's friendless. Callie says she still texts him sometimes, but the friendship has definitely cooled a bit. Bryce sits with us sometimes, and while his aesthetic—if that's what you'd call a T-shirt with a cartoon character and jeans—doesn't vibe, he's a fun, sweet guy, who is clearly madly in love with Callie. And he's got a talent for geometry, which really helps us put together the forced perspective part of the cathedral. Using a 3D model, he maps out a blueprint for us, and after school Callie and I work on cutting and painting foam blocks for the walls while Lenore brings over her stained-glass supplies and shows us how to melt the colored beads between the wire that she's already shaped. It's starting to really come together. I can see the pieces now, hold them in my hands, so I know they'll assemble well. And Callie even managed to reconstruct the old music box melody. She bought another old music box and changed out the reel—the thing that has the music on it, in little cuts of metal—and it wasn't quite the same, but by recording it and slowing it down we managed to find exactly the right level of creepiness. I overlay it with the heartbeat and some faint insect sounds for the graveyard, and it's perfect. For the cathedral, I just go for the sound of rain on glass and a heartbeat. We try to figure out how to make the stained glass look like it's raining, but that would require a lot of screens and all of our budget, so we settle for the light behind them flashing like lightning.

Somehow during all this, I manage to not fall asleep in class, and more impressively, neither does Lenore, who is also working on our homecoming dance outfits. Homecoming is at the end of Spirit Week, when the school mascot, the Headless Horseman, starts showing up outside school and sometimes riding down the halls. We're very lucky to go to a school with such a naturally goth mascot.

We don't even mind high-fiving him as he gallops past us in the halls. No clue who it is underneath, though. Callie says she thinks it's Bryce.

The day before the dance, we finally go over to Lenore's place for our fittings. The circles under Lenore's eyes have gone from haunting to worrying the past few days. But then she takes out our outfits and they're...perfect. Callie has a jacket in the casual skeleton pattern and a giant skirt in gold, like the gilded version of a Victorian school-mistress, but with a black lace button-down underneath and a black tie. Callie has no words, she just smiles in the mirror, glowing.

I'm up next, and Lenore hands me a bright blue velvet jacket. I stare at it, trying to think of a way to be polite, until she bursts out laughing and takes out a black-on-black plaid jacket instead. Some of the plaids have a slight shine to them, so it looks like different shadows are rippling over them. It's short, ending just above my belly button, and she gives me a black kilt to go with it.

"No shirt underneath," she says. "I'm honestly not sure if they'll let you in that way, though, so bring a tank top or something, too. Black, red, or white would be best, I think. But it's meant to be worn without anything underneath."

"I'm not going commando in a kilt," I say.

"It's traditional," she says.

"I don't think pairing it with a crop-top jacket is, so let's throw traditional out the window."

She sighs. "Fair enough. Now go see how it fits."

I change in the bathroom, keeping my underwear on, and it fits perfectly. I go and stand in front of the mirrors in her room and she has me spin, pulling and pinching before deciding it's just right.

"What are you wearing?" Callie asks.

"A surprise," Lenore says with a smile.

Callie and I exchange a look.

"All right," I say for both of us. "Can't wait."

It's not a fancy homecoming dance. I know that. It's the gym and balloons and a student-painted sign I saw them carrying in that says FAIRY TALES ARE REAL. There'll be a DJ playing bubblegum pop from a makeshift platform, if one of the teachers doesn't just do it. Honestly, I'm almost embarrassed to come to school events like this, but it's the only thing that ever feels like a big deal, aside from going into the city, and we hardly ever do that for more than shopping or a concert. I think when we're older and can get into bars and clubs, the city will be cooler, but without reliable fake IDs, this is the best place to show off who we are, even if some people glare at us as we gather in front of the gym.

I show up forty minutes late, like we planned. Callie and Bryce are there already. He's cute, in a regular tux, red hair and freckles looking a little stark against the dark eyeliner Callie has clearly put on him. Callie's makeup, of course, is stunning—gold to match her dress, flaring out from her eyes like wings. She's literally drawn on every quill of every feather. In the dress Lenore made for her and with her long braids down, she looks ethereal, beautiful in a wonderfully uneasy way. I didn't do much for my makeup, just a sheer white foundation and a black lip stain with cat eyes. I don't have the skills to do anything like Callie, so I kept it simple.

Lenore shows up a few minutes later, and she looks amazing. She's used the fabric from both my outfit and Callie's, a mix of gold and black-on-black plaid in the style of an old movie siren. The dress is mostly black, with the gold coming from one shoulder down to the hip like a sash, where it blossoms out as part of the skirt, while the other part stays sleek. It really is like both our looks had a baby. Her hair is up in a messy bouffant, and black pearl chandelier earrings fall like ivy to her shoulders. She wears black elbow-length gloves. Her lips are red, her eyeliner is cat-eyed, and her eyes are pure black, no whites at all. It's wonderful and terrifying.

"You made us all match," I say to her, grinning. "I'd hate that except we look amazing."

"I know what I'm doing," she says, smiling. "Just have a little faith."

"You look like a terrifying and glamorous gang," Bryce says, visibly swallowing.

Callie laughs and takes his arm. "I assumed you knew what you were getting when you asked me," she says.

"I did," he says, smiling at her. "I like it."

"A man with taste," Lenore says with a sigh. "I have to find one of those."

"Maybe he's inside," I say.

Lenore arches an eyebrow. "Unlikely. But let's look anyway."

When we go inside, it is in fact the gym teacher, Mr. Carlson, on the raised platform with a laptop and speakers, wearing sunglasses and a track jacket over a T-shirt, bopping excitedly to Justin Bieber's "Intentions." A bunch of our classmates are dancing, limbs waving joyfully in the air like those inflatable guys outside car dealerships. Some big cardboard stars and white Christmas lights are hanging from the ceiling and walls. There's a table with a water cooler and glasses by the bleachers.

"Okay," I say. "The music sucks, but let's try dancing anyway, I guess."

"Yes!" Bryce says, taking Callie's hand. She laughs and lets herself be led to the dance floor. I look at Lenore and we follow them, doing our best to dance to the pop music. I'm not a terrible dancer, but I am definitely a devotee of the classic goth two-step, where most of the movement is in my shoulders unless I remember to move something else. Lenore is more of a twirler, fanning out her dress and making shapes with her arms above her head. Callie is the only one of us who really knows how to move—and apparently so does Bryce, because within moments on the floor, he is stepping and spinning in a way I did not expect from a science geek. And I don't think Callie expected it, either, because she is wide-eyed, and then her competitive streak kicks in as she tries to match him. Lenore and I step back and they soon have a circle around them, just bobbing and watching until the song ends.

"I'm getting water," I tell Lenore as the next song starts, and I walk over to the table with the cups. Behind it, up on the bleachers and alone, is Malcolm—or, rather, Amanda. I'm honestly kind of impressed he came in full goth drag, and he looks amazing, too, the kind of look I would have liked on Instagram and sent to Callie and Lenore, before I knew him. His wig is black with a white streak up front that falls over his face, and behind that a huge Marie Antoinette–style hair bump adorned with bats. One is even perched as if landing on the very top of the wig. He's wearing a black ball gown with a white sash, but the sash is splattered in red sequins like blood. The sequins continue on his chest, neck, and face, too, a splatter of red sparkle, expertly applied. On the side of his neck without the splatter are two more sequins, like bite marks. His face is contoured, but not so much that he looks alien, and the powdery paleness is clearly intentional. He's drawn a small, bat-shaped birthmark under his right eye. The overall effect is ten out of ten, campy and bloody, like a horror-movie take on historical comedy.

He sees me admiring, and I nod. I may not like him, but I respect the look. Then I turn away. And end up looking right at Steve, standing in a corner with the guys from the soccer team. He's hot, in a dark-gray suit with a skinny blue tie. He pulls a flask out of his inside pocket and takes a deep swig before offering it to his teammates. One takes a drink and then spits it out. Everyone laughs, and Steve grabs the flask back and takes another drink before putting it back in his pocket. He glances up and meets my eyes, and I turn back to the dance floor, where Lenore is twirling by herself. I rush back to join her.

We spend the next hour or so rotating between dancing, drinking water, and asking Mr. Carlson to play some actual good music, which he only does once, saying, "This one goes out to the freaky students," and pointing at us, before playing the Cure's "Friday I'm in Love," which makes us all burst out laughing, because while we requested the Cure, "Friday I'm in Love" is decidedly not freaky. "It's probably the only Cure he has, poor thing," Lenore says, leaning into my ear.

But it is good to dance to.

As the night goes on, people seem to loosen up—I see Malcolm dancing (also the goth two-step) with the punk kids, and the soccer team forms the suburban version of a mosh pit, all of them jumping up and down. Steve is jumping up and down a lot, in fact, crashing into his teammates, until one moves out of the way and he falls. He's really drunk. His teammates all laugh, and he does, too, before heading for the restroom.

I know I shouldn't, but I follow him. This is maybe my fault, right? I never called him or anything after he stopped by the shop, have been ignoring him at school. He keeps trying to talk to me, to tell me something, and maybe it's not just another declaration of love, maybe he's dealing with something and he can only talk to me about it because only I know, and I shut him out, and now he's drinking himself into a public stupor. I can't talk to him, but I might be the only one he can talk to.

The gym bathrooms are violently lit, with white-tiled walls and orange-tiled floors. Steve is hunched over the sink, staring at himself, a fresh cut over his eye. When I come in, he looks up and spots me in the reflection.

I look around. No feet in the stalls, no one by the urinals.

"You okay?" I ask him.

He laughs, one loud bark trailed by softer, sadder ones. He turns around and leans back on the sink.

"Like you care," he says.

"I do," I say.

He shakes his head.

"Just because I ended it," I say, stepping toward him, "doesn't mean I want to see you drink yourself to death. I'm sorry that what I want isn't what you want, that it didn't work, but I'm worried, okay?"

"So you care about me?" he asks, looking up. His eyes are watery.

"Yes," I say slowly, my tone distant. "Not the way you want, maybe, but—"

He rushes forward, grabs me, pulls me into him, kisses me. And for a moment, I remember all the good things again, the days in bed, the funny gargoyle sketch I still have in the back of my drawer.

"We'll call him Butter, after the Butter Tower on the Rouen Cathedral," he told me once.

I didn't understand that at all, but he showed me photos of it, this beautiful Gothic tower, and I got it. I remember putting my head on his shoulder, lacing my fingers through his and him kissing me, like he is now.

And I remember him telling me he needed to date a girl, because his parents were asking questions.

I pull away. "Steve, no, I told you, I—"

"Yeah, you're seeing someone, but it's secret, right? Is it the guy in the dress? Is that what you're into now?"

I roll my eyes. "I would never date Malcolm. He's full of himself, and he was an asshole about my store. So stop.

We didn't break up because of someone else. We're just not right together." I wave my hand between our chests, like I'm tugging on a rope connecting us. He's still so close I can feel the heat off his body, smell the liquor and sweat on him. I look up at him and realize my eyes are tearing up. "You're going to find some amazing guy to build a life with, but not if you drink yourself into a car crash first. Someone is driving you home?"

"You can," he says.

I take a deep breath. "I will drive you home, and there will be nothing else, if you don't already have a ride." My voice is firm. "I care about you, but we're not together."

He stares at me, his face empty. "Nick is giving me a lift." He turns around and walks back to the sink, looks at the cut, rubs the blood away, then spins again, glaring. "Either you want me or you don't, Gray. You don't get to care enough to be like this and then tell me you don't want to be with me. This is messed up. It's like you want to keep hurting me."

"I don't."

"You are." His face gets hard, his jaw clenching, his cheeks pinking. He looks over my shoulder and I glance back, but no one has come in. He starts walking for the door, brushing past me. "Just make a decision. Either be with me, or get out of my life."

"Fine," I say without turning. I feel the door open behind me, hear the swell of music as he leaves. Maybe he's right. Maybe I'm torturing him. But at least he's got a ride. I walk over to the sink and think about splashing my face with water, but it'll wash the makeup off, so instead I just inhale deeply.

212

And as I do, I hear someone else exhale.

I turn around to the bathroom I thought was empty. "Who's in here?" I ask.

There's a sigh, and a rustle, followed by the click of a shoe being lowered onto the tile. And then another. I look at the stalls and spot them—black high heels. A black skirt descends around them. The door opens. Malcolm. I feel electricity spark my blood—fear, embarrassment—but it fizzles. I'm just too drained. Everything Steve just said... I tried to help and I made it worse. And now Malcolm is here. Of course he is.

"Why were you hiding?" I ask.

"I'm in a dress in the men's room at a suburban high school I don't know very well," he says with a sigh, and walks past me to the sink and starts washing his hands. "I waited until I was sure the bathroom was empty, but then just in case, and because skirts are a pain to use at a urinal, I went into the stall and lifted everything else up. When Steve came in, I lifted my feet, too. I don't want to get hate-crimed. Relax, I won't tell," he says, drying his hands with some paper towels.

"Steve's parents are really religious. He could get kicked out."

He turns around and frowns a little. "I'm not going to out anyone. I may be an asshole, but I'm not a monster."

I remember suddenly what I said about not dating him.

"Fine," I say. I could apologize, but what for? "Just don't tell anyone. No one knows. Not even Callie and Lenore."

He looks a little surprised by that. "Sure," he says.

I glare at him.

"What?" he says, pursing his lips slightly. He's got on a purple lipstick that makes his mouth look full and biteable. "Don't believe me?" He raises a hand, two fingers. "Scout's honor. That do it for you?"

I sigh. There's nothing I can do about it now.

He looks like he wants to say something else, but frowns instead.

"You want me to check the coast is clear?" I ask, when he hasn't moved. I may not like him, but queer solidarity, right?

His face softens slightly. "I'd appreciate it, sure."

I go to the door and check the hall the bathroom looks out on. No one. I open it wide and wave him out. He marches past me. He really does looks amazing. Smells good, too, that clove incense smell strong and mingling with some kind of rose perfume.

He nods at me and walks down the hall back to the dance. I wait a moment longer, wondering just how likely he is to out Steve just to make my life hell. He'll definitely lord it over me, little hints, *I know something you don't want me to tell* kind of smiles. I can see all that coming. But I don't think I need to warn Steve. I don't know what he'd do. He just said he thinks I left him for Malcolm. I don't see him getting violent, but using his popularity to make Malcolm feel more ostracized? Spreading rumors about Malcolm hitting on him or something...yeah. He would do that to protect himself. Better not to tell. I'll just trust Malcolm for once. Even if I feel miserable about it. And about Steve. Everything is overwhelming. I take a deep breath. Tonight was pretty awesome until five minutes ago.

I walk back to the dance, where Mr. Carlson has moved on to slow songs—Adele is singing "Make You Feel My Love." Callie has her head on Bryce's shoulder and Lenore is standing against the wall—talking to Cody. I guess it's a night for chats with your ex.

Except she looks a lot happier about hers. She's leaning back on the wall, hands behind her back, and Cody is doing that thing terrible guys do, hand on the wall next to her head, leaning closer.

The thing about Cody is he's not bad-looking. Square jaw, full lips, tall, tan, bright gold eyes, and hair that changes styles and colors enough to be kind of interesting. Tonight it's shorn short, nearly shaved, and dyed cotton-candy pink. He's wearing a red suit with a black shirt underneath, unbuttoned enough to show the top of his abs. If Lenore just wanted to screw him, I'd say go for it. But Cody doesn't like hookups. He likes breakups. At least that's how it always looked from the outside. He likes being loved, likes inspiring adoration and then seeing how much he can get away with before he destroys it. That was always the plan with Lenore. Telling her he loved her and then standing her up, cheating, kissing another girl on the mouth in front of her. There'd be big fights, and from what Lenore implied, great makeup sex, before she finally ended it, and then he'd beg her to come back, and eventually, she would. Until last year. Last year really felt final. But here we are.

"Hey," I say, going up to Lenore, ignoring Cody. "Let's dance."

"Hi, Gray." Cody smiles at me. He likes to flirt with

me, too. He once told me he wasn't gay but wouldn't mind if I gave him a blow job. I declined.

"Hi, Cody," I say, my voice as bored as I can make it. I turn back to Lenore. "Dance?"

She looks at Cody, then at me, and I give her the Look, the *you promised not him again* look, and she looks back at him, and for a moment I'm afraid I've lost her, but she nods and reaches out her hand to me. I take it.

"Bye, Cody," she says.

"Later, sexy," he says as we walk toward the dance floor.

"Thanks for the rescue," she says, wrapping her arm around mine as we wade into the dancing. We take the standard slow dance position, one of each of our hands clasped and my other hand around her waist, her other hand on my shoulder. It feels silly, like playing pretend, and we're both even worse at this than we are at fast dancing, but we sway a little in time to the music.

"You sure you wanted it?" I ask.

"Oh, I am," she says. "It's when he's close it's bad. Like the smell of cigarettes to a smoker, I guess. Or like the sweet smell of opium as you walk by a den."

I laugh, but it sounds about right. Like how I felt when Steve kissed me. "Yeah, I get it," I say.

She narrows her eyes, cranes her neck a little to look up at me. "Do you? You look like maybe you were crying. Are you all right?"

"Huh?" I'm genuinely surprised. I didn't really cry, after all. "Yeah, yeah, just...worried about you, I guess. Kinda wishing my text boyfriend were here."

216

"I'm not a good enough date?" She raises that one eyebrow.

"If I were a good dancer, I'd dip you now, and tell you of course you are, but I think we'd both fall, so let me just say of course you are."

She laughs. "Fair enough. But really, you okay?"

"I'm fine," I say, wishing I could tell her everything that just happened. Wishing I didn't have to deal with all this alone and I could tell her how Steve kissed me and now I wonder if that's like cheating. It isn't, I know, but she knows. She was just talking to Cody. "How about you?" I ask. "You okay?"

"With Cody hitting on me? I'll be fine." She smiles.

We don't say anything else for the rest of the song. Just sway. I know I can't tell her anything, but I'm glad she's here.

"If someone kisses you while you're seeing someone else," I ask her, "is that cheating?"

She looks up at me, eyes narrowing. "Did something happen with Closet Case? Here?"

I nod slightly.

"Mmmm." She looks around as if she's hoping to spot him; then, realizing she doesn't know who he is, she looks back at me. "Did you kiss him back?"

"The way a smoker might inhale if you stuck a cigarette in their mouth," I confess. "But then I pulled back."

"Men are terrible," she says. "But...no, I don't think it is."

"Feels a little like it."

"Then you should tell your text guy. Are you two even exclusive?" She smiles. "Without even knowing him?"

"I don't know. We call each other boyfriend."

She smiles, one of her rare genuine smiles, where the archness of her expression fades and she's just sort of happy, soft, watercolor. Then she leans her head on my shoulder. "You don't know his name or what he looks like, and you're ready to call him your boyfriend and feel bad when someone else kisses you. That's..."

"Stupid?" I ask.

"Brave," she says. "To think it's all true when he's probably some old man somewhere, or a serial killer, or just some teen girl messing with you. But you believe it's this perfect guy. Don't even know his name." She tucks a stray hair behind her ear and glances back at the gym wall, where Cody is now doing the lean thing over some other girl. "I know Cody's name. What did that ever get me? You know—what, this guy's soul?" She turns back to me, eyes wide, genuinely wondering.

"His spirit, maybe," I say. "How he thinks and feels and what books and movies he loves. How he feels about his parents. Who he wants to be."

"I don't know if I know any of those things about Cody. Maybe I should start texting random numbers, see what happens."

"Then we can both end up murdered," I say.

"It's a deal."

10

Bryce offers to drive Callie home, and she has a hungry kind of look when she agrees to let him. Lenore and I giggle as they leave before hugging goodbye. At home, Mom and Mama are waiting up for me, watching *Rebecca*, the old black-and-white one.

"So how was it?" Mom asks. "Was there any good music?"

"He had one Cure song," I say, plopping between them on the sofa.

"'Friday I'm in Love'?" Mama asks.

I nod.

"Well, you're sweaty and flushed, so I'm going to guess you had fun dancing to bad music anyway," Mom says. "Lenore's mom sent us photos of you three all dressed up, that Lenore sent her. The redhead was Callie's date?"

"Yeah," I say. "Bryce. He's cool."

"Good," Mom says. "And they let you in with no shirt."

"Malcolm was in full drag," I say. "So I think there are no rules at this point."

"Who's Malcolm?" Mama asks.

"New kid," I say, shaking my head and remembering him overhearing everything with me and Steve. I hate that he knows. It makes me feel sticky somehow, like gum on his shoe. "I don't like him much, but he can turn out a look."

"Why don't you like him?" Mom asks.

"He's just so condescending, like living in the suburbs is beneath him." I tilt my head, deciding not to tell them he was rude about the shop. "And he's our nemesis in the decorating contest. We drove by his house and he's doing something very good."

"Ah," Mama says. "Well, good. About time you had some real competition."

"I guess," I say.

Mom snorts a laugh. "You guess you wanted to keep coasting to a win?"

I glare at her, and she and Mama both laugh.

"I'm going to bed," I say, not really annoyed, but tired.

"Drink some water," Mama says. "Get some sleep. We have the moon ceremony tomorrow."

"Right." I nod, walking to my room. I fall onto my bed face-first but then pull myself up. I don't want to sleep in this amazing outfit, or with makeup on. I'm washing my face when I hear my phone buzz.

Deer Friend:
You awake?

I stare at it a moment, feeling guilty again about Steve kissing me in the bathroom. I definitely liked it. But Deer

Friend is my boyfriend, right? So...I sigh and wash my face before answering.

> **Gray:**
> Just going to bed

Deer Friend:
Oh okay. Just wanted to say I wish I could have seen you tonight

> **Gray:**
> I wish I could have seen you tonight too

Deer Friend:
It was a weird night

> **Gray:**
> How?

There's a long pause, the dots appearing and disappearing.

Deer Friend:
Just weird. I kind of don't want to get into it. But it wasn't all bad weird. But it would have been perfect weird if you were there.

> **Gray:**
> I am known for being the perfect kind of weird

Deer Friend:
I don't doubt it

> **Gray:**
> I'm falling asleep

I'm not lying, my eyelids are heavy.

> **Deer Friend:**
> Okay text tomorrow
>
> > **Gray:**
> > Absolutely. Good night.
>
> **Deer Friend:**
> Sweet dreams.

When I wake up, I feel gross, my mouth sticky, my muscles aching. I grab my phone and go downstairs and drink a whole glass of water and pour myself another. Mom is making breakfast, eggs. I spot Mama's tall witch hat out in the garden.

> **Deer Friend:**
> Good morning

I smile down at my phone.

> > **Gray:**
> > Good morning

"Who's that?" Mom asks, looking up from the frying pan.

I feel myself blush, caught suddenly. I haven't told her or Mama about the stranger. They would probably make me block his number.

"Just a friend," I say, going to sit at the table, face away from her.

"Someone you want to invite to the ceremony tonight?"

"No," I say, too quickly, probably.

"All right," she says, and goes back to cooking, humming "Friday I'm in Love," while I turn back to my phone.

> **Deer Friend:**
> So how's your Halloween decorating going?
>
> **Deer Friend:**
> Mine is going well I think
>
> **Gray:**
> Pretty good

We've managed to build a lot of the blocks from foam and held them in place to see how it'll look and I think it might be amazing, though it's hard to tell, since we can't just put it all up and glue it in place yet. Callie thinks she might have a lead on cheap screens to create the visual rain-on-the-glass-effect thing, too. Apparently the AV department is getting rid of some stuff. And the soundscape is pretty finished. We found some more pairs of things for the graveyard online. It's coming together. It might be amazing.

> **Gray:**
> I think ours is going to be really special

> **Gray:**
> That sounds so bad
>
> **Gray:**
> But really I think it's cool and I
> can't wait to show you
>
> **Deer Friend:**
> I can't wait to see

For a moment, I think about reminding him about the movie I'm making, too, filming all this stuff. It might be really bad, though, so I don't mention it. I'll see if it comes out worth showing to anyone. I've gone over the footage in my room and it's...okay, I guess. I don't know. It feels silly, but it is sort of like this love letter to—not to him specifically, but maybe to the idea of love. The idea of hope at the end of the world. And to making stuff, I guess. Making the world the one you want it to be. At least for one night.

> **Gray:**
> I can't wait to see yours!

Mom puts down a plate of eggs and toast in front of me, then opens the window and leans out. "Breakfast, my Romeo!"

"Coming, my Juliet!" Mama shouts back, and comes in a minute later. Mom has her eggs ready by then and hands her the plate, and soon we're all sitting at the table.

"So, it's October first on Monday," Mama says. "We need to put up the new window display today. Lure the

Halloween tourists in." Halloween season in Sleepy Hollow is big business for us. We have a Halloween-all-year aesthetic, of course—we are a spell shop—but October is when tourists come up to look at the town, and they want something specific in the windows, something they can buy that says *Halloween*, and so we try to emphasize that. Some fake cobwebs, black candles, and stuff that looks like more than just the tourist souvenirs every other shop will have now. "Can you take care of that, Gray, before you open?"

"Sure," I say. It's usually my job anyway. And ceremony days, I'm in charge of the shop.

"Not too scary," Mom says. "Nothing gory, keep it souvenir-y."

"I know," I say, trying not to roll my eyes.

"Sorry, sorry, reflexive habit," Mom says.

Mama laughs. "You can help him when you're not getting things ready for the ceremony. I'll be in the garden. I want to have as many herbs hanging over the tea desk as possible. Make it look abundant."

"I know Callie, Rose, and Michael are coming tonight," Mom says. "Lenore, too?"

I nod. "We talked about it last night."

"Great," Mom says. "She can take Fire. Callie—we'll give Air. You want Water or Earth?"

"Water," I say. I always have Water. Not because I especially want it, but because the other elements suit other people better. Mom or Mama will stand in the center, and then each of us will stand in the four directions and call down the elements to bless us. It's not really an official ceremony. Mom and Mama have dabbled in all kinds of practices—Wicca was too gendered, Hermeticism too formal, Chaos Magick too, well, chaotic. So they've put together their own ceremony over the years. It's got a basis in Wicca but it's more open, more relaxed. Reform Wicca, Mom calls it.

"Then you may take Earth, my love," Mom says to Mama. "And I will handle the center."

Mama smiles. "The usual layout."

"Unless Rose and Michael suddenly want to do more than watch," Mom says. Callie's parents are cool Catholics, but they don't really participate in the ritual. Lenore's mom came once and said the whole thing reminded her too much of her ex-husband, so she doesn't come anymore. Mom and Mama have other friends, too, even pagan ones, but they're not local, so for just the monthly moon ceremony, we don't do anything big. This one is big to me, though, because it's the first one since Callie and Lenore have been back. The ones over the summer were just me and my moms, and those are always quiet. We didn't even invite them for the one a month ago because everyone had just gotten back and was prepping for school.

After breakfast, I go downstairs and start arranging the windows. We have fake spiderwebbing (we keep it year-round) and it's not hard to rearrange the spookiest, most Halloween-y candles and objects, putting them in the windows. I go outside in my pajamas to check it looks good, and it does, I think. Candelabras, a black skull, a red candle. No pentagrams as part of the Halloween display, Mom says that trivializes our real religion, and nothing too creepy-looking, like the actual bat skeleton. Just tourist spooky.

I'm staring at the windows and deciding if an athame in a skeleton hand might be a nice touch when I hear a voice behind me.

"I like your pants." Malcolm. I can't tell if he's teasing me or being genuine. I turn around. I remember last night suddenly, all of it flooding back, and I feel myself blush. He knows way too much about me now. And about Steve.

I look down at my pajamas. Skull and crossbones on an oversized black-and-gray houndstooth. Just a black tee on top. They're clearly pajamas. So he must be teasing me.

"So, are you open?" he asks.

I shrug. "Technically not for half an hour. I'm just doing the windows."

"Oh." He scratches the back of his neck. He's in a plain black button-down, big enough to fit three of him, and wide-legged black jeans with tears all over them. He starts examining the windows. "They look really good."

I can't tell if he's serious. "For Halloween, it can't be too spooky, we need to get tourists in," I say, shrugging.

"I get that, but it's still really well done. The way the spiderwebbing wraps around that candelabra is…" He leans back a little. "I need to step up my game if this is just how you decorate mere windows."

I smirk, unsure what to do with all this praise. He must want something.

"You think a skeleton hand holding a dagger is too much?" I ask.

He shakes his head and points at the spot where I was

thinking of putting it, his arm brushing my shoulder as he does. "Right there?"

"Yeah, kind of pointing—"

"At the poison bottles? Yeah, perfect."

"Cool," I say, opening the door to the store, then look back at him. "Did you want to buy something?" I assume not, not after what he said last time about the store, but...

"I mean, I wanted to see..." He sighs. "Maybe. I was looking for you, though. Because of last night."

I frown. So that's it. Here to rub it in my face. Maybe blackmail me? What for, I don't know. No, no, that's too much, right? He's not that bad. Though maybe he'll be asking me what we're doing for the Halloween competition. A little information. I could see him trying to do that.

"Okay," I say, and walk into the shop. He follows me, getting close in the doorway, that smell of clove incense strong. I grab the skeleton hand from the desk and fold it to hold an athame and put it in the window while he looks around at everything.

"These are so cool," he says, picking up one of the long poison bottle vases.

"Thanks," I say. "I picked them out." I fold my arms. If he's going to threaten me, I wish he'd just get it over with.

He blushes, very slightly, and keeps his eyes on the bottle. "I...I'm sorry about what I said about the shop, the first time I was in here." He twirls the bottle, and it glints in the light. "I came in, and I saw you, and Lenore and Callie, and I thought, like, *These are cool people my age*. And I wanted to impress you. And I thought, I thought, *No one likes where they work*, so if I made fun of the place..." He glances up, and I nod, briefly, not sure what's happening. An apology, I guess. Not what I expected. "I was trying to be cool. I didn't know it was really your store. Important to you."

"It's my family's store. My parents own it. We live upstairs."

His eyes go a little wide at that. "Oh yeah. You said that before..." His face freezes, like he's thinking of something, then he shakes his head.

"You okay?"

He shakes his head. "Just a weird idea. But yeah. So I'm really sorry." He looks up at me. "I shouldn't have been rude. This place is cool."

I'm not sure what to say, so I just nod. He seems sincere. I guess I sort of understand what he was trying to do, too. It makes a certain sense. Kind of insecure, but...I look at the way he's standing and realize he might be kind of insecure. Hard to imagine Amanda Lash being insecure, though.

"Okay," I say after a long pause.

"And I'm really sorry about overhearing everything with you and that guy last night."

I feel my body straighten out, and I walk behind the counter. "Yeah," I say, not looking at him.

"I promise, I won't tell anyone."

"Can we not talk about it, then?" I say, glancing at the door.

"Oh, sorry." He nods. "Sure, yeah."

He pokes around the store in silence a bit more, but I watch him, noticing the things he lingers over—my favorite athame, this fantastic old clock we found, the anatomical heart lights. He picks out two of the poison bottle vases and brings them over.

"Can I buy these?" he asks.

"Sure," I say, opening the register and ringing him up. I don't give him a discount. The apology is nice, but he's still the competition. And he still knows too much. Part of me can't get rid of the idea that this might be some kind of shakedown. Like him just parading in front of me, reminding me that he knows one of my biggest secrets. Imagine if he told anyone. Imagine if he told Lenore and Callie. It would be bad. He could do that to me, and now here he is, buying some of my favorite vases. That feels like a power play, even if he is smiling kind of shyly while he does it.

He pays me with a fancy black credit card and I carefully package the vases in bubble wrap before bagging them and handing them to him.

"These will be great in my haunted house," he says, taking the bag.

There it is. That's what he's here for. To psych me out. Well, good luck.

"You're going to need more than those," I say. "We have something amazing happening."

He narrows his eyes. "Are we smack-talking? Last time I—Callie said you were but it felt like you were genuinely being mean."

I smirk. I feel a little mean. "You didn't come here to psych me out?"

He laughs. "I'm so bad at that stuff. But okay." He looks around. "I mean"—he puts his shoulders back, throws on a cocky smile—"doesn't look like you have more happening than some spiderwebs. So I'm feeling pretty good."

I stare at him in silence, holding back a laugh. His face falls, horrified.

"I'm sorry," he says quickly. "I thought we were—"

"We are," I say, letting myself smile. He laughs. I guess he really might just be that insecure. I might have been reading him all wrong. I feel sort of bad, suddenly, this weight pulling on my limbs. We should have been friends, maybe. Maybe. "And look, I do want to explain—the thing about using the shop—cheating, I think you called it?"

He blushes.

"Well, there are advantages," I say, stepping out from behind the counter. "We have access to catalogues of stuff, true, and of course we get to sell stuff off after, so the costs aren't as bad. But that's not really that big an advantage considering we have to keep it a working shop until the day before the competition. We have to build our whole decoration scheme in pieces and then put it all up in one night."

"Oh," he says, surprised. "Wow."

I lean back on the counter. "Still think it's cheating?"

He looks around. "I guess, as long as I can buy the stuff you order, no."

"Then I guess we're on equal footing," I say. "And we'll see who wins."

He raises his chin slightly, and then I see it again. The cockiness. He's not insecure. At least, not about everything. But he's allowed to be cocky about his Halloween stuff. I am. "We'll see," he says, a faint smile on his lips as he leaves.

I watch him walk out, and then lock the door, and then scan everything he looked at, go over everything he bought, and make a note not to use them in our decorations unless we really use them well. Maybe I had him wrong, but he's still the competition. He still broke the music box, though maybe it was an accident. I guess maybe he's not a bad person, and he probably won't out Steve or anything—but he'll still do whatever it takes to win. And remembering that amazing Victorian street on his lawn, he could do it.

We're technically not open yet, so I have time to run upstairs and shower. Mom is cooking—that's the best part of the moon ceremony, the food. There's veggie burgers that Mom will barbecue later, but there's also potato salad, pasta salad, chickpea salad, dumplings, mini-quiches. Mom used to cater, and briefly thought about culinary school, she's said, so this is when she gets to have fun. The whole house is filled with scents overlapping and battling: cheese and chocolate, vinegar and vanilla. Paprika, cumin, the watery sweetness of anise. It's everywhere.

I grab my laptop and head back down to the store, officially opening it. I sit behind the counter, going over the footage I have for the film. If I'm maybe going to show this to Deer Friend, then it should be pretty good, right? I go over the footage for the first few hours of the day. Only a few folks come in, mostly to buy the prepackaged teas— some had ordered custom blends ahead of time, which I find under the counter where Mama left them. It's easy to keep one earbud in and close the laptop whenever anyone comes in. Easy to really go over the footage and find ways to splice it together. So much of it is in the edit. Like, me describing what I want, next to the stuff Callie filmed of me saying why I wanted it. Footage of Bryce and Callie showing us a 3D rendering, audio of Lenore talking about how she learned stained glass from her dad over video of her actually doing it. Life is weird and messy, but with editing...things can look more intentional. Less chaotic. Less random.

It's all lies, though, I realize. Life is pretty random, after all. I mean, I'm making this whole thing for a guy who I'm only texting because someone else gave him my number as a fake thing. I suddenly wonder about who that could have been. Our little matchmaker. Some guy at a party. Life is chaotic and bad things happen all the time— but good things do, too, I guess. Or they're both same sides of the coin, because Deer Friend only texted me because some other guy was blowing him off.

It's the beautiful graveyard with the purple light: There's all the stuff, all this chaos, and people either see only the bad stuff and let it depress them, or they try not to see any of the bad stuff and live these fake repressed lives. But if we look it full in the face, the good and the bad, the death and loss, but also the love and beauty—we see they're all related. Vines and flowers growing on graves, the angle of a rain-worn gargoyle, the chats with a stranger because of a wrong number. There's good even in what looks like bad. But if you think a graveyard is a sad place, then you'll never see the joy there. That's what I should be doing with the film, too, I realize. Show the good in the bad.

I put away everything I've done and start again. I turn on the camera on my laptop and record myself.

"Why is this important?" I ask aloud. "Why do I want to make this haunted house? I mean yes, I want to show the hope and all that stuff I said before, too...but also because the world is terrible. But that doesn't mean it's not beautiful, too. The end of the world—that's the story I'm telling in the house. Two hearts that meet and end the world. And that, obviously, is bad. Or a lot of people would consider it bad, not beautiful. But maybe there's beauty in it, too. I have to hope there is. Because there's so much bad stuff happening. All the time, it feels like. But if I can show people the beauty in the end of the world...maybe I can show them that there's still beauty before it ends, too. Like, there's still love. Even as the world implodes there's still love. That's why I want to win, too. Because then—" I stop. Am I really about to say that if I win my online stranger will love me? That is not something I should say aloud. I turn off the camera. I don't know if that's exactly what I mean, either, but at least what I did record is something to work with.

I play with the footage awhile more, making sure to show all the rough edges, all the bad parts, but also all the beautiful things, too. Lenore burned her finger on one of the stained-glass panels—but it left this really cool mark, like it was slightly warped, authentic. I open with that. Her burning herself, the ice pack, the bandages, and her the next day saying her mom made her go to the ER and they bandaged it up with special cream. Second-degree burn, blisters, she laughs as she explains. Then I cut to a close-up of the panel itself. The slight warp. Then I get into what the movie is about. But let's open with that. A burn, and beauty.

The afternoon is packed. Mama was right about the

tourists starting, since several come in and buy some of the little Headless Horseman statues we keep by the counter. Not cheap plastic things—I made sure we got nice metal ones. And our copies of "The Legend of Sleepy Hollow" are all faux-leather-bound, aged, genuinely creepy-looking, with amazing illustrations. I sell a dozen of the statues and two copies of the book before closing, as well as a bunch of other stuff—the anatomical heart lights sell really well, I'm happy to see.

By the time I close up, it's been a really productive day, and yeah, Malcolm coming in was kind of weird, but I guess it wasn't bad, exactly. Maybe after we win the Halloween competition he can sit with us at lunch again. Mama comes in just after I close, huge bundles of herbs in her arms. We spend some time hanging them over the tea counter; by the time we're done, the place smells magical, fresh and green. The herbs will dry, but the scent will remain in the air, turning woodier. It makes the store feel older, even more otherworldly. We always sell more the day after Mama hangs a bunch of herbs.

Then we head upstairs, where Mom has nearly finished off all the food for the day. The sun is low on the horizon when Callie and her parents arrive. Callie's mom, Rose, looks a lot like her, with long braids and wide cheeks. Her dad, Michael, has her eyes, dark and serious. They've brought wine and soda and help us set up the picnic table on the lawn, lighting bug-away candles. Michael helps Mom start the fire in the fire pit. Mama takes Rose through the garden; Rose has an herb garden, too, and they love comparing. I sit on the table with Callie.

"You could have brought Bryce," I say.

"What?" She laughs. "And have him meet my parents?"

"He took you to the dance."

"He *met* me at the dance, and drove me home, and stayed in the car when he did."

I laugh. "So not telling them?"

"They know Bryce," she says, then narrows her eyes. "They know him as the competition."

"How's the makeup coming?" I ask her, watching Rose and Mom laugh over an empty basil patch.

"Really well, actually. I got some samples from"—she pauses, tilts her head, as if deciding—"from Malcolm." She pauses again, waiting.

"Okay," I say.

"Waiting for you to say something about how you don't like him."

I shrug. "He came by today and apologized for insulting the store. Said he thought I just worked there and he was trying to impress us. Too cool for it. So . . . fine. Still the competition, though."

She smirks. "That's good. Yes, agreed, still the competition. But he's really helping me with the science fair. He can write back to some of these makeup people and ask about alcohol content and say it's for a video for his Instagram and they give him numbers. It's great. So I know lots of liquid-based stuff has too much alcohol. Not all of it. But it means if you want, like, decent foundation to create special effects, you need alternatives for keeping it liquid and still creating something that can dry down."

"You find anything?" I ask.

"Oh, sure. Glycerin and oils and lots of stuff. The question now is how well they stay gelled together, so they don't break into little particles in antigravity that get into the filters or anything. Almost need a liquid latex. I've been playing in the chemistry lab a lot during free period. Malcolm has the same one as me, so we hang out. He lets me test stuff on him."

I feel my face scrunch, a little jealous suddenly. "Long as you're not telling him our haunted house plans."

Her eyes flash in the light from the bonfire Mom and Michael have coaxed into life. "You think I would?"

I laugh. "No. But you are being pretty forgiving about how he broke our music box."

She shrugs. "So a music box broke. We fixed it. Here's what I think." She leans forward, both elbows on the table. "The universe is huge. Vaster than our imaginations and growing every moment. You, me, Malcolm, our Halloween decorations? They're meaningless. Pointless. All of humanity is. One day our sun will explode, and what's left of humanity probably won't be around to see it, but the stars up there"—she looks up at the sky—"they'll keep shining." She pauses for a moment, smiling at the thought. Then she turns back to me. "Isn't that beautiful? How little it matters if we decide to be friends with a guy even though we're going to kick his ass in the Halloween competition? Because that's like some dust clinging together, a stray electron hopping onto an atom. That's how meaningless it is when you look up at all that. So why not let it all go? The music box, whatever, right?"

Is that like finding beauty in the graveyard, I wonder.

Part of me wants to agree, let it all go. Malcolm didn't seem so bad today. But I don't want to let my guard down, either. Steve kissed me when I did that, made me feel like a cheater. And I was close with him. Malcolm—he's just some snobby guy from the city. Callie smiles at me, but I don't know how to respond.

"Sorry!" Lenore says, coming around the house and taking a little basket off her bike. "I was working on these forever and they took so long."

When she sets it on the table I open it and peek inside— to find it peeking back at me.

"Chocolate cherry eyeballs," Lenore says happily. "It was hard getting the jiggle just right."

"Wow," Callie says, taking one out. "These really look— and feel—like eyeballs." She pops it in her mouth.

"Wait—" Lenore says too late. Callie has bit down and gone a bit bug-eyed herself. "There's a cherry jelly center."

Callie laughs, covering her mouth, then chews and swallows. "Yeah, when I bit down and it exploded, I was worried it was a real eye. Delicious, though."

"The idea is to bite the top off, suck it dry," Lenore says, taking one out and demonstrating with a small bite, revealing that under the glistening Jell-O–like exterior is a chocolate shell, and within that, a bright red jam. She sips from it like it's a little teacup before she bites. Callie and I both follow her example. They taste amazing, the cherry is so strong and dark that the chocolate is just the background, adding some bitterness and coffee to the fruit.

"This is delicious," I say. "But I think them exploding in your mouth sounds fun, too." I reach for another, but Mom, who has walked over now that the fire is going, swats my hand away.

"Those look amazing, but dessert after dinner, c'mon, kid," she says.

"Sorry," Lenore says, closing the basket.

"Don't apologize. Not your fault Gray has no restraint."

"I have restraint," I say.

Mom snorts a laugh. "Not for Lenore's desserts you don't. Not that I blame you." She turns to Lenore and opens the basket, sneaking an eye out for herself and holding it up to the light. "Amazing work."

"Thank you," Lenore says, looking very proud.

Mom bites into the eye and some of the cherry runs down her lip like blood. She closes her eyes, nods, and makes a sound of contentment, a soft murmur. Then she wipes the cherry away with her hand, licks her hand, and pops the rest in her mouth.

"Really, really good," she says.

Lenore looks like she might die from happiness.

"They need the fridge?" Mom asks.

"If there's room," Lenore says.

Mom nods and Lenore goes to the back door, taking her eyeballs with her. Mama and Rose come back to the table and join all of us, and the adults pour themselves wine as Mama hands out the objects for the ceremony. For Callie, an athame; for herself, a golden pentagram on a chain she wears around her neck. For me, a fancy chalice of water, and for Lenore when she gets back, a carved wand, topped with a topaz.

"Should we start?" Mom asks. "You can participate if you want," she adds, talking to Michael and Rose.

Rose always looks like she's thinking about it, but then she glances at Callie and shakes her head. "I'll let Callie represent us."

"I'm fine just to watch," Michael says.

So the rest of us take our places around the bonfire. Mom is toward the center, walking around it, while the rest of us stand out slightly, facing the four directions: Callie is East, Lenore is South, I'm West, and Mama is North. Each direction is an element, a power. Really, there are more than the four directions that are powers, though. There are countless forces in the world, running through us and around us, like the colors on the surface of a bubble, always moving, running, sometimes together, sometimes apart. Each little line is its own emotion, its own power. Joy, lust, rage, intelligence. Some people think of them as gods, or as mixes of gods, or all of them as one big god. We think of them as all of that. Want to call out to the universe? Think of the whole bubble. Just want help on a math test? Think about the forces that'll help you, maybe they have a name when they're all bunched together like that, Athena, Mimir, Thoth—which one feels right? They have their own associated legends, their own rituals, their own histories. Use those, invoke them, summon those forces into you, and maybe it'll help. It's hard to control the universe. The best you can do is control yourself. That's what this ritual is for: to expel the bad forces that have gotten stuck in or around us, to use the full moon to renew ourselves. And maybe to welcome some good forces into us.

Mom starts. She walks around the fire, arms outstretched to the moon, which is shining bright and full.

The sun is nearly down, so the sky is ink-dark, tinged with pink and purple. The moon is low and white, but shining, almost delicate-looking, like wind could blow it away.

Finally Mom calls out to the moon. Her voice isn't sing-song, or even very melodious. It's more like she's shouting during a rock concert. "We have gathered here to ask your blessing, Moon! We ask you to guide the good forces toward us and drive the bad forces out. Help us renew ourselves just as you do."

She looks over at Callie, who is up first. We don't have memorized lines or anything, but we know what we're supposed to do.

"Hear me, O Guardians of the East," Callie calls out. Her voice is low, melodious, eerie. "We ask that you be with us and bring us your blessing. The genius of the wind, quickness of thought, spritely intelligence!" I nod. Spritely intelligence is new. Nice. "Drive away dullness and grogginess. Help us keep our minds clear and sharp." She stabs her athame into the air and then traces a pentagram with it. "Please come and be with us tonight, and go when you would. Bless us." For a moment, a slight breeze picks up, ruffling my hair, and I smile.

She pauses long enough that Lenore glances over, and Callie nods at her, passing the torch.

"Hear me, Guardians of the South," Lenore sings out. Her voice is higher than Callie's, the melody less eerie and more friendly, a princess in a children's movie. She sways slightly as she speaks, the wand already lifted in her hand. "We ask that you be with us and bring your blessing. The fires of creativity, the heat of passion, the sparks of inspiration! Drive away boredom and malaise! Cast off indifference, and keep intensity burning within us, that we might forever be yearning to create and eager to fight for what matters." The wand is already high up, but now she traces a pentagram in the air with it. "Please come and be with us tonight, and go when you would. And please bless us." I feel warm when she's finished speaking. The fire pops, hot behind me.

She repeated Callie's ending, so I assume that's it, but I glance over at her to confirm. She gives me a nod, and then I'm up.

I look to the west, raise the chalice in both hands, and call out. "Hear me, Guardians of the West!" My voice is not as pretty as either of theirs. I don't sound musical. I think I sound like a teacher trying to lecture over a noisy room. "We ask that you be with us and bring your blessing. The depths of emotion, the tears of feeling, the waters that run through us bringing joy and sadness, love and anger." The West, and water, are about emotions. I try to focus on that, focusing on the positives of what feeling brings us—not just feeling good things, but feeling everything. "Don't let us become cut off from what we feel, don't let us become cold and frozen because we don't have time or are afraid. Let the emotions flow through us, and let us all remember that they all will flow out of us, too." The chalice shakes slightly in my hands and water spills over the side, getting my fingers wet. Water is about magic, too, about mysteries. "Let us feel the magic of ourselves and look into the mysteries of the world." I trace a pentagram in the air with the chalice, using both hands. It's not as fluid or natural-looking as with a wand or a knife, but it works. "Please come and be with us tonight, and go when you would. Bless us." That's apparently how we're all ending tonight, so I thought I should keep it going.

I look at Mama, who doesn't even glance over. She just steps forward, holding out the pentagram in front of her, the chain glittering around her neck. "O Guardians of the North!" she calls out. Mama has a great voice, haunting without being ominous. Powerful. "Roots that feed us, stone that keeps us steady, leaves and plants that bloom and fill our lungs with scent. Nurture us and fill us with your endurance, keep our minds and hearts fertile. Banish the barren spirit, the malnourished soul. Keep us steadfast and make sure the ground never gives way beneath us, that we might always be as strong as you." I can feel my toes squeeze, trying to grip the earth under me. I look over at Mama. She's barefoot. She raises the medallion and traces it in a pentagram in the air. "Please be with us tonight and enjoy our bounty. Go if you must, stay if you will, and let your blessings fill us." Okay, so Mama didn't follow the pattern, she went more traditional. But she's been doing this longer than us.

Mom finishes up by throwing some herbs onto the fire, where they crackle and smoke, smelling of mint and lemon. "Thank you, O spirits," she calls out, "for joining us and blessing us. The feast we now have is in your honor, with your company and with our thanks."

And then we're done. Callie goes over to her parents, and Lenore joins them, but my moms and I take a moment. Mama told me this is the moment when all the elements,

243

all the forces are coming together and joining us, and you should try to hear and feel them, so you can recognize that feeling of good in the world when it reaches for you. So I do. I feel the earth under my feet, the water on my hand, the heat of the fire, and the cool breeze on my face. It feels good, like all the good things in the world are flooding into me and pushing out the bad ones. There's a meditation Mom taught me when I was young and feeling too sad or scared or angry. She told me to imagine the bad emotions inside me like sparks, and then to imagine them flooding out of me and flying to the edges of the expanding universe, where they become new stars to fill it. The end of the moon ceremony is like that, but I don't even have to focus. The good just comes in and pushes out the bad. My body feels cool and warm, tingling with potential, and totally relaxed. My eyes are slightly wet, and I wipe them away before going over to the picnic table to join everyone else. Mom runs in to get the food while Mama lights up the barbecue. I start setting the table for our guests.

"Happy full moon," Callie says to everyone, pouring herself a glass of soda.

"Happy full moon," everyone responds.

I feel good, but suddenly, like I'm missing someone, too. I wish my stranger, my Deer Friend, were here. I want him to be part of this, see this side of my life. Maybe I can tell him all about it later, but...well, maybe one day he'll join us.

Mom comes back out and Mama starts grilling, and I run back inside, just to get my phone, to have that part of him be with me at least.

Gray:
Thinking of you

It goes unread for a few seconds and I put it away. We can talk later. When I come back out into the yard, Callie's dad is hanging out by the door and nods at me.

"Hey, Gray, I was wondering if we could talk."

It's not a request. Michael isn't a bad guy. A little strict with Callie sometimes, high standards, and obviously his being a DA gives him a sort of intense lawyer vibe, but he's always been cool with me. He's never wanted to talk to me alone before, though.

"Um, okay," I say. He doesn't move, so neither do I, and we stand by the door, out of earshot of the picnic table, where everyone else is.

"I just wanted to make sure you know about these missing kids," he says.

"Oh." I nod. "Sure, yeah. I mean we all know about them."

"They were all around your age, all gay men. And now there might be another."

"I didn't hear that," I say. Well, good for Poly Perry.

"We haven't told the press yet, still checking the basics—friends' houses, maybe grandparents. You see, the thing is, normally teen runaways aren't actually this good at vanishing. Unless they get on a bus and just head for the other side of the country, get off the grid—but none of these guys have done that, near as we can tell. We've checked all the train stations, bus stations. They just seem to have vanished."

"Oh," I say.

"Sex trafficking, kidnapping, they're not what they look

like on TV, someone stealing a kid from their home. Usually it's someone pretending to be their age on the internet, getting them to send nudes, then blackmailing them with those. So it could be we have someone like that operating in the area."

"Oh." My phone vibrates in my pocket. He has almost exactly described me and my texter. Except I got nudes back. So it can't be that. Unless those photos were fake. "I'll be careful, I promise."

He claps me on the shoulder. "Good. Especially online, okay? People aren't who they say they are."

I feel strangely numb and I'm not sure what to say. "I'm going to go get some food now." I walk away from him, back toward the picnic table, and make myself a plate. What Michael said was scary, but...there's no way. And besides, I'm going to meet my texter on FaceTime. If he says he's going to send my dirty pics out, I'll...I don't know, I guess tell Michael. Mortifying, but Callie would make me. No wonder she's so scared about all this, if she has to deal with her dad telling her about stuff like it all the time.

I sit down next to Callie and squeeze her hand. She's just scared for me. But she doesn't have to be. We talk and eat for a while, Callie's parents asking all about the dance, and Lenore and I carefully not mentioning Bryce. We show photos and then talk a little about the haunted house without getting into spoilers. When dessert is served, Lenore runs back into the house and comes out with her basket of eyeballs and a smile on her face.

"Callie, Gray," she says, holding out the basket. We sit opposite her, confused. "Happy early holidays." She opens the basket, and inside, among the eyeballs, are two tickets.

Callie plucks them out before I can, and as she reads them her eyes go wide. "The Graveyard?" she shouts.

"What?" I say, snapping a ticket. But they are—the Graveyard. This wild Halloween event that takes over a whole graveyard in Brooklyn for most of October, with performers and music and haunted houses and games. It's like a goth Burning Man carnival thing. We've always wanted to go, but tickets are hard to get. You have to wait online for hours before they even let you buy tickets, and then the only ones left are for weeknights, which don't work when the city is an hour away by train. At least, that's what happened last year, and before that we were too young to go.

"How did you get these?" Callie asks.

"I didn't sleep!" Lenore says. "I was up until about three sewing our outfits anyway."

"That's not healthy, sweetheart," Rose says.

Lenore waves her off. "I'll spend all of tomorrow sleeping, don't worry."

"That's not how it works," Rose says.

"Mom," Callie says. "Please let us enjoy this! We're going to the Graveyard!"

"And I got two extras for our adult escorts," Lenore says, turning to my moms. "Which I thought maybe could be you, if that's all right, because I thought you'd enjoy it the most."

Mom grins at Mama, who turns to Rose and Michael. "Only if you're all right with it."

"It sounds fun," Rose says, then turns to Michael. "But this one would probably ask the age of anyone he saw with a vape, which might put a damper on the evening."

"It's really bad for you, and illegal if they're under eighteen," Michael says, but he's smiling. He turns to my parents. "But I think Rose is right. You'll have a better time."

Mom wiggles her eyebrows at Mama. "We're going to a fancy party, I guess."

"But let us pay you back for the tickets," Mama tells Lenore. "At least ours."

Lenore looks like she might object but then nods. "Okay, it did cut into my fabric budget."

Callie runs around the picnic table to hug Lenore, and I join them.

"This is going to be so much fun," Lenore says.

"It's going to be hard to think about anything else for the next two weeks," Callie says.

"There's school," Michael says. "You can think about school."

We laugh, ignoring him. He, Rose, and my moms laugh and start talking to each other about curfews and rules.

"Thank you," I say to Lenore again. "This is amazing."

"I think it'll be really fun," she says. "Annnnnd maybe a nice place to meet someone."

Callie narrows her eyes. "It's huge. Think you'll find a guy there?"

Lenore shrugs and looks at her feet. "Maybe. I mean, you have Bryce, and Gray has"—she lowers her voice—"his guy." She sighs. "I was the one who wanted to find love this year."

"That was only a month ago," Callie says.

"Yes, but..." Lenore looks up at the moon. "After the

one guy who did ask me out turned out to be a homophobe, I'm just expanding my search beyond Sleepy Hollow."

"All right. But we're vetting them," Callie says, and looks at me.

I nod. "We're excellent judges of character."

Lenore raises an eyebrow at me and Callie bursts out laughing.

"I am!" I protest, but they keep laughing and then we start passing around the eyeballs and Mom's apple pie.

That night, in my room, I take out my phone. I didn't want to check it in front of Callie's dad, not after his little warning. I feel pretty sure Deer Friend isn't a serial killer, but I'm not sure I could convince Michael. Especially if he saw all the messages where we joke about killing each other. Callie says her dad loves discovery during cases.

Deer Friend:
Why are you thinking of me?

> **Gray:**
> Remember the moon ceremony
> I mentioned? It was tonight and
> I wished you were here.

Deer Friend:
I wish I was there too, though I think
I'd be pretty confused

> **Gray:**
> I never really explained it did I?

Deer Friend:
Only sort of

So I tell him all about the ceremony, and about being raised pagan, by two moms who don't subscribe to a specific form of paganism but just kind of make it up. I don't mention the store, afraid that'll make it seem hokey, but I tell him about the ceremony, and scrying and tarot, and how it feels like I'm always sort of dancing with the universe. With different energies. Trying to ride the ones that'll make me the version of me I want to be.

Deer Friend:
So no human sacrifice?

> **Gray:**
> Maybe if you had been here

Deer Friend:
Ah, all this thoughtful spiritual stuff is really just a ruse to lure me to my murder

> **Gray:**
> Not a ruse, I'm being very honest about it

Deer Friend:
True

Deer Friend:
Well I hope I can make it to one of them one day

> **Gray:**
> Me too

> **Gray:**
> Oh! And my friend got us tickets to this amazing Halloween event—if I say the name it'll give away where I am, but it's

> awesome. Like a fair and a
> party all at once.

Deer Friend:
I've been to stuff like that when I lived
in the city. I'm hoping to go again this
year.

> **Gray:**
> I'm so jealous. The best I've
> ever been to is the haunted
> hayride. 😩

Deer Friend:
Oh no that is 😩

Deer Friend:
But this year you can go to the real
thing. The one I went to was amazing.
Way better than a haunted hayride.
Though I did go on one of those when
I was little and got so scared by the
scarecrow that came to life that I
pissed myself.

Deer Friend:
I should not have told you that

> **Gray:**
> 😄 No that's adorable!

> **Gray:**
> Depending on your age

Deer Friend:
5. I honestly barely remember it. But
my mom loves to tell the story. How
scared I was, and I was crying and
then only got better once they took me
to get vanilla ice cream, my favorite,
and then I was happy. She says that's
why I love spooky stuff now. Because
I associate it with ice cream.

Gray:
Vanilla though?

Deer Friend:
Yes and I stand by it. Still my favorite.

Gray:
On someone else I'd be very disappointed but okay.

Deer Friend:
What's your favorite ice cream then, if you're going to make fun of me?

Gray:
I like anything with chips in it, or chunks, and cherries, too. Chocolate and peanut butter. Peanut butter cups? Frozen— delicious. Caramel swirls. A lot more.

Deer Friend:
So everything but vanilla?

Gray:
Vanilla is okay too I guess.

Deer Friend:
And you're not going to tease me or make jokes about me being vanilla in bed?

Gray:
Are you vanilla in bed?

Deer Friend:
I mean, I like some stuff. I don't know. I'm not into anything crazy, I guess. Why, you have some intense fetish or something?

Gray:
I guess not. I mean, I like the trappings of a fetish—sexy black underwear, handcuffs, leather, fishnets, but I've never really done anything. Closet Case's kink was being with a guy. Didn't want to push it further than that.

Deer Friend:
You said he's the only guy you've slept with?

Gray:
Yeah. Not many options. You?

Deer Friend:
A couple. And I've been handcuffed once. It was sort of hot for some of it, but not all.

Gray:
That's vague

Deer Friend:
Bring handcuffs when we meet up and I'll show you what I mean 😈

Deer Friend:
Texting that got me kind of hard so I guess I'm not so vanilla

Gray:
And I guess I'd better get some handcuffs.

Deer Friend:
And I'll get some sexy black underwear. I have a black thong. That work?

> **Gray:**
> YES
>
> **Deer Friend:**
> Hold on a second

    I get up and lock the door to my room, hoping he's going to send me another photo. Even just talking about this with him has me pretty horny. I wonder if this means I should send him another photo, too. The underwear I wore in my last one is probably the sexiest I own, though. The rest are plain. Nothing like a thong. Maybe he's going to find me too innocent and virginal, I suddenly worry. Only been with one guy. Boring underwear.

    A photo comes through. Same crop as last time, almost the same post too, but this time in a black thong. It's really hot.

> **Deer Friend:**
> I can't show you the front, I'm kind of popping out
>
> > **Gray:**
> > This is very hot. I feel bad I don't have a thong to take a photo of myself in
>
> **Deer Friend:**
> That's okay
>
> > **Gray:**
> > I guess I'm the vanilla one
>
> **Deer Friend:**
> Not really

> **Gray:**
> I have black briefs. I can give myself a wedgie.

> **Deer Friend:**
> 😄 You don't have to send me anything

> **Gray:**
> I just feel bad. You're sending me hot photos and I want to send you hot photos.

> **Deer Friend:**
> You have leather pants? Or vinyl? I love those.

I grin. I do have some tight vinyl pants.

> **Gray:**
> Hold on

I feel silly taking a photo in the same pose, but so did he, and without underwear under them, the pants look really hot. I take one of my crotch again, and one of me from behind. My ass looks okay. I send him both.

> **Deer Friend:**
> That's really hot

> **Deer Friend:**
> Wear those for our date

> **Gray:**
> With no underwear underneath, like now?

> **Deer Friend:**
> That does make them even hotter
>
> **Deer Friend:**
> You unzipping them?
>
> > **Gray:**
> > YES
>
> **Deer Friend:**
> Can I see?

I smile and take another photo of my crotch, this time with the fly unzipped—but nothing showing beyond some pubes. I send that.

> **Deer Friend:**
> Yes
>
> **Deer Friend:**
> Is it weird if I tell you I'm jerking off right now?

I slip the pants off and start doing the same

> > **Gray:**
> > Me too
>
> **Deer Friend:**
> I would love to be sitting in your lap right now, with just this thong on
>
> > **Gray:**
> > I want to grab your ass and pull you onto me
>
> **Deer Friend:**
> Would you kiss my neck
>
> > **Gray:**
> > Yes. I'd bite

> **Deer Friend:**
> And you'd be inside me
>
> > **Gray:**
> > Yes, and I'd get up and put you down on the bed, on your back.
>
> **Deer Friend:**
> I want you to kiss me so bad
>
> > **Gray:**
> > Me too

He doesn't text for a moment and I just picture it, sex with him—a shadow where his face should be, my eyes closed, just imagining his body. I finish off very quickly.

> **Deer Friend:**
> I came
>
> > **Gray:**
> > Me too
>
> **Deer Friend:**
> oh good I was worried I was too fast
>
> > **Gray:**
> > I don't know I've never sexted before
>
> **Deer Friend:**
> Me neither guess I really like you
>
> > **Gray:**
> > I really like you too
>
> **Deer Friend:**
> ♥
>
> > **Gray:**
> > ♥

11

The next two weeks go by in a blur. Mostly we work on Halloween decorations, adding texture and paint to the foam blocks and then starting to assemble them the way the 3D modeling program wants. It's harder than it should be—some of the shapes it told us to make were hard to carve and we need to whittle them down a little to fit.

School is pretty boring, aside from Ms. Mullins going from *Dracula* to *Dr. Jekyll and Mr. Hyde*, complete with a beautiful lecture on the darkness in each of us. By the time the weekend of the Graveyard comes around, I can barely focus. All I can think about is how amazing it will be.

That Saturday, we all have dinner together at Calabaza, Lenore's favorite restaurant, where everything tastes good and looks like a painting, especially the little jack-o'-lantern truffles on top of the blackout brownies we always get for dessert. Callie and I treat Lenore and my moms as thanks for getting us the tickets and chaperoning us, respectively. We are all decked out for it, too, including my moms. Mama has a long black gown with bell sleeves and a long black cloak to wear over it. Mom has a bright red suit on over a black shirt, and a black pearl choker with a big black skull in the center. She also has black driving gloves I've never seen before and will have to borrow at some point. Callie is in a suit, with a top hat, her braids back in a low ponytail. Her face is meticulously painted with a mix of gold gears and skulls, a full clockwork picture going from under each eye down her cheeks and neck. Lenore is in a black A-line, fifties-style dress, her hair flipping out at the ends. Her eyes are yellow. On the dress is a large faux-diamond-encrusted pin in the shape of a knife, with a few faux rubies in key spots. I feel the least dressed up in my black-and-red brocade trench coat, over a torn fishnet shirt and black crop top, and my vinyl pants. I've done my makeup the usual way: pale powder, smudged eyeliner, black lipstick, but I should have done something more, I think. Maybe a necklace. Everyone else looks amazing, and I look pretty good, but not nearly as done up.

Mama drives us into the city. We play music the whole time, but over that we look at the Graveyard's website and try to figure out what we should do. The problem is that it's vague. There's no map online, and it's not specific about a lot of stuff. Shows. A haunted house. Dancers, musicians. We decide we have to do the haunted house, but after that we should just wander and see what we see.

It's dark by the time Mama parks outside the event. There's a line filtering in, but not too slowly, and seeing the crowds, I don't feel as underdressed anymore. Some folks are just in jeans and sweatshirts, and others are in full *It* cosplay, so the range is wide.

When we finally hand off our tickets and enter, it's even better than I could have imagined. It's a real graveyard, several acres, with old mausoleum-style crypts dotted throughout. Huge trees twist up between gravestones, and the path snakes up a hill, so we can't see it all right away. We'll have to discover it. The weather is perfect, cool with the softest breeze.

We look around a bit. There's a stand selling apple cider made from the apple trees that grow in the graveyard, and there are tinted lights between the headstones that illuminate dancers balancing on gravestones, or each other. Tinted light in a graveyard. I wish Deer Friend were here with me.

I stop for a moment to admire one of the very good-looking male dancers as he holds up another dancer doing a handstand. The black tatters of their costumes sway. They have on white face makeup and dark eyes. I watch with my parents, Callie, and Lenore for a moment, and then past the dancer, I see someone else watching—Malcolm. Amanda Lash.

His drag tonight isn't as intense as at the dance. He's in a short black dress and shredded black tights, his wig a long black number with bangs cut into a point in the center. His eyebrows have been painted like an old cartoon. The dress sparkles, and he's got an amazing giant red stone in a medallion. Around that he wears a sort of stole, or scarf, of black mesh that must have been spray-glue molded, so it's around his shoulders, but also flying up, bending, twisting, even though there's no wind. He looks like a witch turning into a cloud of mist. It's pretty cool.

Callie spots him and waves.

"Who's that?" Mama asks.

"Malcolm," I say. "I told you, new kid."

"Are we talking to him?" Lenore asks. "I thought he was the competition."

"I don't know," I say. "He did finally apologize for"—I glance at my moms—"the thing he said."

"That's good," Lenore says, her voice a whisper as Malcolm gets closer.

"He's cool," Callie assures us. "Be nice."

"I didn't know you'd be here!" Malcolm says to Callie when he gets close. They hug, and Lenore and I exchange a glance.

"Lenore got us tickets," Callie says, pointing at Lenore, who nods at him. "It's so cool! Have you been before?"

"Yeah," he says, tossing his wig slightly. I can't tell if it's part of the Amanda Lash persona or just that natural condescending thing he has—which maybe is about his insecurity, I guess. He glances up at my parents, a little nervous.

"These are my mom and mama," I tell him. "They drove us."

"Two moms," he says, eyes widening. "Who own the family business..." He looks like he's thinking about something. Sometimes people are weirded out by the two moms thing, but never other queer people. No idea what his face is doing. He smiles broadly at them. "Nice to meet you." His eyes flick down, to my pants, then up again, and for a moment I think he's going to laugh at my outfit, but he just smiles again. Weirdly. Like he knows something.

"Nice to meet you, too," Mama says. "We were about to tell these three that we should meet back at that tombstone"—she points at a large one at the turn in the road—"at ten p.m. You have our phone numbers if you need us before then. Text every now and then so we know you're—" She smirks. "I was going to say alive, but I guess let's just say safe."

"We'll be around," Mom says, taking Mama's hand and walking off down the path into the graveyard.

"They seem cool," Malcolm says to me. "They're like, eldergoths?"

"Yeah," I say.

He nods, a slight smirk on his face. I wonder if he's about to say something about how that explains why my style is old-fashioned, but he doesn't.

"Amanda!" someone calls from farther up the hill. Malcolm turns, spots them, and waves. He starts to head up that way but then glances back at us, eyes lingering on me for a moment.

"Do you want to come meet some friends?"

"I think we're going to look around some," I say quickly. "It's our first time, so we want to see everything." He's kind of weirding me out right now. I'm glad we've gone from disliking each other to friendly competitors, I guess, but now he's acting really strange and I don't know if I want to be around that.

"But we can say hi," Callie says, half glaring at me.

"Sure," Lenore says.

Malcolm smiles and walks us up to his friends. There are three of them: Decker, whose eyes are different colors—one gold, one green—and who wears loose black clothes with a bunch of straps connecting them at weird angles; Joan, with short spiky black hair and a studded jumpsuit; and Anthony, with long wavy blond hair, huge round glasses, and a beautiful brocade jacket.

"These are my country friends," Malcolm says before introducing us.

"It's not like it's farmland," I say. "It's just the suburbs."

Malcolm laughs like I've made a joke.

"Sleepy Hollow seems fun," Decker says. "You ever see the Horseman?"

"No," Lenore says, so bored of that question. "I like your jacket," she says to Anthony.

"Oh, thanks," Anthony says, looking at the ground, then pushing his glasses up as they slip slightly. "I made it."

"That's fantastic," Lenore says, stepping closer and examining the jacket more. "What stitch did you use for the detailing on the shoulders?"

Anthony looks up, a little confused at her sudden interest. "Ladder."

"It looks good. My ladder stitch always ends up looking too tight."

"Oh," he says.

"We should get going if you want to see that show," Malcolm says, taking Anthony's arm. He looks at Callie, then me. "You want to come?"

I glance at Lenore, who seems a little annoyed at having her meet-cute interrupted—and possibly because Anthony and Malcolm are together, based on the way Malcolm was just so possessive.

"I think we wanted to do the haunted house first," I say.

Callie nods. "That was the plan. But we will for sure find you later."

Malcolm smiles. "Great. See you in a bit."

They walk off and Lenore sighs. "He was cute."

"You want to go catch up to them?" Callie asks. "Maybe get to know him more?"

Lenore shrugs, shakes her head. "He didn't seem interested. And from the way Malcolm took his arm, not single. Maybe not even interested in women."

"I don't know, could just be friends," Callie says. "Some friends are like that."

"I'm sure he's got a boyfriend," I say.

Callie laughs. "Why?"

"He's kind of famous, cute, good style."

Lenore raises an eyebrow. "Oh, Malcolm, you mean— I thought you meant Anthony." She smiles. "Should your text friend be jealous?"

I roll my eyes. "No. He just called us country friends. We live like half an hour from the city. Snob."

Callie laughs. "Yeah, his humor sometimes feels like he's not joking, but I'm pretty sure that was him being funny. He's a nice guy once you get to know him, I promise. But who cares? Let's go find the haunted house."

It takes us a while to find it. The graveyard is huge and there are so many performers we stop to watch for a bit. Acrobats, dancers, musicians. One man plays a haunting violin solo in the door to a small crypt, the light behind him set up so he's just a shadow. Some dancers in sparkling green tights slither up and down a large angel statue.

There's a play being put on between graves, there's a pond with someone standing on a boat in the middle of it, singing. There's art, too, huge carved monsters, woven stick charms hung from trees. The place is alive and beautiful and dark and eerie and we love it. I wish I could live in this. I wish I could *make* this.

We finally get to the haunted house after stopping to watch a million other things. It's at the edge of the graveyard, and a plaque out front says it was originally the groundskeeper's house, but it burned down, and they built a re-creation in the nineties, but then added a bunch of rooms to make it a museum. Or, tonight, a house of terror. There's no line, we're just given little buzzers that go off when it's our time, so we hang out nearby until our numbers are up, trying some of the graveyard apple cider (which is a little sour, but not especially different from normal apple cider) and taking selfies with various backdrops.

Inside, it's complete blackness in the first room. I feel other people, waiting with us, all of our breathing seeming extra loud in the dark.

I hear a door close, and suddenly a neon sign comes on above us, on the ceiling: THE DEAD LOVE TO PLAY.

Suddenly, in the light of the neon, the walls all ripple— they were curtains the whole time—and figures dressed head to toe in black emerge from them and start grabbing people. There are shrieks, and people are pulled through the curtains. The light goes out again. I reach out for Callie and Lenore but can't find them. A hand wraps around my wrist and starts pulling me. I'm taken through a curtain, and then another, and suddenly I'm in a dimly lit room.

There's one other person here with me, a girl whose face I can't see, stumbling as if she was just pulled in, too. I don't know if she's another audience member or a performer.

Suddenly, there's noise. Music, almost. The windup of a jack-in-the-box, but too slow. I shudder, looking around for what will pop out. The room is dark, lined in a deep red velvet, floor, ceiling, and walls. The only light comes from a few small fairy lights in the corners of the room.

"Where will it pop from?" the girl whispers. She's got to be part of this.

"I don't know," I say, looking for a seam, anything. There's nothing—I can't even tell where we were dragged in from. It's just a closed box. The light flickers. The music keeps going on, longer than it should. I can feel my heart racing. I start pawing at the walls and finally find a seam. It clicks as I push on it. Is something going to pop out? I stand back and wait. The winding noise continues. The light flickers again. Something feels wrong. I look at the girl, her face still hidden by the light. She must do something.

I try the seam again, and it suddenly flies outward with a shrieking laugh noise.

"We're the jack?" the girl whispers. The door has opened on a dark hallway. It's too small to walk in—I'll have to crawl. I start in and find myself in a tube, with netted windows on either side opening onto other rooms. In one I see Lenore and a bearded guy screaming as a giant teddy bear advances on them. I stop to watch, but the girl behind me whispers, "Keep going, I don't like small spaces," so I keep moving.

We eventually come out in another room, dark, but more furnished than the last one—and in the Victorian style. There's a table with a tea set, a rug, two chairs, and a sofa. On the sofa and chairs are dolls. Old-fashioned ones with porcelain faces and glass eyes, hair in curls, all larger than they should be. The chairs are too tall, the table too wide. I see a door on the other end of the room at the same time the girl with me points at it.

"They're going to come to life, right?" I ask. We walk slowly toward the door. Maybe they won't come to life, maybe it's a fakeout like the jack that never popped. I make it to the door and open it—and waiting there is another doll, a bloody knife held high in her hand. I scream, backing up into the girl, who is also screaming, and we run away, which is when the other dolls finally spring to life, chasing us around the room screaming "Tea party!"

We run for a while, being chased around the room. The girl jumps the sofa and reaches out her hand and I take it, climbing over it to join her by the door, and we escape. It's a long bright room, the walls made out of huge multicolored blocks. It's the first time I can see the girl clearly, and realize—it's Malcolm.

"Oh," I say. We're still holding hands. His thumb is resting on my wrist, a light, pleasant pressure. We both have damp skin from running, screaming, laughing, and I get a whiff of that clove incense smell off him. I let go.

"This is great!" he says, apparently not surprised it's me. He looks around at the walls of blocks. "You were so brave in the jack-in-the-box. I was freaking out waiting."

I laugh, and blush a little that he thinks I was brave. "I thought you were part of the crew, like you were going to pop."

"Pop?" he asks, a wicked smile appearing on his face. I realize how it sounded when I said that and turn away, embarrassed. "So, any thoughts on how we get out of this one?"

"I don't know," I say, deciding to focus on the house and the fun of running and screaming instead of on Malcolm, and how his hand felt. I think his wig has perfume in it, too, something smoky. That can't just be him, right?

I shake my head and look at the room. There's no door. Even the one we came out of has vanished into the blocks. The room seems tiny, too. I walk forward and realize that the way the blocks are set up is covering other parts of the room, depending on the angle. And there are mirrors, too. The whole room could be vast, it's impossible to tell.

"It's bigger than it looks," I tell Malcolm, turning a corner. "It's a maze."

I look back and can't see Malcolm at all until he rounds the corner. And then behind him I see the blocks start to move. A golem of giant blocks pulling itself out from the wall. Amazing costuming, and deeply terrifying.

"Behind you!" I yelp, and start running.

This isn't like the dollhouse, this is so much scarier, because I can't see an exit and don't know if we're just running in circles. The golem moves slowly at least, but each of its footsteps echoes heavily. I briefly wonder how they pulled that off, but I'm too busy shrieking and looking for corners to focus on it.

The room can't be as big as it feels, we must be going in circles. Yes—we're facing the golem again and I turn around, almost knocking Malcolm over, but instead grabbing him for a moment and lifting him up, running and putting him down facing the right way. He's surprisingly light. Or maybe that's the adrenaline.

"There!" he shouts, pointing, and I see a small space between the blocks. He darts in, and I follow, and we find a huge dark circle in the wall. The golem is behind us. We jump in.

It's another crawling tunnel. Again we can see different rooms through dark windows. I spot Callie running from a huge rubber duck with fangs in what looks like a decaying bathroom.

I crawl after Malcolm and notice in the dim light how, as he's bent over, I can see up his skirt, to the skimpy black underwear he has on. He has a nice ass, but I look away— it feels rude, invasive. They should probably say out front this isn't a skirt-friendly haunted house.

We come out in the room I saw Lenore in, covered in teddy bears and matted fur. The tunnel deposits us on the floor, on our knees. The fur feels this unsettling combination of soft and crunchy. It's perfect for the vibe.

"I wish I could study this."

"You should," Malcolm says. "I mean...you should make stuff like this."

"What?" I ask.

"You love decorating your store, and your window displays are good. And your taste. Someone must make places like this, why not you?"

But I barely have time to register the slew of compliments—from Malcolm of all people—much less the idea of making places like this being a job.

One of the bears comes to life and charges at us, real-looking fangs in its plushy mouth wet with blood. Malcolm grabs my hand to help me up and we run, laughing, screaming. Each of the rooms is similar—something big chasing us, haunted toys. The rubber ducky is probably the silliest, though the curved bathtub-like walls make it feel scarier. My favorites are the faceless marionettes that drop randomly from the ceiling as we work our way through what feels like a forgotten attic. There are melted army men zombies and a horrible Barbie-like monster created from pieces of other Barbies and action figures, which cocks its head in a way no normal human in a costume should be able to. It shouts that it wants to play with us; tells us that we have so many good parts for more toys. By the time we make it out of the haunted house, I'm sweating, breathless. It was so much fun.

Lenore is already outside, talking with her haunted-house partner, the tall guy with the beard.

"Wasn't that great?" she asks, grinning when she spots me. "I don't think I've ever screamed so hard."

"No?" the guy with the beard asks. "You seem like you'd be a good screamer."

Lenore laughs.

I study the guy. He's older, college senior or junior, maybe. He's got pale skin and dark curly hair that fades down into his beard, which is kind of pointy. His eyebrows are pointy, too. He's wearing a little black eye shadow and a torn black tee and skinny jeans.

Lenore sees me looking and introduces him. "This is François. We were in the haunted house together." She keeps looking at him, smiling. "He saved me from the duck."

François grins, shakes his head. "Couldn't let you get ducked right in front of me."

She laughs again and introduces me and Malcolm.

I keep my expression neutral, but everything about this guy is giving me bad vibes, and I do not understand why Lenore is grinning at him. Adrenaline maybe. Same reason I'm still kind of thinking about Malcolm's ass in the skirt. But this guy is ... how old is he, anyway?

"How old are you?" Malcolm asks.

"Huh?" François says. "I'm in college. NYU. How about you guys?"

"We're all in high school," I say, smiling.

"Cool," he says, nodding, apparently not at all concerned by it.

I catch Malcolm looking at me. He's frowning. I frown back. We're finally in agreement about something: This guy is bad news.

"Oh my god!" Callie says, stumbling out of the haunted house. Malcolm's friend with the spiky hair, Joan, is behind her.

"That was intense!" Joan says, grinning ear to ear. "And this girl"—she wraps her arm around Callie and points—"this girl is fire!"

Callie laughs. "I just figured that brick monster couldn't turn too fast or see too well."

"She told me to run circles around it and I was like 'What? That's crazy! I don't want to get close to the monster!' but she was like 'Trust me' so I did and we ended up getting it so dizzy it fell on its ass!" She lets go of Callie to make double fists in the air and then high-fives Callie. "Awesome!" She goes over and hugs Malcolm. "Your new friends seem cool. I'm glad you're not alone up there."

"Yeah," Malcolm says, looking sad for a moment before shrugging it off.

"We're going to kick his ass in the haunted house competition, though," Callie says. "Better than what we just went through."

"Oh yeah?" Malcolm says, raising his nose in the air a little. "I doubt it."

"Hey," Joan says. "She's fire. She might. Don't get cocky." She turns to Callie. "But that's awesome you're in it, too. We want to come up for it, but with school..." She sighs, shrugs. "Still, it's all Malcolm has been texting us about. Well, that and—"

Malcolm covers her mouth with his hand before she can say anything else. "No giving away secrets to the competition."

She rolls her eyes but nods and he takes his hand away. "We gotta go find Anthony and Decker, anyway," she says.

"Oh," Malcolm says, looking at me, then glancing to Lenore and François. I nod—he can go find his boyfriend. "Yeah."

"Y'all want to come with?" Joan asks.

I take out my phone and glance at the time. We don't have to meet my parents for another hour or so. I shrug at Callie, who is now looking at Lenore and François, her eyes narrowing.

"Yeah," Callie says. "Lenore, Gray? Let's all go with them."

"Yeah," I agree, looking at Lenore.

"Oh well, François was telling me about some like secret show in one of the crypts," she says. "I thought we could do that."

I know that the missing teens are all guys and all up in Westchester, and I'm almost positive that it's just Poly Perry and his boyfriends, but suddenly I am very very sure that François is the serial killer. Or at least *a* serial killer.

"We can go with you to that," Callie says, walking over. She sticks her hand out. "Hi, I'm Callie, high school junior."

"Hey," François says, again not at all fazed by her mentioning high school. He shakes her hand. "I'm François. NYU. You all seem real cool."

"Okay, well, we'll see you hopefully before we all leave," Joan says. "And if not, send me photos of your decorations on Halloween, too! I bet it'll be fire."

"Fire!" Callie says, matching her enthusiasm. Joan and Malcolm turn to walk off, Malcolm glancing back once and waving and then taking something out of his pocket that seems to magically unfurl into his scarf from before. I shake my head. If he can do that just with a scarf, he's going to make something amazing for Halloween.

Lenore has barely paid attention to all this. She's been talking softly with François, even has her phone out, taking selfies with him—and, oh yes, they're exchanging numbers. Great.

Callie looks at me, and I nod, our mutual concern screaming silently.

"So where is this secret show?" Callie asks. "We should tell Gray's moms about it, too."

Smart. I text my moms, just checking in for now.

"Follow me," François says. He reaches out and takes Lenore's hand and starts leading us through the dancers and tombstones. Lenore and François walk ahead of us, him telling her he's been coming to this for years and knows all the secrets, while Callie and I hang back, speaking softly.

"She got paired with him in the haunted house," I say.

She nods. "Figured. Well. Let's see what happens, I guess. Her life, her choices."

"Yes, but we'll watch so she doesn't get murdered."

We're quiet, listening to François go on about how he met one of the organizers of Graveyard last year and they complimented him on his shirt.

"So you were paired with Malcolm?" Callie asks me.

"Yeah."

"That was okay?"

"Sure. I mean, it was mostly us screaming and running around. It was fun."

She nods, watching as we pass by a contortionist curved into a circle. "I think, you know..." She shakes her head.

"What?"

"Just, knowing him, knowing you, I think if you didn't have your serial killer boyfriend, and you'd met just a little differently, I bet you would be dating by now."

I laugh. "Really?"

She sticks up her chin. "Yeah."

"Well, he has a boyfriend, too, clearly, and hey, I might not be the only one with my very own serial killer," I say, looking at Lenore and François, who are now a little farther ahead of us than I'd like. I try to speed up, and Callie matches my pace.

"I just mean, I just think it's cute. Two goth boys."

"Malcolm and Anthony were pretty cute together," I concede. They were. Perfectly styled, the way Malcolm seemed so much more comfortable with him. "I don't know how my texter dresses exactly," though as I say it, I think immediate of the thong and hope the dim light hides my blush. "But he's definitely culturally goth."

Callie laughs, then looks a little sad. "I wish Bryce were more into this stuff. I invited him but he couldn't get a ticket for the same night. Said it was for the best, that he'd probably be scared."

I laugh.

"I know, it's funny, but does that mean I'm too scary?"

"Maybe?" I say. "But if so, I'm pretty sure he's into it."

She laughs. "Yeah. After the dance, we, uh..." She looks away for a moment. I raise my eyebrows. Callie is— or was—a virgin.

"Wow," I say. "You liked it?"

"Weird at first, but by the end, yes." She shakes her head. "Sorry, this is oversharing. I know Lenore isn't a virgin, so I'd normally tell her, but she's been so desperate for a boyfriend, I didn't want to make her jealous."

"Well, I'm only jealous in that there's a guy I'd love to be having sex with but he's just text messages."

"Aww, don't be sad," she says, patting me on the back. "He's probably also a serial killer."

I sigh wistfully. "If only."

She laughs and we're quiet for a moment.

"I'm not a virgin, either," I say.

"Oh." She looks confused, then nods. "Closet Case?"

"Yeah. A lot. I'm sorry I never told you, I just...I didn't like talking about it because I felt like I was telling someone else's secret. But if you're telling me, I dunno, I feel like I should reciprocate."

She smiles and knocks her shoulder into mine. "You don't ever have to tell me anything you don't want to. I just wanted to tell someone. So it felt real. And so it didn't feel like I was making a mistake or anything." Her eyes dart up to Lenore and François. They've gotten farther ahead again.

"No," I say. "I don't think that. And besides, would you even trust my judgment in that department?"

She laughs. "Maybe not."

We walk past a break in the tombstones, a spray of white petals like a starburst in the center of it, surrounding a kneeling woman in red dress. She watches us walk by and throws out her hand, shooting red petals from it like a fountain.

"Some kind of hose in the sleeve of her dress," I say. "Amazing."

"Not hard to build, I'll bet," Callie says.

"You think I could do this?" I ask, remembering what Malcolm said. "Like, someone must make these things, organize them, right? Could that be, like, what I go to school for?"

She pauses as if it's just occurring to her, too. "I mean, I don't know what that major is...but yeah." She smiles at me, eyes bright in the dim lights. "Yeah, you could."

"Here we are," François says suddenly, lifting a low-hanging branch on a tree that was blocking a little side path. We follow him away from the crowds, and it gets quieter, more like the real graveyard it is the rest of the year. For a moment, I wonder if I can take François. He's tall, and looks kind of muscular, but not too big. I bet between me and Callie we can do it, unless he has a knife or something.

But then I hear the faint strains of a cello, and they get louder as we walk until finally the path opens and we find ourselves in front of a huge crypt. We go inside, and it's almost like a small church. Tombs line the walls, but there's an altar on a raised platform up front, and benches.

And, to my great relief, my moms. They're sitting on a bench in the back and smile and wave at us as we come in, their eyes darting to François, but not saying anything. He, however, drops Lenore's hand. Finally, something that fazes him: older women.

But none of us say anything because in front of the altar is a woman in a white dress, with long red hair, sitting on a stool and playing the cello. I sit next to my moms, and Callie, Lenore, and François take the bench behind us, and we just sit and listen. The acoustics are beautiful. It's like every string on the cello is breathing. I don't know the piece. It's haunting and vibrant, making me feel all the elements at once, like every spirit has gathered here just to hear her play. The music feels tangible, as if it's washing around us, playing with my hair, filling my lungs. When she finally stops, the music takes longer than it should to fade, the final note still ringing.

When the room finally turns silent, my moms start to

applaud. Mama, I notice, is crying. I clap, too, and soon everyone is applauding. The cellist smiles and bows her head a little, then starts packing up the cello.

"Beautiful," Mama says.

"How did you find this place?" I ask. "François says it was secret."

"This tomb is my family tomb," Mama says.

"What?" I almost scream. It echoes and everyone looks at me.

"Very distantly. And obviously full." Mama gestures at the walls. "But these are great-great-great-aunts, I think? Cousins many times removed, distant family. But I still wanted to see it, of course. I've come here a few times. I didn't know they'd be paying it such a lovely tribute." She smiles and stands. "Let's go thank her," she says, drifting past me to the cellist.

Mom grins at me, smiling, then glances past me at François. "Make a new friend?" she asks in a low voice.

"Lenore did," I say softly. "We're trying not to leave him alone with her."

"Go with your mama. I'll handle it." She pats me on the shoulder and walks over to my friends, and I turn and follow Mama, who has approached the cellist.

"Hello," Mama says to her as I come up. She's just done packing up, cello case over her shoulder. "I just wanted to say that this is my family tomb and I was very touched by your music."

The woman's eyes go wide. "This is your family?"

Mama nods.

"And you're not offended?"

Mama smiles and shakes her head. "I think it's lovely. The dead deserve some music, and playing here is..." She pauses and looks around. "I know some people would consider it sacrilegious or indecent, but to me, that music in this place was fitting. It felt like you were honoring them. So thank you." She reaches out for the cellist's hand, and the cellist takes it and shakes it.

"Thank you," she says, looking a little confused. "I honestly thought it was kind of a creepy gig, but thank you."

Mama smiles and lets her go, then glides over to the tombs on the shelves. There are names carved into the shelves, and she traces them with her hands. "It's not like I really know these people, of course," she says. "I never met them, barely know how I'm related to them. But I've heard stories." She points at one of the names. "Marianne was a widow three times. She ran a tea salon and people would come to her for advice. A priest called her a witch, but it was New York City. No one cared much about witch accusations in the 1910s. I've always loved her—or my idea of her—a clever lady with a tea salon making special blends for people. To help them get what they wanted, or maybe— in the case of her husbands, all of whom apparently hit her—what they deserved."

"So she's my relative?" I ask, pointing at the tomb. MARIANNE is carved above it, with little flowers on the sides.

"Your great-great-something maybe," Mama says, hands clasped together. She drifts to the next tomb. "Eleanor was her daughter. One of them. Died young, if what my mother told me was true. Spanish flu. She was a strong advocate for masking during the flu and one day a man didn't like the look of her, so he tore her mask off and spit in her face. She caught it and died. So did the man, from what I understand."

"That sounds like a story from today," I say.

Mama makes a sound, not an unhappy one, like a hum telling me I'm right. "Things happen in cycles. History repeats. Stories are told over and over. The saddest thing about living is how little we learn from the past. How fixed we get in our ways, our ideas. Our brains stop being flexible." She turns to me and takes my hands. "Never be afraid to doubt yourself, to be lost, to make mistakes. You can't avoid bad things happening, become so stiff and scared and set in your ways you don't take a chance. Maybe something bad will happen, but maybe the bad will lead to good." She nods at the crypts. "That's history. Don't forget it."

She's being kind of weird. "Okay," I say.

"Sorry, just feeling sentimental," she says, dropping my hands and walking past me to my friends and Mom. She's standing between Lenore and François, and I'm pleased to see he looks nervous.

"We wanted to buy you kids some candy we saw at one of the stands," Mom says. "And then it's nearly time to get going. That sound all right, or do you want to do your own thing?" She glances between all of us.

"I wouldn't say no to free candy," Callie says.

Lenore glances back and forth between Mom and François.

"You really should see some of these, Lenore," Mama says. "Some of the craftsmanship on the candy rivals yours."

That gets Lenore. Her eyes go wide, as if she's been challenged. "Then yes, let's go get some candy."

"I, uh, I . . ." François rubs the back of his neck with his hand. "I'll text you."

"I'd like that," Lenore says.

I try to think of something to say that'll stop that short, but I'm not sure what. Especially from me. François gives her a hug before leaving, and Mom smirks with triumph.

I take some photos of the tomb, both inside and out, as we leave.

"I know what you were doing," Lenore says to us as we trail behind my moms. "He was nice. And hot."

"And old enough that him hitting on you when he knew your age was sketchy," Callie says. "He gave me bad energy."

"Me too," I say.

Lenore snorts. "Like you should talk. At least I knew his age."

I glance at my moms. They're quiet but don't look back like they've heard this. "I know my guy's age," I whisper.

"You know what he says is his age," Lenore says back, not as softly as I'd like.

"Well, when I FaceTime him, I'll know more," I say. "And if he looks suspiciously old, I will trust my friends. That's what you told me to do, right?"

Lenore frowns. "Yeah." She kicks a stone on the path. "It felt nice to be noticed, though. By someone who didn't seem that terrible. Though his T-shirt was terrible."

"It was," Callie says. "Imagine dating someone who thought that was fashion."

"Well—" Lenore starts, but Callie continues over her.

"And don't say you could have shown him real fashion or something, that's just saying 'I can fix him,' which is never a good thing."

Lenore sighs. "Well, maybe he'll text me." Her phone dings, as if on cue. She smiles. "See?" But then she opens the message and frowns. I peek over her shoulder. It's a semierect penis resting on a tombstone. Lenore deletes it, blocks the number, and puts her phone away without saying anything else. We walk in silence for a moment until all three of us burst out laughing.

"What's so funny?" Mama asks, turning around.

We all shake our heads. "Nothing," I say.

Mama arches an eyebrow, but we keep walking. With my parents in tow, we go slower, and I have time to stop and take more photos of dancers and musicians. It's a beautiful place, and a beautiful night. I'm so happy, I can feel it welling up inside me like all the colors of a bubble.

I pull out my phone.

> **Gray:**
> I'm having a wonderful night. I wish you were here
>
> **Deer Friend:**
> Same
>
> **Deer Friend:**
> It sort of feels like maybe you are

I heart that and smile, putting my phone away. It would be great if he were here, but I'm just happy thinking about him.

We follow my moms to the candy stand—they weren't lying, some of this looks like Lenore could have made it. Licorice spiderwebs with mint juniper hard candy spiders, black dark chocolate anatomical heart truffles with strawberry blood filling, cinnamon marshmallow skulls. Lenore spends twenty minutes just admiring everything and taking photos for inspiration before finally asking if they're hiring. They are, and the woman behind the stand who runs the shop loves some of Lenore's photos of her own work, but they're based in Brooklyn, which is probably too far of a commute for now. But she follows the shop on Instagram, and the shop follows her back, so she walks away happy, and we all walk away with a lot of candy.

We stop at a hot chocolate stand, too, then meander back toward the parking lot as we sip, the paper cups warming our hands. It's gotten colder, I realize. I shiver, which is when I hear a voice behind me.

"Getting cold?"

I turn. It's Malcolm and his friends, watching a harpist playing on a small hill surrounded by gravestones, soft purple lights set up to illuminate her.

"A little," I say, and sip my cocoa. I don't know what to make of him at this point. Sometimes he seems okay, sometimes he seems like he just thinks he's so much better than me. I feel like I could like him if I knew what he was really thinking. I wish I could read him. Then I'd know.

"We're leaving," Callie says, giving him a hug. She waves at his friends. "Nice meeting all of you."

"You too!" Joan says. "I'm going to find you on social. You're fire!"

"You're fire, too!" Callie says, hugging her.

Anthony smiles at all of us before laying his head on Malcolm's shoulder. They're a cute couple. Decker just nods.

"It was really nice to see you," Malcolm says to all of us, his eyes landing on me last. He tilts his head, like he's confused by me, and I wonder if I have some hot chocolate on my lip. I wipe my hand over my mouth. He keeps staring. Weird.

"Good night," I say. "See you at school."

He turns away, with his friends, and we keep walking, finishing our hot cocoa as we get to the car. Mom gets behind the wheel to drive us home, and I must fall asleep because next thing I know, I'm giving sleepy hugs to Lenore and Callie as we let them out at their houses. At home, Mom and Mama both kiss me on the forehead, and I go up to my room and crawl into bed. I dream about soft purple light through tombstones and holding Deer Friend's hand in the dark while my dead and very distant relatives play the cello.

12

Sunday I sleep in a lot, and then have to spend the rest of the day doing homework, but with only about a week left to go before Halloween, I know we have to focus on decorating the store. And on our costumes, I realize.

I'm thinking about it, trying to figure out something that goes well with the haunted house—maybe just a guy with his heart ripped out—in homeroom on Monday, when Ms. Overbury clears her throat in the way that means she's mildly nervous. I look up. She opens the door and a cop comes in. Everyone goes quiet, wondering who's in trouble.

"The sheriff's department says another young man in the area has gone missing. That's four now," Ms. Overbury says. I think her eyes linger on me as she looks around the room. "This is Deputy Greenberg, who's going to tell us all how to be a bit safer."

"That's here?" Malcolm says. He's sitting across the aisle from me, and I look over, confused. The whole room does.

"What?" Ms. Overbury asks, also confused.

He shakes his head. "Sorry, nothing." Then he looks over at me, a little wide-eyed. I shrug before looking away.

Deputy Greenberg takes us through the basics: Don't walk alone, especially at night. Don't talk to strangers, in person or online. If you think you're being followed, go inside a store or restaurant and call the police. Turn off location finding on your phones. Stuff we all already know. We're quiet the whole time, though. Then Ms. Overbury asks if there are questions.

Madison raises her hand. "Aren't all the victims gay?"

"They all identified as part of the LGBTQIA+ community, yes," Deputy Greenberg says in a brisk, professional tone. I'm impressed he didn't stumble over any of it.

"So we don't need to worry," Madison says with a shrug. She turns to me and Malcolm. "I mean, you do. But not me."

I roll my eyes, telling myself to text Poly Perry later and tell him off for the annoyance his orgy is causing me.

"We don't know exactly what's going on yet," Deputy Greenberg says. "We are urging all teenagers to take precautions. Especially with Halloween coming up. Halloween can bring a lot of freaks out, and there are a lot of strangers and people in masks, which can make it confusing. Stay vigilant."

Madison shrugs, unconcerned. Ms. Overbury thanks the deputy, who leaves. As she shuts the door behind him, Ms. Overbury looks at me, and then Malcolm. "You have to be careful."

"Not if I'm the one doing the murdering," Malcolm says.

I laugh. He sounds almost like Deer Friend.

Ms. Overbury frowns. "Not funny, Mr. Gabay."

I almost lean over to tell him it was, but I don't. I still don't want to be too friendly with him. There's something about him I can't figure out, and he's been looking at me so weirdly lately. Maybe he's trying to lord it over me that he knows about me and Steve. A little reminder in his glance.

I'm the first one to sit down at the table at lunch, and my phone buzzes in my pocket.

Deer Friend:
Okay I know we said no details but just in case we could actually meet I am willing to take the chance. So, I'm in Westchester.

Deer Friend:
In New York.

I stare at it a long time, shock turning to joy. I can actually meet him!

Gray:
Me too

Deer Friend:
I knew it! At school this morning a cop came in to talk about the missing guys and I realized oh—we might be close.

Gray:
Us too

> **Gray:**
> They must be doing that in every school in Westchester today
>
> **Gray:**
> But for real? We can meet?

> **Deer Friend:**
> Yes!

> **Gray:**
> What if we've already met?
>
> **Gray:**
> There are over 37 towns in Westchester I know but imagine

The ... appears and disappears a few times.

> **Deer Friend:**
> That would be something

Callie and Lenore sit down next to me, already talking.

> **Gray:**
> There's a restaurant in Sleepy Hollow called Headless. Let's meet there on Halloween at ten.
>
> **Deer Friend:**
> It's a date

I heart his response and stare at my phone a little longer before putting it away. I try to think of who he could be, if I've seen him. If he's really goth on the outside, then it's no one at school. The only other goth guy is Malcolm, and he has a boyfriend. I guess Deer Friend could be secretly goth, maybe some jock, like Steve. I look around the room, trying to see if anyone feels that way. But no, I don't think anyone else is out, and he would have told me if he were closeted. He must be from another town. There's a goth guy I've seen at some of the antique stores, short, with full lips. I wouldn't mind it being him...But no, I shake my head. I don't need to play the guessing game, because I'll know in a week! I'm actually going to meet him. I can feel my smile, it's too big for my face. It must be stretching my head out like a haunted mask.

"It could work," Lenore is saying. She shows me a photo of a dress—a mod black sixties number, with a bow at the neck and a red frill at the bottom that looks like dripping blood. "This is enough for a Halloween costume, right?"

"Is it supposed to be something, or is it just a look?" I ask.

"If I carry a bloody knife, it could be a serial killer," she says, staring at her phone. "Although...that might not be in the best taste after the cops came to talk to us today. Even if it is Poly Perry."

"Yeah," Callie says. "Go with the other one."

Lenore shows me her phone again, this time a photo of her in a more fifties-style dress in black, with a bloodstained apron over it. "Plus some blood on my neck, like I was just bitten. Housewife of Dracula."

"I think that one, too. The other one you can save for a party or something."

She shrugs. "Okay. Anthony says he liked that one better, too, but said I should have used buckram."

"Anthony?" Callie asks.

"Malcolm's boyfriend," Lenore says. "He's been commenting on my videos online. Says I should have used buckram to make the frills on the apron hold more. Some of his suggestions are good, but some he's definitely been wrong, and he was about that, and I told him so. Buckram! I'd break my jaw if I looked down and my chin hit the ruffle. I was up arguing with him last night, but I won. He conceded interlining made more sense." She smiles. "He's fun, though. Makes me like Malcolm more, knowing his boyfriend is so cool."

"Maybe he'll come up for Halloween to support Malcolm's haunted house," Callie says. "So we have to show him how good we are, too."

"Yes," I say, excited to tell them about my date.

"But also," Callie says before I can, "Bryce asked me to do his makeup for Halloween and I don't know what to do."

"Couple's costume?" Lenore asks, excited. "I love those. Remember the time I made them for me and Cody?"

"You were a very chic bride of Frankenstein," Callie says, "and he didn't show up."

Lenore frowns. "Yeah. But it was still nice to have someone to make the costume for. Even if—" She shakes her head. "He texted me *u up* last night. I didn't see because I was telling Anthony how wrong he was, but... I got a little thrill when I saw it this morning."

"No," I say quickly.

"No," Callie says almost at the same time.

Lenore laughs. "I know. Just made me feel lonelier. I don't know. This time of year, all the magic." She shrugs. "And now you get a couple's costume."

"I'm not doing a couple's costume," Callie says quickly. "Just his makeup. I'm thinking of testing some of my space prosthetics on him. Zombie. That too basic?"

"I think it's a good idea," I say.

"You could be a zombie, too," Lenore adds.

"I'm doing my usual witch thing," Callie says. She doesn't do much costume-wise for Halloween. A long black dress with a white collar and black tie, her braids piled up high on her head. She does elaborate beauty makeup, though, and then carries a broom. Says she's a witch. "How about you?"

"I was thinking I want to match the store—try to make it look like my heart has been torn out. Maybe carry it around." I grin, suddenly realizing what else I can do. "And then give it to my date!"

"Give it?" Callie asks, eyes narrowing. Lenore cocks an eyebrow.

"He's in Westchester!" I say, excited. My smile is too big again.

Callie and Lenore exchange a look. They are not smiling.

"So he's definitely the serial killer," Callie says.

"What? No," I say quickly, though just as quickly I can see why they'd think that. "No. There is no serial killer. It's Poly Perry."

"He's in our area? Of all the places this supposedly

random number could be, he's here, and he's going to meet you in person. We talked about this, the odds of that are impossible."

"But—"

"Who figured out you were in the same place?"

"He did," I say, feeling suddenly nervous. "It was the cops this morning, he—"

"And who suggested you meet up?" Lenore asks.

"He did." I swallow. My throat feels very dry. It *is* Poly Perry, right?

"And he only just thought of this a few days before so you can't think too long about it?"

"Yes." It comes out soft. I take a drink of soda and shake my head. "I get what you're saying, but he's not a serial killer. I would know."

"Would you?" Lenore asks. "Four guys are missing, maybe dead. They didn't know."

"But Poly Perry," I say so softly not even I believe it. No, no, my Deer Friend isn't a serial killer. I shake my head. "He's not a serial killer."

"I was already suspicious," Callie says. "But this...no, Gray. No going to meet him."

"You said it was okay as long as you're there, too."

Callie frowns. Lenore tilts her head. "We did say that."

"Fine," Callie says. "But no being alone with him ever. At all. I will follow you all night if I have to."

"I really would prefer you didn't," I say, thinking of how I'd love to be alone with him. I wonder if he'll wear the thong.

"And I really would prefer you didn't die!" Callie almost yells. She bangs her fist on the table.

"I'll be fine," I say.

"I should just tell my dad. Have him take your phone, look this guy up."

I feel cold suddenly, and I know my face is shaking. "You wouldn't," I say.

"To protect you."

"If you do, I'll tell your dad about what you did after the homecoming dance." It slips out of me, almost feral, some animal instinct to protect myself. I feel terrible immediately as she blinks at me, shocked. "Sorry, I wouldn't really, but Callie—"

"I need to go to the bathroom," she says, standing, then marches away.

I look at Lenore.

"What did she do?" Lenore asks.

I shake my head, not wanting to tell her.

"Well, she's worried," Lenore says. "This is scary. And she lives it every day with her dad, don't forget. But I'll go talk to her."

I watch Lenore leave the lunchroom, leaving me sitting alone. Malcolm came in just as Callie was leaving and is looking at me now. He walks over.

"What was that about?" he asks. He's giving me that weird look again. That look that says he's just so amused by what he knows that I don't, about the power he has over me, and my friends aren't happy for me and I'm just suddenly so angry.

"None of your business," I say, sneering. "What do you even want?"

His brow scrunches up and his face falls. "Just—never mind," he says, and walks away. I debate leaving. Lunch is only half over and I still have a sandwich to eat, but now my friends are gone because they're angry with me for what—having a local boyfriend? So I eat in silence instead. Callie and Lenore come back ten minutes later, when lunch is nearly over. Callie's makeup is running and I'm still angry, but I feel bad, too.

"No being alone with him until I say it's okay," Callie says. "Get his full name, I will have my dad run it while you're eating. If Dad says he checks out, then I'll be okay. Deal?"

"You don't get to control my love life," I say.

She sighs.

"No one is trying to," Lenore says. "You can take all the risks you want for love, but we're going to take the risk that you'll be angry and follow you around, because we're *not* willing to risk your life. Got that?"

I go back over the sentence in my head and then nod. "Okay," I say. "I get you're worried, and I will try to get his full name quickly. If I can. If it doesn't ruin the mood."

"And I'm going to keep on you," Callie says. "I'm not leaving you alone with him. Same as we did for Lenore this weekend."

"And you were right," Lenore says. "Though I don't think he was a killer. Just a creep."

They're right. "Deal," I say. "But he's not going to be a creep. Or a killer."

"You hope," Callie says.

"Hope is goth," I say, which confuses her, but she goes back to her food. "There are a lot of scary things in the world," I say as she keeps eating. "Serial killers, war, Republicans, school shootings, plague—being able to acknowledge all that and still have hope is kinda goth."

"That's lovely," Lenore says.

"That's something he told me."

Lenore and Callie look a little surprised.

"Anyway, so yes, please come make sure I don't get killed, but please also maybe have a little hope that this will go well for me? I really hope it does."

Callie nods, looking a little apologetic. "Of course I hope it goes well for you. I just—I'm worried. Because I care about you."

She puts her hand out and I put mine over it. "I get it, and it means a lot to me. But for now, let's have some hope."

"Okay," she says. "But I'm still going to be watching you. And I'm sorry I threatened you with my dad."

"I'm sorry I threatened you with your dad, too."

She snorts a laugh. "I don't know what he could do about it if you told him. He's not going to stop me seeing Bryce or anything."

"Yeah, but he'd probably give Bryce a talk about how he knows every cop in the county and how to frame someone for murder."

Callie laughs. "He might." She shakes her head. "He really might."

"Can we talk about the store decorations now?" Lenore

says. "We have to figure out how long building everything will take."

We spend the rest of lunch planning and meet up after school to plan some more. Almost everything is built, but in pieces. Putting them together overnight is going to be hard. And then on Wednesday, when Mom and Mama look over the plans, they remind us we need somewhere to give out little bags of candy to kids—all wrapped up and tied with the store's business card.

I film everything while Lenore creates a candy bowl made of stained glass. I also film myself talking again about hope being goth. Not sure where to put it in the movie, but maybe somewhere.

I don't really get a chance to talk to Deer Friend again until I'm in bed.

Gray:
So do you want to talk about it?

Gray:
Where we are in Westchester?

Deer Friend:
No

Deer Friend:
We're so close to meeting let's keep it a surprise

Deer Friend:
I'm so excited to meet you and see your decorations and just hang out for real I worry if I know too much it'll be ruined

> **Gray:**
> Same

> **Gray:**
> I'm so excited to see you for the first time

Deer Friend:
You've already seen part of me

> **Gray:**
> 😳 more than that though

> **Gray:**
> I know you but I don't

> **Gray:**
> I want to see the whole picture

> **Gray:**
> Hold your hand

> **Gray:**
> Is that pathetic?

Deer Friend:
No I want to hold your hand too

Deer Friend:
But I do think we should come up with a signal

Deer Friend:
In case we don't recognize each other

> **Gray:**
> You don't think our dark fate is enough?

Deer Friend:
Probably but maybe a backup plan

Gray:
I could wear something

Deer Friend:
I was thinking we could hold
something

Gray:
Like knives? Is that so I
don't suspect anything until you
start stabbing me?

Deer Friend
yes

Deer Friend:
Or maybe just flowers?

Gray:
Like a bouquet?

Deer Friend:
Or just one rose

Gray:
Halloween, people might be
holding roses for their costumes

Deer Friend:
Right good point

Gray:
A black rose?

Deer Friend:
In a book. No one's costume will have
that

Gray:
Which book?

Deer Friend:
Surprise me

Deer Friend:
We can even trade them after so we have something to read

Gray:
I was hoping the date might end in something less solitary than reading

Deer Friend:
 oh?

Gray:
I mean maybe...

Deer Friend:
Well, for when we're alone again

Deer Friend:
Something to remind each other

Gray:
I like that

Gray:
Though your texts are my favorite thing to read right now

Deer Friend:
Soon you won't have to

Gray:

Deer Friend:

That night I feel more nervous than I've ever been. I know it's not just about the store and having real competition from Malcolm this year, it's also obviously about my date, but the two feel linked in a way so that their anxiety cross-pollinates, or maybe it's more like water being poured back and forth between two jars. I decorated the store this way, with these two hearts, for my date, after all. If we don't win the contest, does that mean what I did for him, to show him what I feel, isn't good enough? I don't know. I turn my camera on and try to work through these questions, but the words sound so stupid that I turn the camera off. But it still feels true. I need to win. Otherwise I could lose it all.

Setting everything up is super complicated this year, partly because of the forced-perspective modeling that Callie and Bryce did, so we have to get started right after school. My parents help, but they don't know what's going where, so mostly we just let them order pizza for us and then direct them on how to put stuff together. Well, really Bryce and Callie direct all of us as we carefully assemble the church, the stained-glass windows over the real windows telling the story. In the center of this small church is an amazingly realistic heart Callie and Lenore made, under a glass jar. It pulses loudly, a separate speaker under the foam stone altar we put it on. The forced perspective makes the church seem so much taller and wider than the half-shop area it really is, and when you step out of that into the graveyard outside, the dark walls painted with landscapes feel even more open, because of how eerie and claustrophobic the church is.

Callie and Bryce test the cathedral, adding extra glue to keep things locked in place, while Lenore and I set up the mismatched objects around the graveyard, covering the ground with fake grass sprayed with clear glue that looks like dew. The tea counter is separate, so we can move it into the back room. But the actual counter with the register is part of the shop, and we have to spend another few hours carving and spray-painting mossy rocks to cover it up. But that ends up being the perfect spot to put the other pulsing heart, because we can tuck the battery into the foam. Callie gave this one a light, since it's a little darker in the graveyard area. Then we set up speakers and play the music. Lenore installs all the stained glass on the finished cathedral walls.

I try to film everything, and when we're done, I do a walk-through for the camera, too. I start outside, narrating as I film the three stained-glass windows.

"So this first one is showing two hearts being pulled apart. That's how their darkness was overcome, by separating them. The next window shows the two hearts now far from each other, and life blossoming between them, even as they're yearning for each other. The final panel shows the hearts together again, curving into each other, as all the things alive in panel two die around them. It's this story of a love that's so vast it consumes the world. It's dark and scary but also romantic and wonderful. I mean, these two hearts—these two people—they get to be in love, even if the world is ending."

I bring the camera inside. It's unreal what Callie and Bryce have done, because it feels like entering an actual stone cathedral with arches and a pointed roof. I know it's impossible, and yeah, as I walk along it's easier to tell that it's all an illusion (especially when I look back toward the door), but that first moment of entering—it's surreal, mind-blowing. Mom says it makes her dizzy. I love it. There's the steady beat of the heart over the sound of rain on glass, and faintly, in the background, another beat, too. And everything echoes, like we're really in a big old stone building.

"So this is the cathedral, all done," I say, filming everything as best I can without getting it from an angle that gives the game away. "It's all those foam blocks and the modeling Callie and Bryce did. And here's heart one. It's kept safe by the clerics here, protected, so it can't reunite with its mate. They're keeping lovers apart to save the world, which I guess might seem noble, but maybe a world without love doesn't deserve to exist, either." I turn the camera up to the other stained-glass panels. These just have lights behind them, so they glow softly, not quite matching the ones on the window, which are only lit by the streetlamps outside, since it's past two in the morning now.

"These three stained-glass windows tell another story, of the hearts being torn out of two young men and taken away by the clerics, one kept here, under glass. The other tossed into the sea. But you can't keep good lovers down..." I walk out the open arch behind the altar, into the grave-yard. Here the sound of the rain is louder and the creepy music box plays over it, and there's the faint beating of the second heart, the beating of the first still coming from the cathedral door. There's moss and grass and tombstones and objects put up like tombstones all around. Hanging from the ceiling are sewing needles that seem like falling raindrops when you look up. And just around the corner, far too close and nestled into a mossy rock, is the second heart, beating just as loudly as the first. "There's so many things that belong together in this graveyard, too." I pan over all the objects, ending in two huge candy bowls filled with Lenore's homemade eyeballs and spiders in their neat little plastic bags. "Because sometimes things belong together, for better or worse, in life and death. That's what I'm trying to say. That sometimes, two things—two people—belong together. Even when it's kind of scary. You have to take a risk on the scary things to find who you belong with."

I put the camera down and go outside to the garden, where everyone is putting away scraps and taking drinks of water. Lenore sits at the picnic table, looking up at the stars. "Halloween tomorrow."

"Yeah," Callie says. "It's going to be fun."

"And then winter," Lenore says.

Bryce furrows his brow. "I mean, it'll be November, but that's not winter—"

"It's winter," Callie says.

"The first day of winter is December twenty-first," Bryce says, shaking his head.

"No," I say, sitting down next to Lenore, "after Halloween is winter. End of fall, everything dies—then winter!"

"You guys are weird," Bryce says, mildly exasperated.

"Yeah, we are," Callie says, hugging him. "Thanks for your help."

"Yes, thank you," I say.

"It was a lot of help," Mama says.

"It was fun," he says.

"I think we're going to bed," Mom says, taking Mama's hand. "Any of you need a ride?"

"I have my mom's car," Bryce says. "I'll drop everyone at home."

"Thanks," Mom says, patting him on the back. "Great work, everyone. Try to get some sleep." She and Mama head inside, but no one moves.

"So how's the movie?" Lenore asks me.

"I dunno."

"You think he'll like it?"

"Who?"

Lenore smirks. "We all know this movie is about and for your serial killer boyfriend."

I tilt my head. "No."

"No?" Callie asks, skeptical.

"I mean, I'll bring him back tomorrow and show him. He doesn't need a movie of it."

"No, not that," Lenore says. "But the rest of it. Why you're building it. For him."

I look down at the ground between my feet. Grass and dark soil. "A little," I say. "But I'm never showing him the movie. It's not going to be good enough."

"No?" Callie asks. "After all our hard work?"

I laugh. "Maybe after I edit it so it's just you guys."

They laugh, and Callie kisses the top of my head. "Tomorrow will be great. Or we'll catch a serial killer, which will also be great. In a different way."

"What?" Bryce says.

"We'd get our picture in the paper for sure," Lenore says.

"Brave young women save bad-decision-making friend from certain death," Callie says.

304

"What death?" Bryce asks.

I shake my head. "Don't mind them."

"I'm so tired," Bryce says. "We still have school tomorrow. My parents said I could stay up late to help, but I don't think they realized how late. Can we go home?"

"Yeah," Callie says, taking his hand. "See you tomorrow, Gray." After they're gone, I drag myself upstairs. I'm dead tired, my muscles aching from everything we've done tonight. But we did it. I lie in bed, feeling proud but nervous. What if he doesn't like it? I pick up my phone.

Deer Friend:
TOMORROW!

Deer Friend:
Nervous excited

Gray:
Me too

His texts are from a few hours ago so I'm not surprised when he doesn't respond. I guess he's not that nervous. I lie in the dark, wondering what he'll be like, if he's cute, if he'll think I'm cute, or if he's really some old guy, or a killer or something, and the thoughts swirl and spiral, like a whirlpool that pulls me down into an uneasy sleep.

13

I only get a few hours of sleep, but luckily, our Halloween costume tradition for school is easy. Lots of our classmates come to school in costume. Some just wear animal ears, some full masks, and some try to go goth, though never as well as we do. But Lenore, Callie, and I decided a while ago that no matter what we did it wasn't right. Bigger goth just looked like us dressing up nicely. Costumes always feel silly at school. So what we do is dress normally. Not normally for us, but normally for the world. For one brief shining day, Ms. Overbury, in her annual witch hat with a green curly fright wig, is thrilled when I walk in the door: no makeup, hair slicked to the side, white polo, blue cardigan, pale blue jeans that aren't very loose or very tight. I look adorably preppy.

Ms. Overbury beams at me, then sighs, same as she does every year as she thinks I'm finally turning into what she wants and then remembers it's a joke. My other classmates don't really do more than glance at me, having seen it before, but Malcolm does a full double take.

"I...didn't recognize you," he says. I thought he'd be

Amanda today, but he hasn't dressed up unusually at all—just a black oversized sweater, with the loose knit you can kind of see his chest through, wide black pants, and some minimal eyeliner.

"It's a thing we do," I say. "Wait until you see Callie."

"I'm so nervous about the contest," he says.

I nod. "Don't worry. You're not going to win."

I grin, but he frowns at me. "You're not nervous about tonight?" He looks at me like he thinks I should be. Of course he does, he thinks he's going to win. I'll like wiping that arrogance off his face.

I shake my head. "I'm fine." It's a lie, of course. I can barely focus as the day goes by, thinking too much about the competition and about my date. I shouldn't have scheduled the date for tonight. It's too much pressure from too many things.

"You okay?" Callie asks at lunch. She has a wig, straight black hair to her shoulders, pink headband, matching pink blouse and a pink-and-yellow-plaid skirt. Her makeup is subtle, a little blush, some mascara. Bryce, sitting next to her, clearly got the full force of her talent, though. His face looks like a carved statue of a green man, all grays and curving lines. His red curls make him almost look like a candle. And I don't know where he got the artfully torn black tee—maybe Callie did that, too—but it looks good on him.

"Just not much sleep," I say. "Did you get any?"

"A little," she says.

"I was out the moment my head touched the pillow," Bryce says. "You guys really do this every year?"

"Every year," Lenore says with a nod. She's in a neon green bodycon dress over leopard-print tights, her hair streaked with fake highlighter, and so much bronzer she looks like she's been to a tanning salon. "And every year we say we'll go to bed earlier and never do."

"We gotta stop making it so big," Callie says, opening her second bottle of Coke Zero.

"Well, next year is the last year before college," Lenore says. "Then we might not be able to do it anymore..." She sighs. "So next year has to be even bigger anyway."

"What?" I ask. "We can still do it after we graduate."

Callie and Bryce exchange a look. "Hopefully we'll be in Massachusetts," she says. "College."

"Right," I say, remembering and feeling the world fall out from under me for a moment.

"I'm hoping I'll be at FIT," Lenore says, shrugging. "But I'll come back if I can."

"Aren't you going to college?" Bryce asks.

I shake my head. "I don't know. I mean, I'll apply, I guess, but..."

"I actually figured this out for you," Callie says.

"Oh?" I laugh.

"What you asked me at the Graveyard, if you could do that, make stuff like that."

"Yeah"—I shake my head—"it was a silly idea. You can't major in that kind of thing."

"Shut up," Callie says. "You can."

"You can major in Halloween decorating?" I blink.

"Theater design," Callie says.

I shake my head. "Sets just get seen, it's not the same."

"That's not true," Lenore says, as if suddenly realizing it. "There are so many immersive theater experiences now."

"My parents took me to this immersive theater thing in the city," Bryce says. "It was freaky. This whole house... you guys would have loved it."

"And someone designed it," Callie says, looking triumphant. "Someone designed everything we saw at the Graveyard."

"Huh," I say again, suddenly imagining a world where Halloween is every day.

"I looked them up online, the people who worked on the Graveyard, googled, found their résumés and stuff. Most of them majored in theater design."

"Really?" I ask, feeling some excitement fizzing in me.

"NYU has a great theater design course," Lenore says. "So do a lot of the public universities in New York."

"Oh, you should ask Mr. Ratcatcher, the theater teacher, if you can help do the sets for the show in the spring," Bryce says.

"Our theater teacher's name is Mr. Ratcatcher?" Lenore says, eyes huge. "And I didn't know that?"

"Why aren't we more involved in theater, actually?" Callie asks suddenly.

"Theater people," I say.

Everyone nods quietly.

I stand up. "I need more caffeine." I love everything Callie has figured out, this huge sudden road stretching in front of me, a future I can finally see. It's like puzzle pieces are falling into place, but I don't want to think about that right now, I don't have time. After Halloween maybe. "Anyone need anything from the vending machine?"

Everyone shakes their heads, and I walk off to buy another Coke. Maybe if I go to college for theater design, Deer Friend and I can go to college together. We can make sets together and then move in, build some amazing haunted house to call our own. Or maybe he'll leave me after a year or maybe we'll hate each other. No, I can't think about it right now. My head is swimming, and the Coke doesn't help. It just tastes like sugar.

I don't want to think about what's next. Or, I do, but it's always been just so bleak and empty, and with just one idea Callie has put a hundred futures in front of me and it's kind of overwhelming, scary. I mean, next could be everyone dying in a plague, right? Why think about the future? Even if now I can see so many of them?

If Deer Friend were here, he'd ask me what I hoped for. And suddenly, there's a lot.

Steve walks up to the vending machine and puts in some money. No one else is around. But he's avoiding looking at me. Pointedly.

I sigh and push myself off the wall.

"I miss you," he whispers as his bottle of soda clangs to the bottom of the vending machine. I stop for a moment, wanting to tell him to move on. But instead, I just keep walking back to my table. I feel bad, but what else can I do?

Back at the table, talk of the future has faded and instead we talk about setting up for tonight. The competition officially begins at sundown, and the winner is announced at the Headless Horseman statue at nine. The identity of the judges is kept secret, so everyone who enters the haunted house is a potential judge and has to be amazed.

When school is over, we all go home, planning to meet up for an early dinner at the shop and then open up at sundown. I think about getting home fast and showering, trying to get my hair back to normal, but with my planned costume of a guy with his heart ripped out, I decide staying kind of norm looks even better. Which means I have time to kill, and though I'm exhausted, I'm also too wired to sleep, so another idea strikes me: checking out the competition. I know it's going to be good, right? I may as well get my expectations in check. I feel almost guilty getting on my bike, and my heart starts going really fast. I don't know why. I shouldn't be freaking out. It's not cheating. His house is going to be great. So is ours. But as I pedal over, I feel this thrum in my body, this strange fear. What if his *is* better? Obviously, outrageously better?

I swallow as I turn the corner and his house comes into view. Some people are already headed into it. And it really is sort of a house—he's built a full enclosed box on the lawn, painted it black, with spiderwebs all around it and an old-timey-looking sign over the door that looks like a black cat arching its back, the words LUCKY STREET underneath it. A few costumed kids are going inside, hands held by adults, and I follow them.

Inside, it's like I've been teleported. What before looked like a replica of a Victorian street now *is* a Victorian street, at night, shops on either side of me, brick walls. And in every window are symbols of luck, good and bad. And you can go into them! He thought us decorating the store was cheating, but he's built a half dozen stores himself. Above me, the stars twinkle. There are streetlamps and a cobblestone street, cobwebs, a few jack-o'-lanterns, but it's not scary, exactly. More eerie.

In each store are shelves full of things: Horseshoes—some with ends up, some down. Rabbits' feet, not the little plastic ones, but ones that look like real taxidermied feet (that I hope are fake), on fancy stands with the genus of rabbit listed underneath. Wishbones, silver dollar plants, white elephants, hamsas, but then in the same store, black cats—not taxidermied, thankfully, but in framed black-and-white photos—and broken mirrors and statues of ravens. One store even has an open ladder just inside the door that you have to walk under.

I pick up one of the horseshoes and feel its weight in my hand. Real.

"It's amazing the stuff you can rent," says a voice behind me. Malcolm. I turn, a little embarrassed to be caught here, but he doesn't seem to be mocking me. He walks closer and takes the horseshoe and puts it back. "Prop rental companies have everything, but I'm on the hook if anyone walks away with any of it."

"I wasn't going to steal it," I say, frowning.

"I didn't—" He shakes his head. "Sorry. Trying to be funny. I didn't expect to see you here so early. And then I almost didn't recognize you again."

"Thought I'd check out the competition before I go home to get into my real costume and open up."

"I had a free last period," he says, nodding. "So I came

back and put everything out and just opened up. I thought the kids who are out early might like it." He nods out the window at a pair of girls, maybe four or five, who walk by in princess costumes. "The last shop has bags of candy for them."

"That's cute. We almost forgot about the candy."

"The candy is the best part," he says with a smile.

I look around, suddenly aware of how close he's standing. "So...luck?"

"Luck." He grins, shoving his hands in his pockets and looking around. "Yeah. I know it's not the most Halloween thing. But I wanted to think about luck, chance—I almost did a haunted casino, but that didn't feel so kid-friendly."

I nod, suddenly wondering if a beating anatomical heart on an altar in a cathedral is kid-friendly. Can the judges be kids?

"So just"—he shrugs—"shopping for luck. Getting lucky." He laughs at his own joke.

"Why, though?"

He narrows his eyes at me a little, then turns around and walks out of the shop. I follow him onto the street. The cobblestones are painted, flat, but they look real. He must be quite the artist. "Luck has kind of changed me a lot this year. One chance sort of...encounter, I guess. And now I feel so lucky. In love at least."

"What, you and Anthony had a meet-cute under a coffee-shop awning in the rain or something?"

He turns around slowly, his face genuinely perplexed. "What?"

"You know, 'cause luck."

He laughs. "Anthony is not my boyfriend, no, no." He pauses. "Wait, does Lenore think Anthony is my boyfriend?"

"I think so?" I shrug, feeling like I've done something wrong.

"Oh boy." He shakes his head, then laughs. "No. Anthony is completely smitten with Lenore. That was the word he used. *Smitten.* The moment he saw her. And he told me they've been texting every night so I thought it was going well."

"I think they're mostly talking about sewing," I say.

"And she just thinks they're talking." He nods and then bites his lower lip. It's kind of hot. "Okay, wait, we can fix this." He takes out his phone and starts typing. "I'm telling him to ask her out and to be very very clear that it's a date. Right now. They can't go on like this."

"Um," I say, unsure of what I've started here.

"Well, she doesn't hate him, does she?"

"No," I say quickly. "And she did think he was cute. They might have some disagreements about"—I try to remember but can't—"some sewing thing."

"Oh god, I bet he thought that was flirting. He's not great at this stuff. Not that I should talk." He stares at his phone a moment longer, then texts something again, and waits, and smiles. "Good. He's doing it right now."

"He's asking her out?" I ask.

"Yep. I think they'd be good together, right? I mean, I know I don't know her well, and you don't know him well, but—"

"Is he an asshole?" I ask. "Lenore's ex is not a great guy. Like lots of cheating."

Malcolm shakes his head. "Anthony would never. His last boyfriend cheated on him, too, and it was terrible."

"Well, then, yeah." I nod. "If he's a good guy, I'm in support of this."

Malcolm looks down at his phone. "Good. Because after some clarification and similar confusion, she said yes, apparently."

I smile. Lenore finally finding a boyfriend? That would be really good.

I walk the street toward the exit, Malcolm following. It's a really amazing street. It's beautiful and pulls you in and has a theme and just feels real. Magical. I'm nervous now. Imagine pulling up to my date tonight saying I lost after all my talk and bragging. I've practically made this thing everything about me in our texts. What would I be if I lost?

"I gotta go," I say to Malcolm. "To kick your ass, I mean."

He smirks, rolls his eyes. All the goodwill of matchmaking vanishes and I'm suddenly so annoyed at him again. This is the guy who could be standing between me and the perfect date tonight? No. "See you later," I say.

And then his face does something strange. He smiles, nodding, but looks surprised, too, eyes widening, and a slight shudder, like I've said something that relieves him. Like I've said something big.

"When they announce the winner," I clarify.

"Right," he says, his face changing back to a smirk. "That." He laughs. "Sorry. May the best of us win, I guess?"

"Yeah, me," I say, taking off.

I hadn't meant to be there so long, so I need to rush to

change into my costume. The white shirt with a torn hole over the heart and a prosthetic Callie made me that looks like a gaping chest cavity, broken ribs and all, is pretty easy to slip on, though. I use a faint sheen of white powder on my face to make me look drained of blood and then dab a little fake blood at the corners of my mouth and use it to stain the shirt where it's been torn. My hair stays preppy, though. I look like a kid from a fifties horror movie after the monster gets him. It's great.

Then Lenore knocks on the door, in her Housewife of Dracula costume, looking fantastic, and also grinning, ear to ear.

"Guess what just happened?" she asks when I open the door.

"Anthony asked you out," I say.

The smile falters and her eyes go wide. "Are you a witch?"

I shrug. "I mean, you know I am. You've been to my rituals—"

"Gray!"

I laugh. "I went to look at Malcolm's, to see the competition, and we were talking and he said something about how Anthony has been smitten with you since first sight."

Lenore does something I've never seen before: She blushes. "Smitten?"

"That was the word used," I say.

"I mean, he's really cute, and he knows a lot about sewing even if he's wrong about a few things. But that's fixable. I…" She pauses, still stunned. "I am very glad you went to check out the competition."

"So am I," I say, and she hugs me.

"I have a date!"

"Me too!" I say.

"Mine's not with a serial killer!" she says in the same joyful tone.

I laugh and she releases her arms just as Callie and Bryce round the corner.

"I have a date with a cute boy who sews!" Lenore repeats, hugging a surprised Callie, who now wears a long flowing black coat, a black top hat with a skull atop it, and a black tie and button-down. It's not so much a costume as it is Callie in formal wear. The makeup is what's most exceptional, with gold filigree down her cheekbones and shadowing that makes the planes of her face almost sharp, metallic. She's wearing contacts that turn her whole eye gold, too.

"You do?" Callie asks. We catch her up. By the time the sun sets, Lenore has told us about the pros and cons of six possible outfits for the date and repeated the word *smitten* seven times.

When the sun hits the horizon, we turn on all the sound, run through checking the store one last time, and then open the doors.

A lot of people pour into Sleepy Hollow for Halloween, so we always get crowds stopping by the store to see what we've built. October thirtieth is always one of the best days of the year, sales-wise, and I bet if we didn't do the haunted house, we could do even better tonight, but it's good advertising, and the business cards with the candy have our website, too, so people can order stuff there if they head back to New York tonight—though on a weekend, I'll bet most of the tourists will be back tomorrow, when we're a shop again.

But tonight, it's all about the Best Halloween Decorations. And people know we've won every year for six years, so they're already lined up by the time we open the door. And then they come inside and are wowed. I only have a few moments inside before it starts getting crowded. Mom and Mama take a place in the cathedral and courtyard, respectively. They're done some makeup and are wearing black, but they're more in uniform than costume, there to talk about the store if needed. I mostly wait outside, watching, filming, and sometimes walking through with Callie and Lenore.

I hear screams and laughs of delight from inside. I peek my head in, go in and out now and then. People are definitely impressed. They point and take photos.

"Tag us," Mom says, "at CeremonySleepyHollow." We may not sell anything tonight, but it is damn good publicity.

A few little kids who come in do run out screaming when they see the pulsing heart. But for the most part, it's a really good night. It's so amazing to see people react to our work, to be touched by it, or scared by it, or have any kind of feeling about it. In the graveyard, I watch a woman spot the heart and say, "So the end of the world is close," and her friend, another woman, says, "Yeah, but it'll be nice that they get to be together again," and it just feels so good to have everything be seen like that. To have people understand what I'm doing here. So even if some people run out, and some look confused, or grossed out, at least some people really get it. And that makes me feel like all the work, everything we've made, is completely worth it.

We rotate watching the store and reminding people to tag us and making sure they only take one bag of candy, standing outside to lure people in, and running upstairs to eat pizza, so there's not much time for any of us to talk for a while. Bryce leaves eventually to go hang out with some friends, promising to meet Callie later. By a quarter to nine, the crowds have faded, and I am so tired. It's always exhausting—staying up hours the night before to put the thing together and then being on our feet for a few hours, watching people react to it. But I feel energized, too. People really liked it, and I have a date and tonight is going to be amazing. I can feel it.

"We're going to win," I tell Callie and Lenore as they join me on the sidewalk at quarter till nine. Mom and Mama stay to watch the stragglers as we walk over to the Headless Horseman statue to claim our award.

"Don't get too cocky," Callie says.

"Yeah," I say, kicking the sidewalk. I'd almost forgotten how good Malcolm's Victorian street was, seeing how people loved ours. "Still." Ours was better, I'm almost sure. I don't think I could stand it if he won. We might be in a better place since he apologized, and I guess we're kind of heading toward being friends, but if he wins, I just feel like he'll hold it over all our heads. He'll say he doesn't mean it that way, but of course he will.

There's a small crowd around the statue when we show up. A guy taking photos for the town's social media, the mayor, and some people in costumes waiting to see who wins. I spot Malcolm, too, looking up at the statue. He's alone, which is sort of sad. I guess none of his city friends made it up here for this. Callie waves at him and he comes over to stand next to us.

"Is this weird?" he asks. "We're competitors."

Lenore shrugs. "It's over. One of us will win, and then we won't be competitors anymore."

"And we can all sit together at lunch," Callie says with a grin. "Time to really dig deep on my prosthetics." She points at my chest. "This is the latest."

"Oh, nice," Malcolm says, bending slightly and putting his face close to my chest. It feels weirdly intimate, like he's about to lick me. It's kind of hot, and I feel myself blushing slightly. And Lenore sees it. She raises an eyebrow. I frown at her as they study the prosthetic on me and Callie talks about a particular type of rubber she used.

"I think this is great for the prosthetics. It's the blood that's still the problem."

"Yeah," Malcolm says, straightening up, his face once again at a normal distance from me. "But we can try more solutions next week."

"Thank you," Lenore says to him suddenly. "For, you know, talking to Anthony. I really thought he was unavailable and I'm very pleased that's not true."

Malcolm glares at me. "You told her?"

"You didn't tell me not to," I say. "What's the harm?"

"It makes my friend look bad."

"Actually, I think it makes him look good," Lenore says. "A guy being slick isn't a good sign. Not to me, anyway."

"Which I knew," I say.

"Ah," Malcolm says. "Okay, sorry, yeah. Just…defensive of my friend for a moment."

"You two always think the worst of each other," Callie says. "That's the issue."

"What?" I say. "That's not…" I look up at him. She's kind of right. And he's nodding.

"You're both cool. Give each other a chance."

Before either of us can reply, there's a squeak of a loudspeaker as the mayor steps up in front of the statue, one of the uplights hitting his face so he looks like a kid with a flashlight trying to be scary.

"Thank you all for coming. As usual, the Sleepy Hollow Halloween Decorating Contest brought out the marvelous creativity and ingenuity of our little town. We were delighted and scared, and deeply impressed by the work and imagination that went into some of these decorations. Thank you all for participating and know that it was very close this year. Everyone was impressive." He stops to applaud, and the crowd claps along for a moment. I can feel my heart start to beat faster, and a trickle of sweat rolls down the back of my neck. "Now, without further ado, the winner is"—he takes a folded piece of paper out of his pocket and reads it—"the Gabay family."

There's applause, but it sounds like it's coming in through thick cotton. That's Malcolm's last name—Ms. Overbury has called it every day in homeroom.

Malcolm lights up and heads toward the statue, hands already out for the award one of the mayor's assistants is handing to him. He stands with it for a moment, everyone clapping. That's it. We lost.

14

I look around at Callie and Lenore, who look disappointed but not devastated. What I feel more than anything is embarrassed. This fancy famous goth came in from the city and won our prize. I feel small, somehow. Just shrinking and shrinking, ready to be crushed under one of Amanda Lash's heels.

Callie pats me on the back. "Hey, he still needs to win five more times before he even ties our record."

I force a smile. She's right. But still. When Deer Friend and I meet up tonight I'll just be some loser. He probably won his contest. He'll hear about how I lost mine and about me going to school with this goth semicelebrity who beat me and I'm just so little. Why would anyone want to go on a date with me?

Malcolm comes back over to us, holding up his trophy.

"Okay, you get one dig at us," Callie says.

Malcolm grins. "I don't want to. You pushed me to make it bigger and better. Every time I went into the store, I was inspired and realized I had to make my decorations even more extravagant. So, yeah, I won. But thanks."

"Come on," Callie says. "One dig."

Malcolm laughs and waves the statue in her face. "Fine. Smell my victory pumpkin. Smell it!"

Callie laughs but sniffs and he holds the statue out to Lenore next, who rolls her eyes but inhales, and then he turns it to me. I sniff, suddenly feeling like I might cry.

"Are you okay?" Malcolm asks, looking at me.

I make my face happy, hold back the tears. "Yeah, just annoyed the judges didn't recognize our art."

"I bet it's amazing," he says. "I was sort of hoping to see it later." He pauses, expectant.

"Well, we're going to take it down tonight," Lenore says. "Sorry. They have to make it a store again in the morning."

"Oh, right." He nods, but he seems unconcerned. "But it'll still be up for a little longer?"

I was supposed to show Deer Friend. We were going to tour each other's houses, provided Callie and Lenore declared him not a serial killer. I don't know if he'll still want to see my loser house, though.

"Yeah, it'll be up a little longer," I say. My voice is soft, too sad. I sound so pathetic, or like a sore loser.

"You can come by now if you want," Callie says, too enthusiastic, covering for how sad I am. I look down at the concrete.

"Oh..." I can feel his eyes still on me. "Um, not just now. But later, I promise. How late?"

"Well, we'll be around. Gray might not be," Lenore says, elbowing me.

"Or he might," Callie says. "Or we'll all be talking to my dad."

"Your dad?" Malcolm asks, confused.

I take a deep breath, look up, forcing a smile. "She's joking."

"You hope," Callie says softly.

"Congrats," I tell him, reaching to shake his hand. He takes it. "Your street was really something."

"We should go see it," Callie says. "Tomorrow maybe? Or tonight after you see ours?"

"Sure," Malcolm says, looking at his phone. "Oh, I need to get home, my parents are asking if I won. I'll see you later?" He looks up, eyes darting between all three of us.

"Yes," Callie says, smiling. He walks away as the crowds start to clear. It's a nice night, the moon is nearly full and shining brightly down on the Horseman.

"You okay?" Lenore says.

"It's stupid," I say, "but I felt like, if we won, then that would mean the date tonight would be good. And if we lost..."

"No," Lenore says quickly. "Your date tonight is going to be amazing."

"If he's not a serial killer," Callie adds.

"Maybe even if he is," Lenore says. "Especially, maybe."

"I thought we agreed not to joke about that anymore."

"We're going to be there," Lenore says. "It'll be fine." She wraps her arm around mine. "He's going to be some sexy, age-appropriate guy who absolutely wants you, and you're going to see each other and he's going to take your arm and pull you in and kiss you. I just know it."

"I don't know if we should be telling him—"

"Let him imagine the best possible scenario," Lenore says.

I nod. "Let me hope." I smile, trying to take that in. Hope. So what if I lost? I still can hope to meet my cute boy, I can even hope to win next year. I take a deep breath and the feeling inside me, being small, it seems to fade. I inflate. "I bet there was some scared kid who was a judge this year. Ours was pretty scary. His isn't scary. But it *was* cool. We can still take him next year, right? I mean, we don't want some fancy Instagram star stealing our thunder again."

"We'll go a little softer next year," Callie says, nodding.

"Creepy as opposed to horrifying," Lenore says. "That'll be the energy. Maybe something with potions. I really liked the stained glass, but I kept thinking it would be so much more fun if we had glass bottles."

"An apothecary," I say, walking back home. Callie takes my other arm, so we're *Wizard-of-*Oz-ing down the street. We pass people in costumes, fewer kids now, more teenagers in their ironic costumes, or just animal ears. Everyone is still vibing with Halloween, shouting and laughing. The night is really just starting.

"I like that," Callie says. "I can make bottles overflow with foam every few seconds, maybe even put them on a shelf with a vent, make it work like a fountain."

"Oh, that's good," I say.

We have a whole plan for next year by the time we're home. Mom and Mama are still inside, a few teenagers marveling at the beating heart in the first room.

"How'd we do?" Mom asks as we come in.

"Broke our streak," I say with a sigh. "Sorry."

"Don't apologize," Mom says.

"We don't mind," Mama says. "We still get all the publicity from people being amazed. But I'm sorry you didn't win. With all this, you definitely deserved it."

I wave them off. "It's all right. The guy who won—it's impressive. But we'll beat him next year. And besides, we have so many years of wins. It would probably look bad, us winning again."

Mama laughs, putting her hand on my shoulder. "You're sure you're all right?"

I shrug. "Disappointed. Feeling kind of...small? But I'll be okay, I think."

"You will," Mom says. "Everything has its season, even disappointment, but all seasons pass. Let's close up, put our feet up for a little bit before we have to start taking everything down." She turns to Callie. "It'll come down easier than it went up, right?"

"Yeah," Callie says. "Just be careful taking the windows and glass down, and then everything else you can yank. But we were going to show it to someone, so we'll tell you when we're ready."

"Plus we have to be somewhere soon," Lenore says, looking at me. She's right, my date.

"I'm just going to use the bathroom," I say, running upstairs to check myself in the mirror. The costume is still cute, the makeup has held, but it's chilly so I put on a coat over it. I grab a fake black rose (I have several for wardrobe options) and a copy of Silvia Moreno-Garcia's *Silver Nitrate* that I just finished and I think Deer Friend will like. I shove them in my coat pockets, then go back downstairs, where Mama is turning around the OPEN sign and Lenore and Callie are waiting for me with different looks: Lenore, in love with love again and excited for me, and Callie with arms crossed, ready to call her dad.

"We'll be back in a bit," I tell my moms.

"Okay," Mom says, already walking upstairs. "We'll be on the couch."

I laugh and then leave with Callie and Lenore.

"So here's how it's going to go," Callie says once we're outside. "We go in first. You wait. What's the sign? How do you know it's him?"

"How do you know we—"

"How else would you recognize him?"

"A black rose," I say. "In a book." I hold it up.

Callie frowns and pulls the rose from the book and puts it back in my jacket pocket. "Don't flash that, it says *victim* in loud letters."

I roll my eyes. "So I hide it?"

"Separate pockets," she says, putting the book in the opposite pocket. "If you see him, and you like him, you put them together and sit down with him. But like I said, we go in first. We look for the sign. We evaluate. Then we'll come back outside and decide what to do."

"When do I get to go inside?" I ask.

"When we okay it," Lenore says, her tone light. "Just to be on the safe side. You promised, right?"

I sigh. I did. "So then we all go in together and you sit nearby?"

"Maybe with you if I don't like the look of him," Callie says. "With my finger on my phone to call my dad the moment it goes south."

"And if he's old or creepy we won't even let you go inside," Lenore says. "Obviously."

"Okay," I say. "That's all fair. But if he's okay, do I get to be alone with him? At all?"

"Not tonight," Callie says at the exact moment Lenore says, "Maybe." They didn't talk this part through.

"Get his full name," Callie says. "I will ask Dad to run a check. If he's for real, then maybe tonight." She looks at Lenore. "But maybe not. I mean, who puts out on the first date? Isn't that tacky?"

"Was homecoming your first date with Bryce?" I ask.

Callie blushes under her makeup. I can only tell from the way her eyes open slightly and from knowing her for a decade. "That's different, we've been flirting forever, friends for ages, it was like a fifth or sixth date, really."

"What do you think all my texting is?"

"Yeah, but you still haven't met him," she says. "Just be careful, okay? And I'm running background. And sticking nearby."

I sigh. So much for alone time.

When we arrive at the door to Headless, it is crowded and noisy. Maybe I should have chosen a better spot, but Callie and Lenore wanted public, and this is very public. Yellow light shines out of the fogged glass windows printed with large black letters. HEADLESS. There's no Headless Horseman imagery. It's cooler than that somehow. Music is playing and we can hear laughing and shouting from inside.

"Okay," Callie says, looking at me. "You wait here." She turns to Lenore. "Let's go."

I sigh but stay put as they go inside. The noise is louder as they open the door and I peek in, hoping to see a rose in a book, but it's so filled with people, I'm not sure I'll be able to spot it even once I'm inside.

I wait. It feels like it's taking forever. I keep wondering what he looks like, how it'll be. Part of me is so sure it's just going to be magic and perfect and then part of me feels small again and thinks he'll see some suburban loser and part of me worries he really could be a serial killer, but then maybe he'd be older? Can you be a young hot serial killer who wears thongs? I guess there's no reason why not. I try to imagine him my age but, like, ugly. I've seen enough of him that I know he has a body I like—although I like all kinds of bodies, so that was never going to be an issue. But what about his face? I try to picture him with weird features—bulging eyes, a too-tiny upturned nose, chipmunk cheeks, a receding chin—he becomes a cartoon character, but then I think about texting him and it doesn't matter. He's going to be hot no matter what. I know it.

Lenore and Callie come back out after what feels like forever. They look a little stunned. A little amused. Suddenly I'm worried. What if this was all some prank or something?

"Okay," Callie says. "He's not a serial killer."

I feel my eyebrows raise. "You're that sure?"

"We're going back to the store," Lenore says, taking Callie's arm. "Have fun. We'll see you in a while."

"What?" I ask. "All that, and now you're just leaving?"

Lenore is pulling Callie down the street. "Have fun!" Lenore repeats, waving. And then they're around the corner and gone. What does that mean?

I stare up at the door. I guess there's only one way to find out.

I pull it open and go inside.

It's so crowded and loud, I'm so overwhelmed that for a moment I forget what I'm even looking for. A black rose in a book. My eyes take in everything: crowds at tables, waitstaff going from table to table. At one table, I spot Steve and the soccer team, all dressed like crayons, with T-shirts in different colors, crayon wrapper patterns printed on them, and matching conical hats. They're passing a flask around and look like they've been doing so for a while. His eyes are bleary, even as they look up and catch mine. I look at the table. No black rose in a book. So I look away.

I walk a few tables down—the restaurant is long, and thick with people. I'm not even looking at them, though. I'm looking at the tables, for the book, the rose. I finally spot it in the corner, a small table for two. The book is a hardcover, black fabric, far enough away that I can't read the spine. But there's a black rose stuck between the pages.

And next to it, a trophy: a jack-o'-lantern. My eyes dart up immediately. Malcolm.

I feel a million things at once, like the surface of a bubble, swirling with forces. Humiliation, that the universe has put me in front of him, like this. I'm so exposed. If I take the rose out he'll know everything about me. He already does. And I didn't know it was him. And that makes me feel like a fool. How did I not know? Did he know? If he did, was he happy about it? He's been acting kind of weird lately, and today at his Victorian street, when I said I'd see him later... I think he knew. And then he beat us, so he knows he won, he bested me, and now, I'm what, supposed to be happy to see him? Anger bleeds into me, red-and-black swirls on the surface of the bubble. His expectation, expecting I'd be glad, maybe, that it was him.

Except... I *am* kind of glad? I've always thought he was cute and sometimes he's really annoyed me but sometimes he's been funny and nice, too—knowing everything he said in his messages, knowing that was all him, it's like I can see all of him at once, see the part of him he was hiding because he was nervous and they make the parts he showed me that felt condescending or rude make more sense. Red-and-black rage are pushed to the side and something lighter swirls in, pink and green. But it's all swirling so fast around me that the bubble feels ready to pop.

I feel my feet stop moving. I look at his eyes and I see him start to get up a little, a faint smile on his face, not a superior one, but this soft vulnerable joy starting to spread over him, and I know I have to go to him and maybe it'll be messy and weird and awkward but this is him. This is my boyfriend. And I'm so glad to see him.

I take a step forward and then feel a hand around my wrist, pulling me slightly back.

I turn. Steve. He smiles, sloppy, so drunk. "I was the black crayon for you," he says, slurring a little.

And then he leans forward and kisses me.

15

I pull my wrist back with enough force that I almost fall into a waitress behind me.

"What are you doing?" I ask, looking around at everyone. A few members of the soccer team are staring, whispering to the others. "Everyone saw that."

"What?" he asks.

I swallow and look at Malcolm. He's looking down now, his eyes on his phone.

Steve takes my wrist again, and I think I see Malcolm's eyes flick up, then back to the phone, but I'm not sure.

"Everyone just saw you kiss me," I hiss. Over at the table of soccer bros, the rest of the team is staring. He's drunk. This is not okay on so many levels and I know it's what he did but I suddenly feel so guilty and then I look back at Malcolm and feel a different kind of guilt and confusion and it's like every color on the bubble has turned bad, rotten. It's so loud in here. Everyone is so close. Steve's cheap vodka breath is making me sick.

I pull my wrist away and head for the door. I need to get out of here. I need to breathe. I need to think and decide what to tell Malcolm. Do I tell him anything? Do I want to tell him everything, the truth? Will he be happy about that or will he hate me? He always seemed to think he was too good for me. Surely he won't think I'm good enough to be his boyfriend, right?

Outside, I run around the corner and lean against a wall of the store next to the restaurant. It's baby clothes. Closed, and the window has a display with a jack-o'-lantern with little baby mannequins popping out of it in various costumes. I look at them, faceless and stiff, and realize my breath is coming in short, loud puffs. I try to slow it down. It takes a minute, but it sounds normal again, and then I don't know what to do. Go back? I don't know what the soccer team is thinking right now, or Steve. And what do I say to Malcolm if I sit down in front of him for our date? I just kissed someone in front of him. Someone he knows I've been with because of the conversation he overheard. And I don't even know if he really wants me. He looked maybe a little hopeful in that moment, but then—

I take out my phone.

> **Gray:**
> I can't make it tonight.
>
> **Gray:**
> I'm sorry.

I watch the . . . of his message show up and vanish four times before disappearing for good. Suddenly I want to cry. I want to slide down the side of the baby clothes store and put my face in my arms and cry and I don't know if that's because I'm sad or relieved or both, and I feel like I've done everything wrong and have no idea how I could have done anything right.

Nothing is happening tonight the way it was supposed to.

For a moment, I hope the baby mannequins will come to life, shatter the glass, and swarm me, zombie style. That would be the death I deserve in the moment. But nothing happens. A few people walk by across the street in costume, laughing. Their footsteps echo loudly.

I wipe the tears from my face with my hands and walk home.

I walk into the shop, and there are Callie and Lenore, who throw black confetti on me before they actually look. Then they look behind me, then back at my face.

"Did he say no when he found out it was you?" Lenore asks. "I'll kill him. Painfully."

I shake my head. "No."

"Don't tell us you decided to tell him you weren't interested because this stranger you've been crazy about for months is actually a guy you're kind of lukewarm about," Callie says, glaring.

"If that's how you feel," Lenore say carefully, "then that's your choice, of course."

"No," I say again. I'm here. I'm safe. I sit down on the floor and look up at the stained glass.

Callie and Lenore exchange a look and then sit down next to me.

"What happened?" Callie asks.

I take a deep breath. "I saw him there, and I didn't know what to think, but I think I was going to sit down and tell him and I think maybe it would have gone okay except then Steve grabbed my arm and kissed me."

"Steve?" Lenore asks.

"Did he have a black rose in a book?" Callie says.

I shake my head. "Steve is—was—the closet case."

"Oh," Lenore says, leaning back a little.

"I'm sorry I lied, but he told me he only wanted to use you as a beard so we could hang out publicly and I didn't want to out him but didn't want you to get used like that, either, so..."

"That's"—she shakes her head—"a lot. But I get it."

"So Steve kissed you, in front of everyone?" Callie asks. "And Malcolm saw?"

I nod. I can feel the tears again. "So I ran away."

My phone buzzes and I take it out.

> **Deer Friend:**
> Ok. I hope you're all right.

I sigh.

"What's he saying?" Lenore asks.

"I told him I couldn't come, so he says he hopes I'm okay."

Callie says. "This is bad for him, too."

Lenore reaches out and puts her hand on my leg. "What do you want?"

I blink, my eyes watery. "What?"

"Do you want to be with Malcolm? Steve? Neither? We'll support you no matter what."

"I mean I think you and Malcolm would be cute together," Callie says. "But I don't know anything about Steve."

"He was drunk," I say. "I hope he doesn't get in trouble for that."

"So he only kissed you in public because he was drunk?" Lenore asks.

I nod. "I don't think he meant to come out."

"Well, that feels like a no," Callie says. "No on Steve. But how about Malcolm?"

I stare up at our fake cathedral. The sound is still on, a faint fake pattering of rain on windows, a loud thumping heartbeat.

"I think we should clean this up," I say. "The rest of it—I don't know yet."

"You're probably breaking Malcolm's heart," Callie says.

I shake my head. "I'd break his heart if I went to him right now and said *Hey, it's me, the guy who just kissed his ex in front of you and who's been snarking at you for months. The guy you fought with, who you beat in the competition, who—*" I take a deep breath.

"I thought Steve kissed you?" Callie said.

"He did, but I don't know if that was clear to anyone looking." I shake my head. "What does it matter, anyway? Even without Steve, there's a lot of past there."

"And in the texts," Lenore says.

"Yeah." I think about the texts, imagine him typing them in, moving to this weird little town, feeling alone, and talking to me. Telling me about his day, helping me see the hope in things I thought were hopeless. Two Malcolms. Two pasts. Two Grays, too, I guess. I should have been nicer to him, once he apologized for what he said about the store. Who knows how he sees me?

I want to scry, I realize. I want to ask the gods for just a little guidance and hope they help me out. But first, I know, we have to tear down this cathedral.

"I'm going to sleep on all of it," I say. "There's just too much in my head. But first we better take everything down."

"You don't want to leave it to show him?" Callie asks.

I sigh. I do. But I can't. "We need to open the store tomorrow. It's one of our highest-selling days of the year. And I filmed it. I have all of it on film. Everything I wanted to tell him."

Callie nods. Both she and Lenore look sad. I probably look worse. I feel miserable. It's like the ache of a terrible flu in my whole body, and in my chest, too. It's like I need to cough but can't. How I feel is making me sick. And I don't know how to cure it.

But the tearing things down feels good. Pulling foam stones off each other with a pop. The foam squishes in my fists, and it's like I'm actually doing something to the world instead of the world doing something to me. We don't even bother to go get my moms, we just pull and break and cart things outside, where Callie gathers them all in trash bags, saying she'll figure out how to reuse or store them, or else dispose of them. By the time we're done, it's close to midnight, and the store needs a good sweep, for things to be put back on shelves, for dried herbs to be rehung—but it's good enough.

I go upstairs, where Mom and Mama have fallen asleep in front of the TV, the "are you still watching?" pause still waiting to be clicked on-screen. I nudge them awake and they look at me bleary-eyed.

"You're covered in dust," Mama says.

"We took everything down," I say. "But we haven't put anything back into store formation yet."

"Why didn't you wake us?" Mom asks, stretching.

"We didn't need to," I say. "But you can do the sweeping and putting stuff back if you want." I try a smile, but it's only half there.

Mom snorts a laugh. "Sure. We can do that tomorrow. You get some sleep. You've had a long couple of days."

"Is there something else?" Mama asks. "All day I felt there was something else going on."

They look at me, still half asleep but curious. When both your parents are witches, it's hard to hide things. But I just shrug. I don't want to tell them everything, especially not the part about me meeting a stranger online. "I'm going to go wash off and go to bed."

"All right," Mama says, going to kiss me on the forehead, then stopping. "Maybe when you're not covered in dust."

Mom ruffles my hair and I go to the bathroom and rinse all the dust and tears off me. By the time I'm done, the house is quiet and dark, so it's easy to grab a Coke and a bowl and go back to my room. I fill the bowl and lie naked on the floor, staring into the dark liquid, unfocusing my eyes and asking myself what do I want.

It takes a minute for me to really lose myself. My muscles ache, and it's harder to forget about them and just see the colors in the soda, listen to the hiss of carbonation. But then eventually, I do. I'm gone and it's just me and the darkness, and in the darkness are colors, and suddenly things get so clear. I can see the bubble, all the forces and gods, like ribbons of color, and I can see four in particular, and I know what they are—there's a purple-and-red ribbon, twined together. One is me—or the version of me in my texts—and the other is Malcolm, Deer Friend. Our texting, our relationship, already so woven together. But running parallel to them through the black liquid are two more ribbons in yellow and green, not at all tied together. They're scrunched, facing off like angry snakes. I need to tie them together, make them match the other braid. Balanced.

I need to make real-life Malcolm and real-life Gray into friends so that we can see which set of ribbons we are. Maybe all four can be tied together. Maybe not. And I can't keep lying to him, either. But I can wait to tell him the truth. Just the weekend, I think. The weekend to win him over before I tell him everything. And then—I smile as I blink and the colors all vanish and I'm in my room again.

Then maybe we can be happy. Because Malcolm, Deer Friend, whoever he is—I'm in love with him. I want to be with him. I just need to make sure I give him a chance to feel the same way. So I'll do that first thing tomorrow.

I wrap myself in my comforter and turn out the light. I can feel myself smiling. Today was a mess. It was chaotic and terrible and things were destroyed. But there's beauty in that, too. At least, I have to hope there is.

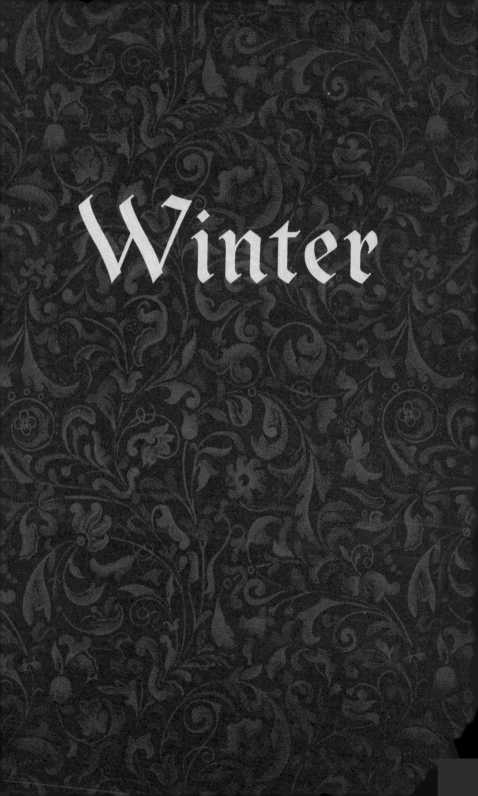

16

"Gray, there's a boy here to see you," Mama says, knocking on my bedroom door.

I bolt up in bed, ribbons of color playing at my vision.

"Malcolm?" I ask, getting up and throwing on some clothes.

"No," Mama says.

I open the door. Standing behind Mama is Steve, eyes red. His arms are folded tight in front of him, and he won't look me in the eye.

"It's about our science project?" Steve says.

I sigh. "Right." I step to the side so he can walk past me into my room. Mama raises an eyebrow. "Thanks," I tell her. She nods and walks away as I close the door.

When I turn, Steve is looking at my room like he would a graveyard. He hasn't been in here in months.

"So?" I ask.

He takes a moment to meet my eye and flinches when he does.

"This is about you kissing me in a crowded restaurant last night?"

He nods and then starts crying. "I was drunk, I'm sorry, I don't know…" He takes out a wadded tissue and blows his nose, then shakes his head. He looks up at me. "I told the guys you kissed me."

I sit down on my bed. Of course he did. "And you want me to back you up?"

He looks away and nods.

"So I look like a crazy gay predator and you look like a straight guy who thought it was funny?"

He nods again.

"You think they're going to beat me up?"

He finally looks me in the eye, startled. "No, no—maybe tease you, but I wouldn't let them do it. I said it was funny. Said we were friendly and I always thought you had a thing for me, and I guess you were drunk and got the nerve up and…" He blows his nose again. "I'm sorry. I didn't know what else to say. If my parents found out, then—"

"I know," I interrupt. "Fine. I'll be the sad gay joke you want me to be. Two conditions."

He nods, takes a deep breath.

"First," I say, "I'm telling my closest friends. They're going to want to know what's up, and I'm not going to lie to them. I will swear them to secrecy."

"No," he says. He looks terrified. "If they know, then they could tell other people, and then—"

"You kissed me in public, Steve. You messed up, not me, and you're asking me to clean it up. These are my conditions. Otherwise I do nothing, and if people ask I tell them the truth. So it's either my close friends get to know, or everyone does."

344

His eyes are so wet. "You don't mean that. You wouldn't."

"I would." I think it's true. He did this, not me.

He swallows. "Okay. But they can't tell."

"They won't," I promise. I know Callie and Lenore. And Malcolm, too, who I'll have to explain everything to. But he already knew anyway. "Second, take out your phone."

He looks confused, but he does what I say, showing it to me.

"Unlock it," I tell him. He does, and I take it from his hand. "What am I under?"

"What?"

"My phone number. I'm deleting it. What do you have me under?"

He's quiet for a long time. I don't look up. I keep my eyes on the screen. I know I'm being cruel—but so is he.

He sniffles. "Lab partner," he says finally.

I scroll down to it, my hand hovering over the delete button, wondering if he'll say something, if he'll ask me to stop. He doesn't. He knows there's no coming back from this. Yeah, he can find it again in the student directory, but he won't. He gets it now. It's over. It's sad and terrible and I am so sorry for him and how he has to live. But I have to live, too. I delete it.

"A third thing I can't really require, but I recommend," I say, handing back his phone, "is that you stop drinking. I get why you are. And I'm sorry if I added to that, but clearly alcohol isn't going to help you. I think what will is focusing on your plan. College, coming out, going low-contact with your parents until they accept you. Right?"

He nods. "That was our plan."

I shake my head. "It's *your* plan. A good one. You included me for a little while, and..." I reach out and take his hand, wait until he's looking at me. "Steve, I loved that you included me. But that's not what the plan is anymore, okay?"

He nods, still sniffling.

"You need a plan that's just for you. One you can always go back to no matter who else comes or goes."

"Just for me," he repeats. "A studio apartment."

"Or one-bedroom." I smile. He's messed up, but there's a great guy under it. Not my great guy. Maybe if I'd met him when we were older, it would have been different, but I didn't. A lost chance. A beautiful graveyard. "Your plan. It's about you. Not us."

He nods again. "I'm sorry."

"It's all right. I'm lucky. I can be out. And hey, one day, when we're ready, we can be friends. And if you want to come to the store and talk to my moms, they're good at this stuff, they won't tell your parents."

He stops sniffling, his eyes already on the door, and nods. "Thanks. Maybe."

"Sure. See you later."

He nods again and leaves without saying anything else. I lie back in bed, but the smell of pancakes wafts in through the open door, and I pick myself up again and go to the kitchen, where Mom and Mama are sitting. They're a little dusty—Mama has her hair up in a bun by the stove, and Mom is wearing overalls. They must have been setting the shop back to normal when Steve showed up.

"Everything okay?" Mama asks.

"That was Steve," I explain. "He got drunk and kissed me in public last night and came over to ask me to say I'd initiated it."

Mom snorts a laugh.

"Poor child," Mama says. She takes a pancake from the pan and puts it on a plate and hands it to me. "What did you say?"

"I told him yes, with a few conditions," I say, sitting down with the plate.

"Really?" Mom says. "Sounds like his problem."

"It is. But I'm a lot luckier than him. His parents..." I shake my head and grab a fork, knife, and syrup.

"Ah," Mom says. "Well, good on you, then, taking one for the team."

"Yeah," I say. "I could use the good karma."

"Oh?" Mama asks.

I put some pancake in my mouth and nod.

Vanilla ice cream. His favorite. I know he only told me that in text, so bringing it might be sort of a clue, but I don't care. He thinks he was stood up last night, and that's my fault. So I'm bringing him something I know he will love.

There's an out-of-the-way ice cream shop just outside town, opening just as I bike over. They have vanilla, but they also have, for Halloween, Horseman's Vanilla, which uses extra smoked vanilla and throws in some charcoal for color. It's my favorite vanilla, rich and smoky and pitch-black. I buy two pints and bike over to his place.

The Victorian street is still set up, so I walk through it, but he's not here. It's still so impressive, and I'm not shocked he won. His was friendlier, while still being amazing. Ours was technically more impressive, with the cathedral and the hearts, but it didn't invite people in as much as this does. Mine showed. His shared. Maybe it was because I was trying to tell a story just for him, and he was trying to show our story to everyone.

I walk up to the house behind the street. There's no car in the driveway. I hope he's home. I walk up to the front door. There's a little garden to the side of the house I didn't see before, and bushes all around the front. The door is yellow. It's a friendly house. I ring the bell and wait. A moment later, Malcolm opens the door. He looks like he's been sleeping, in just a huge black sweatshirt that falls off one shoulder and a pair of pink gym shorts.

"Um...hi?" he says. I stare at him a moment in silence, trying to figure out if he's happy to see me, but he just looks confused.

I hold out the paper bag with the two pints of ice cream. "For you," I say, and then realize I have no good reason to give him ice cream. I swallow. "For winning."

He looks even more confused but takes the bag and looks inside. "Vanilla ice cream?" he asks.

I nod.

"It's my favorite. How did you know?" He leans against the doorframe, examining me. I move my eyes away from his face and they land on the bare shoulder. His skin looks so smooth.

"Who doesn't like vanilla?" I say. "Plus, this is special, only in Sleepy Hollow, only around Halloween."

He's quiet for a moment, still looking at me. "I saw you last night," he says. "At Headless."

I nod. I'm not going to lie if he asks, but I want him to like me more before I tell him.

"I saw you kiss Steve. You two back together? He came out for you?"

I shake my head quickly. "No. Gods no. He was drunk and this morning he came over to tell me he was telling everyone I kissed him, when he kissed me."

"So he's lying to stay in the closet?"

"His parents are very conservative."

"But everyone's going to think you just kissed him."

"I know."

"That's quite a thing to do for a guy you're not dating."

I look up again to meet his eyes. They're narrowed, searching.

"I made him delete my number. Really end it. I feel bad for him, but that's not a reason to be with him."

"You're hoping for something better?"

I smile. "Maybe."

He turns and walks into the house, leaving the door open. I wait, not sure if I'm invited in.

"Come on, what are you, a vampire?"

"I wish," I say, following him in and closing the door.

"Don't we all," he says.

It's a big house. I follow him down a beige carpeted hall into a big black-and-white-tiled kitchen with a little eating nook that looks out on the garden. It's so peaceful, so suburban.

"I know what you're thinking," he says.

"Really?" Are we about to finally reveal ourselves?

"That this isn't the kind of house Amanda Lash belongs in."

I shake my head. "Nah. I wasn't thinking that. I know you're from the city originally."

"My parents wanted a lawn," he says, opening a cabinet and taking out bowls.

"It always sort of intimidated me, the Amanda Lash thing," I say. "I thought you were so fancy, better than us suburban kids."

He sets the bowls on the table and sits, motioning me over. "Yeah, I don't usually lead with it. Sometimes I try to keep it a secret altogether. Some people can be weird about it. Ask me for stuff, or expect me to be a certain way, or..." He shrugs.

That's why he never wanted to exchange photos, social media, names. Because he was afraid I'd know who he was. I sit down.

He dishes out the ice cream into bowls, smiling at the color. "This is pretty cool."

"See, suburbs have some good stuff."

"I don't mind it," he says. "I mean, I did at first, but"—he looks out the window—"I kind of like it up here now. Sort of. I miss the city, too, but it's not so far." He turns back to me, shaking his head. "But I'm sorry if I came off as a snobby city kid. I was just—"

"Nervous, you told me. It was my fault, too. I feel bad about it. And now that we're not competitors anymore, I wanted us to"—he looks up, eyes flashing—"be friends," I say.

He smiles. It's a nice smile. A very kissable smile. "I'd like that, too. I kind of thought we already were?"

"We are," I say. "I just wanted to make it official. And apologize if I've been kind of cold."

"So have I." He takes a bite of the ice cream and grins. "This is good vanilla."

"Know your vanillas?" I ask.

"Oh, I'm a vanilla expert. That's what they call me in the city. The vanilla queen."

"That's a compliment?" I ask, laughing.

"Hey, vanilla is great if you do it well."

We stare at each other in silence a moment. I lick my lips.

"So," he says. "Why were you at Headless last night, then? If not to meet Steve?"

I swallow and look down at the ice cream. The bowl is a little white dish with rose trim. The black ice cream looks delightfully out of place in it.

"You don't have to tell me."

"Can I tell you later?" I ask.

I look up at him and he narrows his eyes. "Why?"

"Because I want you to like me before I tell you."

"What makes you think I don't like you?"

"I just feel like I haven't shown you my best self."

He takes a spoonful of ice cream and puts it in his mouth, letting it melt, slowly, before swallowing. "Maybe I like what I've seen anyway." He knows. And he knows I know he knows. This is a game now. But it's important to me. I want him to see me as the best me before I tell him. Not as the guy who kissed some other dude in front of him and then ran away.

I smile. "Please?"

He takes another spoon of ice cream, swallows it. "Why don't we take the day?"

"The day?"

"Let's go do something together. You show me your best self. And then at the end of the day, you tell me why you were there. And why you left."

"I left because Steve kissed me and I didn't think that was the best time to..." I shake my head. "I left because I thought everything I was there to do had just been messed up."

He finishes his ice cream and closes the top of the pint. "You make assumptions a lot."

"I do?"

"That I'm some fancy guy from the city who thinks he's better than you. That an ex drunkenly accosting you can't be explained in the moment. Small things, but you turn them over in your head until they become big."

"I guess...yeah," I say. "I do that."

He grins, flashing teeth stained slightly gray by the ice cream. "So do I. Although I admit what I said about the store probably didn't help. That was me making assumptions."

"It's okay."

"It is a really cool store. I'm sorry I didn't get to see it decorated."

"Yeah." I frown. "I have video of it, though. I can show you that."

"I'd like that."

"Okay so...one day," I say. "I'll end with that."

He laughs. "Already making an itinerary?"

"Yes," I say proudly. "And I know where we should go first."

"Okay." He combs his hands through his hair. "How about I meet you there, then. I gotta shower if we're going to go on"—he pauses—"if we're going to hang out."

"Okay. Then meet me at the entrance to the cemetery."

He grimaces. "I can't ride a bike, so"—he shakes his head—"I'll get an Uber. Give me an hour and a half?"

"Sure," I say.

He stands up and stretches, his sweatshirt riding up to show just a hint of his stomach. I pull my eyes away and realize he caught me staring. We don't say anything. I stand up and head for the door.

"See you in a bit," I say.

"Later," he says.

Outside, I take a deep breath. He almost called it a date. A do-over date. Maybe. I don't know. But a chance to get everything right. I sounded very confident when I said the cemetery, but actually I have no idea what I'm doing. I pull out my phone.

Gray:
Lenore, you have any of those eyeballs left over?

Lenore:
Yes! Why?

Gray:
I'm meeting Malcolm at the cemetery and I want to prepare a picnic for us.

> **Callie:**
> DO-OVER DATE?!
>
> **Gray:**
> I haven't told him it's me yet
> but I think he knows
>
> **Lenore:**
> How long until you meet him?
>
> **Gray:**
> Hour and a half?
>
> **Lenore:**
> I can do better than just some leftover
> eyeballs. Come over.
>
> **Callie:**
> Me too! I want to help!

By the time I get there Lenore is already in the kitchen, a large picnic basket to one side, something delicious-smelling in the oven, and HorrorPops playing softly from somewhere. She smiles when I come in and gives me a big hug.

"I like this do-over idea," she says.

"It was his. He said—well, he asked me why I was there last night, if not to see Steve, and I said I didn't want to tell him yet."

"So he knows," Lenore says.

"I think so."

"He knows!" comes a voice from a speaker somewhere. "Can I tell him, then?"

"No!" Lenore says.

I look for the source of the voice and find her laptop

open in the corner, facing us. On-screen is Anthony, his long hair pulled back in a messy bun.

"Sorry, I told him everything last night as we were leaving," Lenore says. "I didn't think it would all go sideways."

"He's crazy about you," Anthony says. "Or...well, the version of you he texts with. *You* you he talks about more...nervously?"

"Yeah, that's what I was afraid of," I say. "That's why I have to make him like *me* me before I tell him I'm the one he texts with. Even if he already figured it out."

"That's romantic," Anthony says, grinning. "Still, what a world. Of all the towns he could have moved to. So random."

"A dark fate," I say. "Destiny."

"Awwwww," he says, then his eyes dart behind me. "You put the cookies in ten minutes ago, Lenore, they're probably ready."

"Thank you," Lenore says, putting on a bat-patterned mitt and opening the oven. She pulls out a bunch of black, cinnamon-smelling cookies studded with chocolate chips and cherries.

"How did you make this already?"

"I had some dough in the fridge."

"We were baking together last week," Anthony says. "Same recipe, same time. Like—"

"A date?" I ask.

"No," Lenore says. "I thought he was with Malcolm and we were just doing friend stuff. Our real first date is next weekend. He's going to come up here and we're going to go to the cemetery and then to your shop."

"Is it as cool as she says?" he asks.

"Of course it's as cool as I said," Lenore says, smiling. "You don't believe me?"

"I'm just gathering outside opinions."

"I'll try to make it special for you," I say, laughing. Their first date, but they already feel like an old married couple. This is so much better than Cody.

Lenore inspects the cookies and nods, setting the tray on top of the stove. There's a knock at the door and Callie comes in a moment later, Bryce with her. She's surprisingly not done up, no makeup, just a band tee and black joggers. He's just in a tee and jeans.

"Hello," Lenore says, looking them over suspiciously. "Casual day?"

"I hadn't showered yet, leave me alone, I wanted to help," Callie says.

"And Bryce was with you?" Lenore asks.

Bryce turns strawberry red, so bright I almost don't notice Callie blushing, too.

"Can we help?" Callie asks.

"Hi!" Anthony says. "I'm Anthony."

"Oh, hey," Callie says, noticing the laptop. "This is Bryce, my boyfriend."

"Boyfriend?" I say.

"Shut up," Callie says. "I'm here to help you get one, too. What can we do?"

"I have it all under control," Lenore says, just as one of the cookies on the stove catches on fire. "Dammit!" She smacks it out with a towel, then turns off the burner she had on.

"Is something burning?" Lenore's mom calls from upstairs.

"It's supposed to!" Lenore calls back. We all laugh.

For the next half hour, we help Lenore prepare an amazing picnic lunch of eyeballs and cookies, black bread cheese sandwiches and a few cans of dark cherry cola.

"Not my best work," Lenore says, closing the basket. "But not bad on short notice."

"Go get your not-serial-killer," Callie says.

"Don't make him sound so boring," I say, hugging them both. "Besides, we don't know, maybe I'll get lucky and it's been him the whole time."

"Actually," Callie says, eyes plummeting to the floor, "they found the guys."

"Oh?" I ask.

"Yeah," Callie says, not looking up.

"They're okay?" Lenore asks.

"Aside from the bad breakup," Callie says, giving a slow shrug and looking up at me. "Of their polycule. Please don't look too smug."

I laugh. "Poly Perry's boyfriend's rules strike again."

Lenore is cracking up. "How'd they find them?"

"They all went to live in this cabin owned by one of their grandparents. The last one, Dad said, that's how they put it together. No one even knew they were a thing, but then the cops searched the place and found all four of them fighting and... anyway. No murders!"

"Poly Perry," Lenore says. "He had his tongue in someone's mouth for too long."

I laugh. "I will not gloat," I say, smiling in a way I know

is gloating. "And hey, just because there wasn't a killer doesn't mean there can't be one! Maybe I can be Malcolm's first victim."

"That you know of," Bryce says. Everyone goes silent, staring at him. "What? Did I do it wrong? I was trying to joke like you guys."

Callie kisses him on the mouth and I grab the picnic basket, laughing, and leave.

The Sleepy Hollow Cemetery is beautiful, with bridges and little paths. It's not as big as the one in the city, but it has its own charm, and some famous dead people. There are headstones with statues of angels and small mausoleums. The leaves are bright orange in the afternoon light, and the whole place looks golden. I wait just inside the stone arch, picnic basket in hand.

A car pulls up and Malcolm gets out and I suddenly feel underdressed. He looks so good in a black shirt with net sleeves, loose black pants, and an actual cloak, black but lined in red, that falls to just above his knees. He dressed up. I'm just in torn jeans and a black V-neck.

He sees me looking him up and down and smiles. "So, where's the best spot?"

We walk into the cemetery and I show him the various sights—the graves of Washington Irving and Elizabeth Arden, our favorite angel statue, the delightfully Gothic memorial to Owen Jones, a man we only know from the memorial. We talk as we walk, but it's safe, easy talk: classes and essays, Callie's prosthetic experiments. I suddenly wonder if the magic we had in our texting was only in our texting. If being in person has somehow ruined it.

Or maybe everything else has. Except then we walk in silence for a moment and I glance at him out of the corner of my eye and see him looking at me and we both smile and start laughing.

"It's kind of weird," he says.

I nod. "Follow me." I take him to our favorite spot and sit down, a few worn headstones around us. "We watch the Fourth of July fireworks from here."

He smiles. His eyes scrunch; I don't think I've noticed that before. It's really cute.

"It's really nice," he says, looking at everything. Then he looks at me, and then quickly looks down. His hand starts drawing a circle in the dirt.

"Did you hear they found the missing teens?" I ask. "They were in a polyamorous foursome, ran away to try being together. Didn't work out."

He laughs, but then his expression turns more melancholy. "It's sad when things don't work out."

"I know."

"I was really hoping I could be the next victim," he adds, flashing a smile.

"Hey...," I say, patting his leg. "There are a lot of serial killers in the world. You could be sitting next to one right now."

"Oh yeah?" He raises his eyebrows. "Gonna murder me on a bed of rose petals? Because I want to go out with style."

"First he wants to be murdered, but then he needs rose petals." I shake my head. "So picky."

He nods. "I won't deny it. I'm very particular."

I laugh and we look at each other for a moment and I want to kiss him. Because this is the guy from my texts. I don't just know it anymore, I feel it. The threads have woven together, and all it took was a few jokes, a little conversation, a smile. But I have to tell him. I take a deep breath.

"I was there to see you," I say.

He smiles. "I know."

I put my hand next to his, my finger sliding up and down a blade of grass. "But I didn't know it was going to be you and then Steve kissed me and I thought about how you had heard us in the bathroom at the dance and then about how I'd thought you were like, lording that over me—"

"I wasn't—"

"I know, that's just how it felt, because I didn't know you and we were competing and..." I shake my head. "A lot went through my head, and I kind of ran away, and I'm sorry."

"I was so sure it was going to be you," he says, looking out at the headstones. "And I wanted it to be you. I know I might be awkward and condescending sometimes, but I like you. I've always thought you were hot—"

"Me too," I interrupt. "I mean, always thought you were hot."

He laughs. "But then Steve kissed you and you were gone and I was worried I got it wrong and you were going to be with Steve, or worse, you had come in, and seen me, and decided I was ugly or not what you wanted and—"

I lay my hand over his on the grass. "I'm sorry. I didn't mean for you to feel any of that."

"It's just so unbelievable. Both of us. Wrong number. Same town. I realized then that me hoping it was you meant that I was going to be disappointed if it wasn't. So actually, I left right after you. I was going to text you that I wasn't ready. Because"—he turns to me—"I wanted it to be you."

"It was me," I say. "It is me."

"We're so lucky," he says. "That's what my Halloween decorations were about. Luck. You."

"Mine was about you, too." I pause, my voice nervous for some reason. "You want to see it?"

He nods, and I pull my phone out and show him the video of the haunted house, explain the story.

"I don't know how that didn't win," he says with a laugh. "That's insane. The forced perspective is otherworldly."

I shrug. "Yours was amazing, too, and more interactive and kid-friendly. I think yours was more open. You were like hoping people would find the luck you had. I was just being dramatic about mine."

He leans his head on my shoulder and I almost pull back for a moment, afraid to actually feel him touch me like that. Then I reach out and take his hand again.

"It's messy, isn't it?" he says. "You, me, phone-you, phone-me, competing, insults, flirting."

It doesn't sound like he's saying anything good. I feel queasy, suddenly. Is this it? Are we over before we really get to start?

"Yeah...," I say.

He's quiet. I want to sink into the ground and join the dead.

"We could start over," I say.

He pulls his head off my shoulder and looks at me. "Start over?"

I stick out my hand. "Hi, I'm Gray. Do you like Night Club?"

He takes my hand, squeezes. Then he pulls me close and kisses me. If my soul is a graveyard, at that moment it explodes in purple light.

17

Monday at school is a weird mix of high and low. I have Malcolm with me finally, holding his hand, but I also have a lot of people looking at me weirdly, and Jenny stage-whispers in science class that "he totally threw himself at Steve, like full sexual assault. He's lucky Steve isn't pressing charges."

By lunch, apparently everyone else has heard about it, too. I can feel eyes on me as I sit down with Malcolm, Lenore, and Callie. Lenore and Callie are looking at me funny, too, but a different kind of funny. Like I'm a baby rabbit or something.

"Stop it," I say.

"We're just happy you two are together," Lenore says.

"That you worked it out," Callie adds.

Malcolm rolls his eyes and squeezes my leg under the table.

"Can we just be normal?" I ask.

Jenny is walking by as I say it, holding her tray, which just has a bottle of skim milk on it. "No, you're a freak," she shoots at me, and keeps walking, laughing.

"How long you think it's open season on me?" I ask.

"It's the Steve thing," Callie says. "It'll pass."

"Nah," Malcolm says. "We can do better than that." He stands up and hops up onto our table. Everyone in the lunchroom looks at him, confused.

"What are you doing?" I whisper.

"You made a deal. I didn't," he says back.

"Just an announcement," Malcolm says. "About my boyfriend. And that kiss he shared with another guy on Halloween. It was a bad choice, for sure. An apology was made." I swallow. He's telling the truth, just not saying whose choice, whose apology. "And yet everyone keeps gossiping about it and accusing my boyfriend of being a predator? Which is funny because my understanding is Jenny Applebaum kissed Jerome Cohen at the end of the summer, despite him having a girlfriend, and no one is calling her a predator. How many of you have gone in for a kiss and found out you messed up, apologized, and went on your way? I'm not saying it's cool, but it's not being a sexual predator, either."

I look over at Jenny, who is bright red, with embarrassment, fury, or both, I can't tell.

"I wonder if maybe you all just like calling gay people predators. I'm new here. Is that the kind of place this is?"

From the back of the room I hear a clap. Esme and her punk bandmates—Jerome included—are leading the applause. A few more join them, then most of the room, if half-heartedly.

Malcolm smiles and gets down off the table. The clapping fades. I look around and meet eyes with Steve. He looks away.

"Was that really the best thing to do?" I ask.

"He put you in a bad situation. Sometimes when there are no good choices, you make the best choice you can and just hope."

It sounds like what Mom said. People are turning away from us now, the murmur of the lunchroom swelling back up.

"How did you know about Jenny kissing Jerome?" Callie asks.

"Esme told me. We text. She's cool."

"I appreciate it, but maybe next time can we run plans like that by me first?" I ask.

Malcolm thinks for a moment and nods. "Sorry, you're right. I just—I felt angry. But you're right, I should have said something."

"I didn't think you were the kind of guy who stood on tables and yelled at people," Lenore says. She looks impressed.

"I am," Malcolm says, smiling. "Sometimes. When I feel...like me. And I think I finally feel like me again, here." He takes my hand. "Since I know someone here really knows me."

"Should we talk about what you said, though?" I ask.

"What? About Jenny? I don't really care, I mean she's a total—"

"No," I interrupt. "I mean, you called me your boyfriend."

Under his makeup I can see him turning pink. "Oh, well, I mean, I guess—"

"I like it," I say.

He breaks into a grin and squeezes my hand. "Me too."

"Awwww," Lenore and Callie say in unison.

"Shut up," I say.

The day goes on and people leave me alone more. Malcolm's table speech seems to have had some effect. By the time we all meet outside after school, I'm feeling like the attention isn't on me anymore. At least, no more than usual.

We walk our bikes over to the store, because I still need to teach Malcom how to ride, and then we fall into the day, like he was always part of it, like he's always been there. It's easy, how well he fits into my life. We go over our next big project: Callie's science fair entry. She and Malcolm know more about it than Lenore and I, but Callie has brought samples and starts applying them to all of us as I ring up the occasional customer. I'm not going to pretend I understand the science stuff, but I can tell her which of her formulas drips the most like real blood.

When my shift is over, Lenore and Callie walk home, but I bring Malcolm up to my room, where we do some more kissing before I get off the bed and take out my video camera.

"Kinky," he says, "but also illegal until we're eighteen."

I laugh. "No, for the interview."

"Interview?"

"Remember, when we first started texting, and I told you I was making this documentary about the store, and about us, and I asked when it was all over, could I interview you for it, and you said yes?"

He nods after a moment. "Yeah. That'll be quite a story, I guess. But I don't think anything is over yet." He puts his hands on my hips and pulls me into another kiss. "I hope it's all just starting."

We do a lot more kissing over the next few days, and some other stuff, too. I finally get to see the thong in person. And we do the interview, too. It's funny, asking him how he felt about me when he didn't know I was the texter— cute, standoffish, always so quick to judge him. But he's not wrong. That's what I was. He was trying to be cool; I couldn't get over the things he said about the store. Our own little Regency drama. Our own little happy ending.

Mom and Mama love Malcolm almost immediately, possibly more than they love me. He does an Instagram post about the store as Amanda Lash, calling it her new hangout, which drives up the online business almost immediately, so much that we have to order a lot more stock. Plus he and Mama swap makeup tips. Apparently she'd been looking for a new red lipstick since her favorite one was discontinued, and he knew exactly where to find the right shade. We all help Lenore pick an outfit for her date, too; a black-and-blue houndstooth pencil dress with a pin she made in the shape of a giant jeweled spider.

"He loves spiders," Malcolm assures her. "Because they sew."

"Weave," she says. "But I'll correct him."

When she and Anthony show up at the store on Saturday night, we're all already waiting. I've dimmed the lights, and I close the store once they come in so they have some privacy to wander it, and then I leave them to make out on the chaise a little as I go help my moms set up for the moon ceremony. Callie, her parents, Bryce, and Malcolm arrive after the sun is down, and I knock politely on the store door. Anthony and Lenore emerge a moment later. Mom and Mama pretend not to notice anything, but I spot Callie's dad narrowing his eyes.

"So, this is real witchcraft?" Malcolm asks me, sitting on the picnic table as Mama gets out the athame, chalice, wand, and pentacle.

"Paganism," I say with a shrug. "Just sort of calling down all the elements, all the forces in the universe, and saying, *Hey, we love you, thank you for everything you've done for us, and maybe keep doing it, please.*"

"Everything?" Malcolm asks, taking my hand.

"Everything. Good, bad, sad, happy, life, death."

"Luck. Hope."

I smile and squeeze his hand tighter. "Yeah."

"Then I want to thank them, too."

I let him stand next to me as we perform the ceremony, and quietly explain everything as it's done. When it's over, Anthony applauds like it's a show, and we all laugh.

"That was really beautiful," Malcolm whispers in my ear. "Thank you for inviting me."

"You'll always be welcome," I say, wrapping my arms around him. He turns, keeping my arms in place, and leans back into me. His hair smells like smoke from the fire and a little like moss.

"Is this what life will be like now?" he asks softly. "You and me, and all our friends and bonfires and magic?"

I watch the fire burning. I know it won't, of course. Things change. There's college to consider, and applications to theater design schools to look at. We could break up, even though it feels like fate brought us together. There could be another plague, or a bomb, or an environmental disaster, and we could all die. Or we could grow old together and our graves would be right next to each other, the moss on our headstones connecting them like a bridge. It could be good, or bad, or both. But it'll always be beautiful.

I hold him closer and softly kiss his ear. He giggles, then turns to kiss me on the mouth. I love him so much.

"I hope so."

RACHAEL SHANE

L. C. ROSEN

writes books for people of all ages, including the Evander Mills series, which began with the Macavity Award–winning *Lavender House* and continued with *The Bell in the Fog*, *Rough Pages*, and *Mirage City*. His most recent YA novels are *Emmett* and the Tennessee Russo duology. He lives in New York City with his husband and a very small cat. He invites you to find him online at LevACRosen.com and @LevACRosen.

MORE FROM
L. C. ROSEN

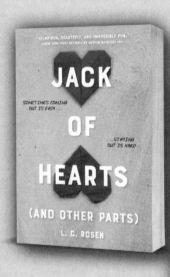

NOVL theNOVL.com